The Heart Is a Burial Ground

Tamara Colchester

SCRIBNER

LONDON NEW YORK TORONTO SYDNEY NEW DELHI

First published in Great Britain by Scribner,
an imprint of Simon & Schuster UK Ltd, 2018
This paperback edition published in Great Britain by Scribner,
an imprint of Simon & Schuster UK Ltd, 2019
A CBS COMPANY

SCRIBNER and design are registered trademarks of The Gale Group, Inc.,
used under licence by Simon & Schuster Inc.

1 3 5 7 9 10 8 6 4 2

Simon & Schuster UK Ltd
1st Floor
222 Gray's Inn Road
London WC1X 8HB

Simon & Schuster Australia, Sydney
Simon & Schuster India, New Delhi

www.simonandschuster.co.uk
www.simonandschuster.com.au
www.simonandschuster.co.in

A CIP catalogue record for this book
is available from the British Library

Paperback ISBN: 978-1-4711-6574-0
eBook ISBN: 978-1-4711-6573-3
eAudio ISBN: 978-1-4711-7503-9

Typeset in Garamond by M Rules
Printed and bound by CPI Group (UK) Ltd, Croydon CR0 4YY

Tamara Colchester has written for film and various publications, including *AnOther Magazine*. *The Heart Is a Burial Ground* is her first novel.

'There is an addictive pungency to this exotic tale of lives lived loudly' *Sunday Times*

'Sensual, evocative and rich with observational truth, this is a vivid and intricate portrait of three extraordinary women' Jeremy Page, author of *Salt*

'Evocative' *Good Housekeeping*

'An elegant rumination on the impact of a life lived far outside the conventions of her time. This story is one of love, desire, glamour, and also neglect, abuse and a legacy of shame' *AnOther Magazine*

'Evoking the writing of Kate Atkinson and Tessa Hadley … you'll be swept along with their fanciful lives across centuries and continents' *Irish News*

*'Le guerre non fanno la pace,
i popoli fanno la pace.'*
Caresse Crosby

*(War does not make peace,
people make peace.)*

The Heart Is
a Burial Ground

Prologue

This is a story about a woman I never met and the lives she created. Examined from the outside and imagined from within.

It is as though I live on the ground floor of a tall house and she lives at the top. On the floor above me lives my mother.

On the floor above that my grandmother.

And way up above, in impossibly large rooms crossed with sun and shadow, lives my great-grandmother, Caresse.

I long to go up and meet her. I wish I could walk in those rooms. Lights go on and off. Sound filters down (often only the empty scratch of a gramophone needle going round and round and round), sometimes voices – laughter that could be the cry of a seabird, or the high pitch of weeping that clings too long to one note – but might only be the sound of the wind. The bang of a door moved by that wind, shocking the silence out of itself.

Mostly though, there is nothing.

My mother describes things as best she can, when I ask.

1

But there are some things that make her hands go cold where she holds me, and I don't like to press her there.

So it is inwards that I go to meet them. For they are in my blood, these women, in my bones; there is no choice in this matter. Led by a twisted gut feeling, I walk in the overgrown garden of my imagination where remembered tales grow tall. This is private, family property where I can search uninterrupted, away from the cold facts and ordered paths of chronology and into the darker corners, unvisited. Here I can collect the dropped stones, half hidden in the past, that led nobody home and lay them before me until a pattern begins to emerge – a mosaic of fractured images cast in the hard light of my present experience.

I will describe it as best I can.

This is their story.

Or perhaps just mine.

Let us begin, again.

Hotel des Artistes, New York, 1929

They had to break the door down to get in.

And there they were, lying fully dressed like brother and sister with only their feet naked, her stockings like two shed snakeskins in a heap on the floor. The tattooed suns on the soles of his long, gentle feet gave the police cause to raise their eyebrows but it was his ochre-painted toenails that really got them talking. Every newspaper mentioned it as though it meant something, as if it were a clue or even an answer. For many it was evidence enough. BOSTON BANKER AND HIS BRIDE IN SUICIDE PACT, said the headlines.

Well, they were wrong on two counts.

Harry was a poet, not a banker, and that girl was not his wife.

Roccasinibalda, Italy, 1970

Damn. She knew she should have brought a coat.

Diana slammed the car door, cutting off the man talking in the front seat. She looked up at the walls of the castle that straddled the low mountain and felt the wind move through her dress, making her shiver like the tops of the cypress trees just visible above the battlements. The sound ran through the forest that covered the hills around them – a river of *shh shh shh* – and Diana turned her head and sniffed the air. Someone was burning dead leaves, the rich smell sinking quickly into her hair and the soft wool of her cardigan.

A white flag flapped in the wind.

She had a flag now? Christ. Well, the sooner she organised things ... the sooner she could leave. She wrapped her arms round herself. Why the hell was it so cold?

The other door to the car opened and the man got out, still talking. 'This needs to be handled with care. Your mother is very ...'

Diana looked at the lawyer's face, still thick with sleep, and the greying hair sticking out over one ear. She couldn't stand people who showed signs of the night before.

'That's enough, Roberto. Besides,' she leaned across the roof of the car, 'you didn't care about all that earlier, did you?'

His eyes travelled down to the low neck of her dress. She rolled her eyes – too bloody easy – and began walking towards the vast wooden doors that stood wide open before them.

'Who was it for this time?' Diana sat in a low chair by her mother's bed, inspecting her hands. There were the beginnings of some pale brown marks on their backs – sun damage – and she stretched her fingers and looked at them appraisingly. Still pretty good.

'For all the young,' her mother said in a Boston drawl as long and elegant as the curve of Back Bay, though roughened a little to a cat's scrowl now, as she rested her head back against the banked pillows. Diana could tell the eyes were closed behind the dark glasses as she remembered. 'We decided on a masquerade and had a great sugar-crusted cake covered with little flags to announce the different nationalities present.

'At midnight there was a symbolic cutting of the thing and then a collapsing of each of their kingdoms into a sweeter world. There was a yoni – carved in rose marble by a new arrival, a most invigorating Lebanese – in front of each girl's plate and a lingam for the men. A man from Japan sang a weird tragedy and there was a long recital – rather too long in Ellis's case. I think his last poem might need a little edit; people were becoming somewhat restless towards the end. But the fireworks were wonderful. One girl screamed like a

5

banshee – it might have been Paola, the baker's girl – every time one went off, or perhaps she was just making love, I don't know. And the Japanese singer drank everything in sight and kept shouting "Banzai!" at the top of his lungs for no clear reason. I could hear them all shrieking till dawn. Oh, it was marvellous, Diana, we were just on velvet.'

'And what did this one cost?' Diana asked in a voice that was not unlike her mother's, but that drifted towards English, the vowels a little French.

'What a prosaic question, in the face of a night that was pure poetry.'

'There is a great distance, Caresse, between good poetry and bad.'

'Well, this was good.'

'As good as yours?' Diana asked with a raised eyebrow.

'Oh, you're impossible. Hand me my glass.' She held out a hand.

'Isn't that why I'm here?' She fixed her mother with a level gaze as she handed her the water. 'To see the lay of the land?'

'You're here,' her mother said quietly, 'of your own volition. I'm happy to see you, of course, but you didn't need to come.'

'The doctors said that you—'

'I know what the doctors said,' Caresse interrupted, and they were both silent.

'It's looking very well, the place.' Diana got up and looked out the window, her stomach dropping at the sight of the trees so far below. She stepped back. 'You should come and see the house in Ibiza. It's looking spectacular. It's just been photographed for a book called *The Allure of Interiors*. The photographer was the most hopeless fruit. He stayed for a week and kept drifting about in velvet flares calling everything "*charmant*" and drinking "fizz". I thought I would strangle him with my belt.'

'Yes, I must try and visit . . .' Caresse said in a vague voice. 'Perhaps next winter, when the storms come.'

'Yes.' Diana looked at her elderly mother where she lay in bed, her face unusually pale against the pillows. 'Perhaps.' She turned and ran her hand along the curved back of a chair upholstered in faded rose silk. 'Strange to see these here.'

Her mother looked over. 'I did wonder if the furniture wouldn't be dwarfed by the space, but it looks quite right.' The two women often returned to politely furnished conversation like this. It was the Boston in them, the dollar-bill green that still coloured their blood. 'We've now decorated thirty-two of the rooms and the frescoes we're uncovering are quite astonishing.'

Diana watched her mother as she continued speaking, but her mind was moving with her hand over the curve of rough silk, picturing him seated in the very same chair, untying his shoelaces with vicious movements and then pulling his inked foot free.

'I have new shoes, Rat.' He reaches into a cloth bag and removes two hard black shoes, looks at them for a moment, then puts them to one side before picking up the battered old pair with the tender care of the newly bereaved. 'But these have been my faithful friends since I returned from the dead in 1919. How many hundreds of thousands of steps have I walked in them? How many stairs have they mounted? How many rendezvous have they taken me to, how many storms have they passed through?' He looks down at them and they

7

seem limp and worn as the dead rabbit she'd watched floating past in the current of the stream while the grown-ups ate and laughed on the far side of the garden. 'I shall bury them.' He smiles. 'They must be exhausted.'

'. . . I shouldn't be surprised if we uncover a Michelangelo or a Raphael.'

Diana looked up, startled to hear her mother still speaking.

'The eternal optimist,' said Diana, her throat dry.

'Bars or stars, darling. It is a choice, you know. And you've arrived just in time – the roof's almost finished. What a thing. I've promised a huge dinner to all the workers.'

'A dinner for all of them?'

'I'm hardly going to invite some and not the others. Each of their hands have contributed to the warmth and security of this castle and we must honour them for that service. I'm planning an Umbrian feast with an extraordinary recipe for roast turtle doves. You can stay for it.'

'No, I won't. I have to get—'

'As you wish.' Caresse shrugged the sentence off and smiled at the nurse who had quietly entered the room.

'I have to get *back*,' Diana continued, clenching her fists, 'to finalise the divorce. Anthony's being difficult. He's retreated to his frigid country house to bang away at all the birds he likes. Takes absolutely no interest in Elena and has allowed himself to be snared by one of his secretaries. A ghastly little something called Anita.'

'Bruised male ego *and* a jealous woman. Jeepers. I hope you've got a good lawyer, darling.'

'Yes,' Diana looked pointedly at her mother, 'I have.'

Her mother returned her gaze levelly.

'Anyway,' Diana gave a little toss of her head, 'I have my own guests arriving . . .'

'Well, you'll do what you will, as always.' Caresse leaned forward as the nurse pushed up the pillows behind her. 'Those endless divorce papers,' she said fondly. 'Such a bore.'

Diana picked something invisible from her sleeve and said nothing.

'Don't be cross with me for not writing to you,' Caresse said after a pause. 'Your letters can be so gloomy.'

'I'm not cross with you. I know you don't like my letters.'

'Those listless sheets you used to send from school,' Caresse continued.

That weren't intended for you, Diana thought, watching the nurse roll up the draped sleeve of her mother's heavily embroidered dressing gown, revealing the pale softness of the once strong arm. She wrapped a thick black band round it.

'I'm not angry,' Diana said. 'I was only upset to hear about your heart. The doctors said—'

'Well, what's done is done, isn't it.' Caresse reached for her diary with her free hand as the nurse pumped one, two, three and then released, carefully watching the dial. 'Let's look at today, that's much more interesting. You're staying for what, two weeks? A month?' Diana glanced at the nurse uncertainly, but she made no sign, so she looked back at her mother.

'Let's say . . . a month.'

'Wonderful! You can have the run of the summer palace across the courtyard. It's quieter over there – I know you need your sleep. I'm sad Elena couldn't come with you, she was so charming when she was here last. There was a poet who was wild for her. How is she? Grown into a beauty?'

'Of course. She has your breasts.'

Her mother smiled. 'Good.'

The door opened again and an olive-skinned girl in a simple cotton dress entered with a tray holding a bottle of wine and two green glasses.

'Elena's a mystery,' Diana went on. 'Never *speaks*, but it's as plain as day there's something getting at her. She gives off a sense of continual disappointment, like a whipped dog. Eats absolutely nothing. What she *does* say is that I was wrong to get rid of Inés, which is absurd.' Diana drank from the glass that had been placed in front of her. The wine was good and cold. 'Whenever she's down from Oxford she retreats to Inés's little flat in Battersea. I had to practically threaten her with violence to get her to come and spend some time in Ibiza.'

'Who is Inés?' her mother said vaguely, bending down the top of the manuscript she was half-reading.

'My old Spanish housekeeper. She lives in England now. You've met her several times.'

'Ah, of course.' Caresse brought her hands up to her hair to wave it back off her forehead. 'How old is Elena now?'

Diana thought for a moment. 'Nineteen?'

'You were very fond of that awful Belgian, despite her being a reprobate.' Caresse raised her eyebrows as she swallowed the pills handed to her by the girl.

'Mette wasn't awful . . . I loved her rather. And I was still a child, Caresse. I needed someone.'

Her mother said nothing and the silence hung heavily between them.

'Well, Elena should have come here.' Caresse broke the silence. 'Tell her to come here.'

Diana shook her head. 'She's writing a paper about contemplation or some other whitewashed juju.'

'Has she a lover?'

'Yes, another one who wants to marry her. I picked him up from the side of the road in Ibiza. Terribly handsome.' Diana smiled and Caresse laughed. 'It won't last though – she maintains a cool distance with all her men. Enough to catch a chill.'

'Perhaps she's trying to communicate something.'

'Like what?'

'Maybe she's a lesbian.'

'Perhaps. Though I'd be the last person to know if she was. Inés has the keys to that kingdom.'

'Well, all will be revealed in time,' Caresse said.

'And has ... Leonie been in contact with you?' Diana asked, looking over her shoulder at the view through the window.

'Yes,' Caresse said quietly, 'she has. She called me from the hospital in New York a few days ago.'

'And ...'

'And she doesn't want to see you, I'm afraid.'

Diana's eyes glittered. 'She told you that?'

'In as many words.'

'Well ... she's old enough to do what she wants.' Diana could not look at her mother and focused instead on the arch of her foot. She had wonderfully high arches. Sculptural, really.

'The doctors say she's recovering very well. No lasting damage, slight scars.'

'It's good that I didn't flog all the way over there, then.'

'Yes, she mentioned that you hadn't.'

'Is that why she won't see me?' Diana's voice rose in anger.

'It's not easy is it, darling, getting it right?' Caresse said thoughtfully. Then her voice changed, surging in a new direction. 'Children are strange things. I wonder why it is that *we* have to have them – women, I mean.'

'Some kind of punishment, I suppose. They certainly take it out of you.' Diana finished her glass and then looked around the room, stopping when she noticed a portrait hung between the two windows.

'You've kept it,' she said, surprised.

'Yes.' Caresse turned to see what she was looking at. 'I've always liked it. I think he got you very well.'

'I thought you'd got rid of it.' She smiled and turned to face a mirror, arranging her hands in the same position and tilting her head, until she caught her mother's amused glance in the bed behind her.

'Why would I do that?' Caresse said mildly.

Diana looked at her in the reflected glass and then shook her head, turning away. 'I don't like this place,' she said decisively. 'It's too big. These thick stone walls keeping nothing out or in. Your houses are always too big.'

Her mother looked at her over the top of her glasses. 'Places are just people, Diana. Places are just you. Why are you so touchy anyhow? Who's your lover?'

'I saw your flag flapping about outside.' Diana ignored the question. 'How is the great political party?'

'It's not political, it's anti-political.'

'Flags are always political.'

'This is a place of true democracy,' her mother declared. 'A Republic of the Arts.'

'And were you elected as divine ruler?'

'Oh, Diana,' her mother laughed. 'You're impossible. The Città della Pace is a peaceful philosophy that Ezra and I—'

'Peace? Really? Why, that's as worthy an aim as happiness. Far better to make peace with war, Caresse, it's the only constant. And that old bastard Pound was always trying to get me on the stairs outside the nursery with his horrible scratchy beard. What the hell does he know about peace? It had hardly been two weeks . . .' But something in her mother's eyes seemed to block the words, so she changed tack. 'He barely waited till you were out of mourning before throwing his horrid checked hat in the ring.'

Her mother looked at her for a long moment, but then, seeming to decide something, laughed. 'He wasn't that bad. And when the thoughts are as good as that, well . . .' She held up her hands. 'Anyway, when you've lived through two wars, you see that peace is the only thing *worth* fighting for. And peace *is* possible where people refuse to judge . . . Besides,' she said lightly, 'I remember you quite liking some of those kisses.'

Diana's nails dug into the familiar tenderness of her palm as, from somewhere below, the round metal sound of the gong signalled lunch. She stood and smoothed her skirt down.

'You know,' she turned at the door and eyed her mother, 'I did live through two wars.'

Caresse looked up, eyebrows raised in question.

Diana nodded. 'Hitler, and you.'

A look of pain briefly crossed her mother's face. But the remark did not penetrate; it was only the comparison that hurt.

*

Everyone was already gathered around the large stone table set in the middle of the walled garden. The spreading branches of lemon trees threw shade across the people as they chattered, their faces flickering in the dappled light. The garden was surrounded by crumbling walls, veined with capers and lichens; and although these walls contained the group around the table, the empty blue sky above gave rise to the sense that they were seated on a plateau at the top of the world. The air was clear and there was no sound except the occasional call of the birds flying way below, soaring straight-winged over the tops of the trees that covered the hills.

Diana took them in. They seemed nice enough (despite the ridiculous little white flag pins they all wore) but were hardly worth breaking concentration on what she knew would be a very good meal. She didn't always care for her mother's menu choices – a gastronomic confusion of caviar, puttanesca and marshmallows – but the cooking here was excellent. She sat back and smiled vacantly at the bespectacled young man talking earnestly at her left elbow. There was that poet Ellis thingummy who looked as though he'd been asleep in an ashtray; a few young people wearing T-shirts, a Canadian in a lilac kaftan who'd written a strange book of poetry about the migratory pattern of flamingos; that English art historian who was meant to be something of an expert on restoration (her hair in a severely ill-advised middle parting), the film crew from the BBC – she nodded in greeting at the raised glass of a bearded man in a paisley cravat, yikes, she must have met him in London somewhere – and an admittedly interesting-looking woman from Haiti, an artist with a shaved head who spoke quietly in a scattered French patois.

As she raised her own glass in salute to her, and the gesture was returned, Diana recalled an ugly voice speaking across another dining table long ago in the purple-painted dining room at Rue de Lille.

'Negroes,' the wine-stained stranger spat, causing the other guests to turn towards him. 'Running all over the country like cockroaches.' His lips searched for his glass. 'In my opinion, the only thing a gentleman should do to a Negro is knock him down.'

The guests had looked over to her mother at the head of the polished table, dark hair cut in a sharp line above her eyes. She had crossed her arms and looked straight down to the other end of the table where her new husband sat. Diana had watched them as they smiled at each other, wondering why they didn't speak; she *hated* it when they didn't speak (she gripped the sides of her chair, tears pricking her eyes), it was *rude* not to share their jokes.

Eventually her stepfather leaned back in his chair and caught the man in his hard blue stare. 'And what do you suppose,' his hoarse voice silenced the room, 'we should do with the *Negress*?' He glanced at her mother, whose mouth had stretched into a slow smile and Diana had wished, wished to death, that she knew what it was they should do with the Negress.

He tapped his pipe against the sole of his shoe, one two three. 'Knock her *up*, I suppose?' And her mother had laughed, laughed even when everyone had gone home, even when Diana had been sent back downstairs and she could only hear the sound of them moving across the ceiling of her nursery.

A word at her left brought her back to the table. Nodding

in agreement at the man without hearing a word he said, she continued to look around at the group, her eyes stopping on a boy whose hair shone white in the sun. At that moment he looked over, and despite the pretty girl nestled in the crook of his arm, Diana met his gaze with a kick of satisfaction. *Later*, she thought, as the table was distracted by the arrival of a girl wearing a short dress made of silver discs that shimmered like a tambourine. She was almost as irritating as a tambourine, Diana decided as she listened to her regaling the company with a story of how she'd got stuck in Rome with an old count.

'He'd left all his money to his dog. Said if he was going to leave it to a bitch, it might as well be one he liked!'

Diana observed her for a moment and sat forward.

'You know my mother bought me a dog when I was a child.' Her voice was low and clear, her painted mouth giving out each word like a gift. The table turned towards her and she nodded as someone filled her glass. 'She was a little pearl-grey whippet that was to be a companion to my mother's magnificent dog, Narcisse Noir. One day my mother took Narcisse to meet Picasso at his studio – she wanted him to illustrate one of their books – and the great beauty of the dog stirred the Spaniard,' she caressed the word until it came to life, 'to demand that Mother bring him one of his sons. Well, Narcisse never did breed – too fancy to fuck, you might say – but one of his brothers did and this animal was brought to *me* as a gift. Its name, my mother decided, was to be Clytoris. (I was told it was the name of a Greek goddess.) So from that day on, much to my delight,' she smiled, 'I had a little Clytoris to play with.'

The ashtray poet laughed long and hard, and everyone followed. He looked at Diana across the table and wiped his perspiring face with his linen napkin. He'd been waiting to meet this daughter for a while and no, she definitely didn't disappoint. She looked as expensive as her mother and wore her age well, particularly that mocking smile that lifted the corners of her mouth. He'd like to wipe it off her face with this very fine rag. There was an ass worth visiting beneath that swishy skirt. The waist was thickening a bit, it always did at that age, but the proportions were still a honeyed ratio. What was he thinking though? He shook his head as she glanced over him and turned towards the man on her left. She looked cold as hell. The torture of rich pussy – may he be delivered from this tumorous obsession. A fish nibbling at the fingers of a sick old lady. What was wrong with him? A tumour tuna. A tumour sandwich. He laughed, delighted and disgusted. A disgusted boy. A custard pie. He would go down to Rieti and fuck a girl from the port, he decided. This place wasn't good for him.

'To your mother.' He stood with a sudden movement and raised his glass. Diana flicked her eyes over him and then nodded and everyone followed.

'Her mother, what?' Caresse came through the stone archway into the garden with Roberto beside her as tender and careful as a groom. Though her hair was now brilliant white in the sun, her hips still swayed with the knowledge of the sex between them. Everybody stood as she took her place at the head of the table and she laughed, thick and throaty, patting them all back into place.

Oh, she loved to see her table full! Look at all this colour, the shimmer of that little dress, the bitter scent of the capers that clung to the walls of the castle and the smell of pine high on the wind. *It's like a bouquet*, she thought. A magnificent bouquet gathered in the arms of this castle.

'Diana was just telling us about her Clytoris,' someone said.

Caresse smiled. 'Such a sweet little dog.'

Diana laced her hands tightly together and watched the girls from the kitchen carry out two huge pans, the rich scent of the *rigatoni alla pajata*, the milky guts of a calf in tomato sauce, drawing everyone towards their glazed pottery plates.

'Thank you, Roberto.' Caresse indicated where he should fill her glass to. 'Now I want to hear everything.' She sat forward, ready to hear the first person speak. 'What have you all been *doing*?'

Diana leaned back in her chair and put her face to the sun. Aware that the young blond man that she'd noticed was glancing occasionally towards where she sat, she allowed the words to wash over her. She'd done her bit.

Later that night she made her way slowly down through the dark corridors and out onto a terrace. Someone was attempting a tremolo, and she sat down on a stone bench beneath the bent shape of a tree, amused by the ineptitude. The guitar stopped with the whack of a palm against wood.

'Have you got a cigarette?' the young man asked.

Diana nodded, pointing at the wicker bag that lay curled at her feet, then watched as he set the guitar down and approached her. He was thin and very tanned with lightly freckled skin stretched taut over the bridge of his nose, hair in tangled sun rays round his head. She noted his eyes on her legs as he crouched down and held the case up to her. She took one between her fingers and withdrew it slowly.

'So what brought you here?' She gently bit the tip between her teeth.

He sat back on his haunches and moved his hands in the shape of a woman, or was it a guitar? Diana put her head to one side.

'Sculptor,' he said.

She turned her face slightly so that he could see her profile. 'I'm surprised you're English. You look American somehow.'

He smiled. 'I'll take that as a compliment to my good health. Very much improved by a month in this rather beautiful place.'

'How did you come to be here?'

'Your mother came to see me at my studio in Rome. She just appeared one afternoon out of the blue and asked to see my drawings. We drank some wine and had a long discussion about Brâncuşi. Apparently, he once roasted a pullet for her in his studio and then carved it with a sculpting knife. The way she told it made me laugh and that was it, we've been firm friends ever since. I very much liked that she didn't ask me where I was from or where I was going.' (Dig; Diana smarted, but the boy didn't seem to have said it with any intent, so with a roll of her shoulders she let it go.) 'And I appreciate her philosophy. Citizens of the World. A City of Peace. That feels about right.'

'Yes, she's always been full of ideas.'

'I hear you live in Spain?' He looked up at her from where he sat, tanned arms round his knees.

'Ibiza mostly. I like to sail.'

'So do I. I sailed the Bay of Biscay with my father when I was a child. He got beaten up by a port master for insulting a plate of *angulas*. I've had a special love for them ever since.'

Diana laughed. 'Spain's a fascinating country. They have a relationship with violence that is very life-affirming.'

'And why not Italy?'

'Spain suits me. The sun's hotter, shadow colder. Plus they make better wine.'

'And I suppose your mother got Italy first.' He inhaled deeply on his cigarette.

Diana looked into his eyes as he said this, but again saw no malice. Just a light moving like a torch in the dark. She felt the thrill of pursuit begin to beat.

'Do you like bullfights?' she asked.

'I've never seen one. You?'

'Very much.'

'And here you are in the Città della Pace.' He laughed.

'Is peace really one of your ideals?' Her tone was less mocking than usual.

'Yes, I think I aim for that.'

'Well, you're still young.'

'Your mother's not.'

'My mother's always been younger than me. It's a fact physics has no answer for.'

The boy, whose name was David, laughed. 'She's certainly a one-off. They don't seem to make women like that any more.'

'How are you so sure?' Diana sat forward.

Lowering his cigarette, he squinted at her through the smoke.

'Which room are you in?' she asked.

He pointed towards one of the dark ground-floor windows. 'We sleep in there.'

'We?'

'My wife and Pierre. We picked him up on the way here.'

'Wife? You're too young to be stuck in that mud.'

He shrugged. 'Twenty-eight can feel awfully old.'

'Well then.' Diana stood and pulled her cardigan over her shoulders. 'You'd better come with me.'

Boston, 1920

'There's that Crosby boy, just back from Verdun. Apparently he refuses to wear a hat.' Diana stood on tiptoes to see where her grandmother discreetly indicated and saw it was the man that had stared at them all through church. The women allowed their eyes to stray briefly in his direction before returning to the centre of their little group.

Diana's grandmother turned to the pretty young woman whose smile seemed to be taking a bite out of life's cheek. 'You never did tell me how you got on chaperoning his beach party.'

'Oh, did I not? I must have forgotten.'

Diana recognised the lie in her mother's voice, as high and irretrievable as the ribbon of a let-go balloon, and staring up at her, she bit her lip.

'I thought he was terribly interesting really, not to mention brave. He came back with the Croix de Guerre, you know.'

'Awfully odd, some of his antics,' a blonde woman said lazily. 'He crashed his father's Bugatti into the Porcellian Club.'

'I find that intensity rather attractive,' another one put in. 'There was that scandal at Harvard . . .'

Leaning out of the circle, Diana watched the man walking around the side of the church towards the graveyard at the rear, where she could just see him pacing back and forth between two tombstones. He seemed like the bird that had flown through her nursery window, darting madly about causing screams and breakages.

'I heard he was seen with Bessie Pulborough on the shore early in the morning before her wedding. Her husband has threatened to . . .' The other women murmured their interest and five flowered hats gathered in a closed bunch.

'Maybe he just doesn't care about hats.' Her mother's voice was a cry that silenced the women. They narrowed their eyes towards her and Diana gripped her hand a little tighter.

'I think we'll go,' her grandmother said, holding an arm out towards where their driver waited.

'You and Diana can go,' her mother said, pulling her hand free. 'I need some air.'

And Diana's hand was taken up in the dry leather grip of her grandmother's while five flower-laden hats watched in silence as the young woman pulled hers from her head and walked slowly around the side of the church towards the graveyard, long skirt trailing on the ground, before ducking away out of sight.

Roccasinibalda, 1970

One foot in front of the other, Diana's ribbon-crossed ankles flickered over the old stone ramparts as the sun lowered itself beyond the line of hills in the distance. Below her, a sheer drop, the tops of the trees – Diana faltered for a moment, tipped a fraction and split: watched her body fall, only half interested by the possibility of her dying. She completed the circuit of the roof, the last heavy rays causing her to half-close her eyes, the angled roofs of the town below tucked in shadow now, like a shy child holding close to its mother's skirt. Carefully ignoring the men at work on the sea of tiles that rose and fell around her, she turned away and looked out across the valley gilded by the evening light. Oh, it made her mad, she would not look at it. A million dollars. A million dollars!

'An investment, a legacy,' her mother called it, the cloudless sky reflected in her glasses. Diana had shaken her head. 'We don't choose our own legacy, Mother, it's decided by the people doing the remembering.' She'd looked a little perturbed by that and made a note in her diary.

It shamed Diana somehow, this late altruism. It was all so *meagre*, with the meetings, and flag pins, and the eager teenagers doing dance routines. Why did she bother with all this now? Frittering what little remained on this absurd flea circus. It had been so huge, and this was so ... pathetic somehow; just look at it. She stared with folded arms at the tiles spreading between the battlements, the wind blowing her skirt against her legs. This roof was nothing more than a lid on a steaming pan. A load of hot air. She smiled condescendingly, pleased with her metaphor. Perhaps that was it: denial. Nothing more than the simple fear of death. *Well, we all have to face up to that*, she thought, with the brusque clarity of one who wasn't. But why did her mother bother with all these *ideas*? Why couldn't she just be brave, like he had? He hadn't cared about roofs and political reconciliation. He'd just done it. He'd smashed on out of here instead of this endless birthing of all that was new. New ideas, new life, new friends. She gripped the wall, the weight of loss inside her as heavy as stone. Coming back was always a mistake. As she stood there, she slowly became aware of the press of someone's gaze and, turning her head, saw that a few of the workmen, large men, sweating and covered in dark hair, were indeed staring. Without altering her expression she arched her back slightly – a better line – and shook her hair back as she gazed, open-eyed, into the last of the sunlight. Biting her bottom lip, she bent further over the edge of the battlements to look down at the streets winding below.

'*C'è un fico maturo*,' one of the men murmured, causing the others to laugh.

'*Attento, che ci troverai dentro una vespa*,' another said.

'*Morirei per una così.*'

She watched a boy kicking something along the road that ran beneath the south wall and then, hearing a shout, moved slowly, her hand trailing the stone, feeling the men's breath rising and falling in her own chest, to where the winding walkway of the entrance unfolded beneath her. Through the archway she saw the wide circle of her mother's jade parasol making its swaying descent, the fringed silk cutting side to side as she was carried in her sedan chair – a man in front, a man behind – down the steep winding entrance of the castle towards where the large doors stood open. Strange thing to do with a fortress, Caresse, she'd said to her mother. This place was built to keep people out. And her mother had smiled that infuriating smile. 'I like a bit of subversion.' She leaned further over to watch her mother going forward with arms extended to greet the driver of yet another car, suitcases tied to its roof. Who were all these people? Always people ... guests, guests, guess who's in your bed tonight. But then look at this place. She shook her head and turned back, the sole of her shoe rasping the grit. Living in a castle was *asking* for an invasion.

They would talk today, she decided, after her mother had finished filming.

'*Always yes, Caresse.*' Diana rolled her eyes at the sky so that blue met blue.

'*So much better, don't you think, darling? So much bigger than the sad finality of no. A yes always fissures into a thousand possibilities.*'

But Diana knew what that really meant – always saying yes was to forever promise nothing.

*

26

Pressing her foot down, Diana pushed her mother's car faster so that the trees either side sped to a blur. Down to her left she could feel more than see the lake, dark-rimmed with trees and sky blue at its centre – an inverted eye.

David's slender arm lay across the back of her seat and, as Diana deftly steered the car along the winding road, she glanced over at him, at his tangled hair blown back from the tanned face.

Under her gaze he turned and though he could only see his reflection in her cat's eye sunglasses, they both smiled and felt the moment closing around them with the simple motion of a sheet pulled over two heads; a memory that would be pulled apart, separately and together, countless times over the years to come.

The lake was quiet, the water's edge marked by a thick line of trees and a strip of muddy sand, a single boat tied to a broken jetty that stretched a small way into the water. The season was not yet ripe for tourists and it was still too early in the morning for locals.

They swam right out to the centre, naked bodies pushing through the water, and as Diana moved, her breath coming in rhythmic gasps, she noticed with appreciation David's ability to remain silent with someone he still hardly knew. It was rare in the young ones. Her arms pushed through the warm surface of the water, as her legs kicked into the dark coolness beneath. She wanted to be alone here. Alone but accompanied; someone keeping an outside eye on things while she dug into her thoughts.

Pulling herself up onto a pontoon, Diana sat up straight-backed and looked into the sun. A fine, straight stare that hurt her eyes.

27

'Look at it, Rat,' he'd say. 'Keep your eyes open. Look at her, giving us everything and everyone too blind to take it. That's the Sun of God right there.' And she'd look and look and look until she could see nothing at all.

She lay down on the warm wood of the pontoon and pictured herself, seven maybe eight then, climbing up the tower to sit with him, the noise of the babbling guests far below, her mother's laughter softened by distance. She would sit and listen to him talking, face held in a profile that was a single line of beauty, watching his inked feet and hands move with slight, blind movements, his words riding close to his thoughts that were always actions so that listening to him was like running alongside a moving vehicle – let go and you were left behind, hold on and you would likely come to harm. They would lie side by side until Diana's skin started to hurt. But it was better to burn. If you got up for water or to sit in the shade, he was always gone by the time you came back. She felt the sun weaken and shadow cover her body. Opening her eyes, she saw her mother standing over her, her face dark in the shadow. Harry lay with his eyes half closed, watching her. 'Caresse,' he said, and put out a hand. Without a word, she lay down and circled her arms round him and the back of her hand was cool against Diana's hot skin.

'Hey.' She felt David's hand cover her own and turning to him she saw he was watching her uncertainly.

She smiled and put out a hand and he came forward and rested his head on the soft sweep of her stomach. He turned on his side and with his ear pressed against her, right where she had begun, he listened to the mysterious movement of her insides. Above those soft, inner sounds, David became aware of a whispered stream, and glancing up he saw her mouth moving gently with the insistent cadence familiar to him from countless services in a cold church on top of a hill in the Sussex downs. She was praying. He lifted his head up, waiting for her to finish. But the feverish voice was whispering something he did not recognise, the words cutting and dipping in a staccato rhythm too quick for the steady tread of Protestant prayer. When she finished and was quiet, he stroked the curve of her breast, causing the nipple to grow and harden, bringing her back to him.

'What was that?' He frowned, his voice a little hoarse.

She curved towards him. 'Habit.'

'Do you believe in them? The words?'

She shook her head, her hand guarding her face from the sun.

'Why do you say them?'

'I believed in him.'

'What do they mean?'

'It's not something that translates.'

His eyes moved over her face, wanting to know more, but it was some time before she spoke.

'Once in India there was an old man they called the Sun-Gazer whose eyes had been burned out by his endless staring at the sun's rays. Every morning he would be carried down the steps by his brothers to his accustomed place by the Ganges – he couldn't walk as his legs had withered away from years of inactivity – so that he could turn his face towards the east. Slowly he'd open his eyes to greet the morning sun as it raised its head over the temple tops of the Holy City. He'd remain there the whole day with his eyes fastened on the blazing disc without once turning them away or closing them for even an instant until the dying sun had sunk once more below the horizon.' She moved her hand in a slow arc that came to rest on the side of his face. She turned his face towards hers. 'Ritual is important, David, it gives shape to things. You create the structure; time provides the meaning. Leave working it out to the others.' She waved her hand away.

He reached up without understanding, distracted now by a different need, and pulled her towards him, and soon they lay together as quietly as sleeping children.

'Roberto?' Diana knocked on the door of his study. It was the only one in the castle that was always closed.

Hearing his voice, she pushed it open and on entering the room, stopped short. Surprised to find a boy standing in front of his desk doing up the top button of his shirt. Both he and Roberto turned towards her.

'Diana.' Roberto rose hastily. 'Alessandro was just trying on the shirts your mother has bought for the new choir.'

He spoke to the boy in quick Italian who, with a scornful glance at Diana, flicked down his collar and walked from the room, closing the door behind him.

Roberto tented his fingers and sat back down. He wore a pale blue shirt, expertly ironed. 'Would you care to explain where the car has been?' His manner was different today, and as Diana took a seat, her wet hair combed back from her face, she looked over the carefully tended plants, the large Picasso, the inlaid walnut desk; and realised that Roberto was a man who benefited greatly from being seen in context. There was something in the room – the boy, his collar – that caused a sheet-tangled memory to surface (Roberto's face just before he lost control) and Diana had to cross her legs. She was just considering reaching forward, when Roberto rose from his seat again, came round and sat on the edge of his desk, causing his trousers to ruche round his groin in an unflattering shape. Adjusting her dress, she sat up.

'I wanted to swim.' She smiled. 'I would have asked, but you were still asleep. A *very* relaxed start to the day, I must say. Caresse normally likes her staff up and at it in the morning.'

Roberto stiffened. 'I always take breakfast in my bedroom and work there until midday.' (*Don't rise to it, Roberto*, he chastised himself.) 'But I was meant to collect your mother's prescriptions from the pharmacy in Rieti this morning, alongside a visit to the bank and the notary . . .'

'Oh well, if I'd known it was for something as urgent as all that . . .'

Patronising bitch, Roberto thought.

'Diana, it is, in fact, serious. The pharmacy is now closed and she will have to spend an uncomfortable night until they can be collected tomorrow. You are aware that your mother is recovering from pneumonia. Her last heart attack was very recent and she needs to rest without any complications. The scar tissue has made it stronger, but she is still very unstable . . . One day the importance of health will perhaps mean something to you. You will go and tell her what has occurred, please.' He held his arm straight towards the door.

'She's having her interview, Roberto. I'll tell her afterwards.'

'Yes. Of course. After.'

'No, actually, I'll go and see how they're getting on now.

Something's made me change my mind. What fun—' She stopped suddenly. 'But I did come for a reason, Roberto.'

'What?'

'Come to the bar with me?' She smiled, looking for a moment exactly as she had when he'd met her on the day of her first wedding to that old French aristocrat almost thirty years ago. He had only met Caresse a few weeks before and had been surprised to be invited at all to the wedding of this wonderfully vital widow's daughter. 'Oh, but you must come,' Caresse had said. 'I can tell you are going to be in my life for some time and I don't believe in doing things by degrees. If you're in, you're all in, so don't stand on formality.' The night before the wedding they had all eaten a vast meal of black sausages and galettes with raspberries and thick cream, along with bottle after bottle of Clos de Vougeot. He'd paid the price in the inn's outside toilet in the early hours of the morning, bent over as though in prayer while a nightingale sang in the wood. It had been unclear to him why this woman had so taken to him until they sat together surrounded by the detritus of the wedding breakfast. He had only just completed his final legal exams and this seemed to please Caresse. 'You're still untouched by that dreadful system. You know it, which is important of course, but you haven't become wired to it. I like outsiders who know how the insides work. You'll be a great help to me, I'm sure.' She'd patted the chair next to hers and he'd moved tentatively closer. 'My late husband couldn't bear lawyers. He felt they wasted time with their technicality-spotted bird brains.' Roberto had laughed at that, safe in the outside position she had placed him in. 'But my time in this life has shown me that it helps to have those around whose feet are firmly in the filing cabinet, even while their heads are full of dreams. You do still believe in your dreams, don't you?' And she'd looked at him with a face as fresh and open as a lily on a pond.

'I was born in the mountains so was brought up with my head in the clouds,' Roberto had said, pleased with the words that fell from his mouth. 'So, yes, signora. *Io voglio*. I do.'

He'd been surprised at the daughter's choice of husband – he'd been old enough to be her father, in fact. She looked sinfully young in her stiff little dress as she made her way down the aisle of the chapel, trying to smile at everyone. He smiled to himself. If only the old boy had known what he was letting himself in for.

'Why do you want me to come to the bar, Diana?' he said, his voice softer.

'I want to talk to you.' And her voice was higher and softer too, as though she was following his thoughts.

'No, Diana.' He shook his head and walked behind his desk and firmly sat down, drawing pen and paper towards him. 'Not again.'

'No?' she said sharply.

'What happened in Rome was a mistake. A common mistake, but ... inappropriate. We must revert to the previous contours of our relationship. It's better that way. To draw a clear line, I mean. And you are a woman who needs very strict lines.' He glared at her from beneath the storm of his grey eyebrows.

'Well, *I* don't make mistakes. But, you're right, I do love a strict line. It's always nice to know the exact moment one's overstepped it. Oh relax, I just want to talk, you'll be perfectly safe in the bar.' She placed her finely boned hand on his large white one sprouted with dark hairs. *Beast*, she thought, and then noticing as though for the first time the gold wedding band circling her fourth finger, tugged it off and tossed it onto his desk. 'I don't need that any more. You can consider it a bonus.' She smiled and rapped the desk. 'You have some time to get ready. See you at six.'

Boston, 1922

'What's divorce?'

'Divorce . . .' Her mother knelt by the narrow nursery bed and looked into Diana's eyes. 'It means the end of something old. And then the beginning of something new.'

'Is the end for ever?' The child's hands played wonderingly over the delicate embroidery of her mother's flower-sprigged dressing gown.

'Yes.' Her voice was low.

'Is it like when you die?'

'Nobody's going to die.'

'What about Father?'

'He's going to hospital to dry out.'

Diana blinked. She knew about that. Her father was a soak. She'd heard the housemaids talking on the stairs.

'What about us?' Diana whispered fearfully, looking again at her mother's pale face.

'Us?'

'Yes, will we have to get divorced too?'

Her mother smiled and shook her head, running her fingers through the silk fronds of the lampshade that blushed rosy pink on the bedside table.

'No, Diana, you're staying with me. Now sit up and drink your milk. We need to make you strong.'

Alderney, Channel Islands, 1993

Elena hadn't slept. She leaned towards the small plane window until her forehead met its coolness and looked below her at the island beginning to shape itself out of the surrounding grey sea.

Another try.

She peered through the rain-flecked glass as one drop met and merged with others until the whole window was running.

Home.

She shook her head. *Hardly, Elena* . . . And smiled wryly at her own sentimentality as she looked down at the scant island, beset by the waves. There was something of the left-behind about the place, with its disinterested islanders, the net-strewn harbour littered with diesel cans and green-bearded lobster pots, and the empty concrete forts that knuckled its edges. Pretty too, though, with the cobbled streets that ran like rivulets through the small town and the nettles and wild flowers growing round the war memorial.

In front of her, her husband turned round in his seat, their two sons next to him. One dark, one fair, both wearing rough woollen army jumpers in dark green, their legs bare. He smiled at her.

They took one another in for a moment and then he turned away again and Elena listened to him talking earnestly to the boys.

'. . . nothing was left to chance.'

'Who did the work?' The blond little boy, Tom, spoke.

'A vast number of prisoners. Russians, Spanish, also French. Political prisoners in the majority. Not soldiers. The few who survived and returned to their own countries were often shot as traitors.'

'But they didn't want to work.' Jake the elder, darker boy frowned at his father. 'That's unfair.'

'A rule of war – you can only be on one side. And whether they wanted to or not, those men had helped the enemy.'

'But why did nobody rescue them?' Tom asked anxiously.

'The defences they were building for the Germans were too successful. Essentially, the men built their own prison, denying any hope of rescue. Thousands died. A terrible irony, really.' Elena could just make out the largest of the forts standing alone on the north edge of the island, where the land heaved itself, white-faced, out of the sea.

'After the war,' her mother was fond of saying to the occasional person who still came for lunch, a glass of wine held loosely in her hand, 'the lobsters the fisherman brought in weighed as much as small children.' And closing her eyes, Elena began to murmur to herself a measure of words that ended in palm-pressed supplication.

Another try.

She moved back in her seat and her reflection appeared, vague and pale in the scratched glass. She habitually turned her head slightly to the left, following the contours of her face, searching for the familiar changes. What would her mother see? She peered closer, but then thought better of it and closed her eyes, denying herself the reflection. *Still, Elena?* Something shifted beside her and Bay, her youngest child, leaned across her to look out the same window, pressing against Elena's rounded stomach.

'Bay . . .' she gently lifted her away, 'careful, darling,' and without looking the child tucked herself round the bump, and Elena wrapped an arm over the small body and held it tight.

'Will she be wearing her tied-on shoes?' Bay asked, looking up.

Elena looked down at her. The little girl wore a small army jumper the same as her brothers, but rather than boots her thin bare legs were punctuated by a pair of red jelly shoes.

'I doubt it. She doesn't get out of bed much any more.'

'Why?'

Elena pressed her hand to the window and at the island below them.

'Because if your grandmother doesn't like something, then sure as champagne, your grandmother doesn't do it.'

As the plane circled, Bay pictured the square house with its garden of trees whose fruit always seemed to be lying on the ground waiting to be stepped on, soft and wet.

Inside there was . . . she tried to picture the inside . . . but it kept collapsing like the walls of a failed den.

39

She tried again, concentrating.

Inside there were closed doors . . .

A cupboard crowded with big men's coats that were never worn . . .

A hallway with a telephone that never rang.

A big dark green drawing room that was like being inside a bottle, heavy silk curtains good to hide inside . . .

A room upstairs full of books.

And then, of course, there was her grandmother . . .

Lying, like a strange animal, in the darkness of her bedroom.

Bay felt her mother shift beside her and she remembered what she'd said in the car that morning on the way to the airport, turning in the front seat so that Bay and her brothers could see her eyes, her sunglasses on top of her head holding the short lengths of her dark hair back from her clean face.

'It's *your* home too. You must remember that.' And her brothers had nodded and Bay had nodded too, without knowing what any of it meant or why they even agreed like that.

She pressed her hand into her pocket, feeling the shells she had collected last year. As her thumb touched the hole at one of the shell's openings, her tongue also felt into the softness of the hole in her gum, and she felt a little wave run through her body as she probed the wobbling absence where her tooth had been. When, she wondered, would the sharp white tip of her grown-up tooth begin? Thumb and tongue felt blindly in the darkness, the dip of the plane making her tummy slip wildly. Hearing her father speaking to her brothers, she sat forward and tried to listen over the searing drone of the landing plane.

'It's hard to imagine *now* what could have been so important about this little island . . . ' they all looked below them as the plane flew so low its shadow could be seen on the rain-soaked field beneath them, 'but back then it was of the greatest strategic importance.'

Paris, 1923

'Are we going to stay here?'

'Yes, Diana. We've escaped.'

'From what?'

'From the big black beast of boredom. I thought I didn't want to give birth again, darling, but I do. I want to give birth to life each and every day. With the moon guiding my tides, and his arm pointing true to the sun, we can make our own world. Sunrise and moon-tide, each of us holding today taut as a rope between us.'

Diana stared at her mother as she drank. She grimaced. There was something wrong with this milk.

'Look out that window, Diana.'

She put down her glass and stood up, heaved uselessly at the solid frame. 'I can't open it.'

'It doesn't matter, look through it.'

'It's stuck closed.'

'Never mind, Diana, what do you see *beyond* it?'

'A pigeon on a roof.'

'Behind that.'

'The Eiffel Tower.'

'Well, I can see the cosmos spread above us like a great starred blanket, and we're lying beneath it in a tangle of happy bodies.'

'When will we go back to Boston?'

'Diana.' Her mother turned to look at her, and her eyes were darker than ever. She had been biting her lips and they were bruised dark. 'There's no going back. And furthermore, we are each our own home now, as marvellous as a castle or as mean as a shed.'

'Perhaps I can be a kennel like the one we had at home?'

'It's forward now, darling. No more looking back.'

'But Father still lives in Boston.'

'Nobody is living in Boston. They just settle, like fog. Obedient clouds that stay in their cages, forgetting the bars can do nothing to keep them in.'

'Why are the clouds in cages?'

'Because Bostonian clouds have very sharp teeth. Now snuggle into your bed, it's time for your dreams to come true.'

'Will you be going out?'

'For a little while. When you wake up in the morning, I'll be there. Worry not, everything is going to be glorious.'

Roccasinibalda, 1970

In an arched portico, Caresse showed the men where they could sit and then arranged herself in a chair where, unbeknownst to her, her daughter had knelt between the young man's legs the night before. The silk was becoming rather frayed. *How beautiful decay can be*, she thought, looking through the large stone archways covered in a mosaic of lichens, to where the upright pines could be seen, dark against the scrub-covered hills that played across the horizon.

'Now, Mrs Crosby, I'm going to be speaking to the camera, here.' She turned back and the man with the Hermès scarf knotted neatly about his throat (Martin, was it?) indicated behind him. She nodded, eyeing the cameraman who was waiting patiently. He looked just like Canada Lee, Caresse noted. A Negro boxer from the Bronx, he'd been one of the gentlest men she'd ever known. (No, she wouldn't share that anecdote. She knew enough about men like Martin to know you could trust them about as far as you could . . .)

'All right then, Mrs Crosby, let's begin.' Martin waved his

pen. 'And three, two ...' He twirled a finger in the air and began, his voice seeming to melt into the shared space between the two of them.

'Mrs Crosby, your feelings for the arts and the role you played in shaping the work of Joyce, Hemingway, Picasso, Fitzgerald, Dalí and others is well known. As we sit here in the remarkable environment of the fortress of Roccasinibalda, do tell our viewers about how you came to turn this place into a fortification for the arts. For many are convinced that the most peculiar, and in many ways envied society, is living here in these walls where art and literature are the essence of everything.'

'Well,' Caresse rested her arms on either side of the chair, 'I found this castle in 1950 after it came to my attention through an artist friend who'd shown at the gallery of modern art that I started in Washington. I had begun my campaign for peace by that time and this friend told me that his mother had been born in a little town in the foothills of the Abruzzi and that in this town had been built the most amazing castle, like something from a Grimms' fairy tale. He said to me, "Caresse, you must go and see the place because it's just the thing for you to start your Città della Pace." He thought that artists would love to live in a place like this.' (*No shit*, thought the cameraman. But there was something about this old lady that stopped him mocking. Something pure.) 'So when I came to Italy I came to visit and arrived at that hill there,' she glanced behind her, more sky than land, and thought it was absolutely beautiful. It was towards sunset and the castle was ablaze with light. 'I love to say yes and so my answer to the castle was yes.'

45

Her hooded eyes looked directly at the two men and she smiled as someone does who is used to giving in to pleasure. 'After I bought it, I lived here alone for over a year and was happier than I ever had been anywhere. Alone at night, I could wander through the echoing halls, circle the deserted battlements and stand in the bare and brilliant solitude of the courtyard . . .'

She was silent for a moment as she remembered drifting in her silk dressing gown followed by her own tapping echo. Lazily undoing the wide ribbon at the front so that the cool night air moved through the mere idea of her nightdress, making her shiver. She was like a flag herself then, white silk rippling in the dark, witnessed only by the humped shapes of furniture lying in wait in the shuttered rooms. She smiled. 'That solitude was important and the fruit of it was my plan that the best of the spiritual life of the world would meet yearly here, preaching freedom of spirit and soul and standing above narrow-mindedness and dogmatic thought. I found this ancient fortress and I started again.' She looked at the men. 'Who knows where this will lead . . .'

'So.' Martin leaned forward. 'Born into the upper echelons of Boston society, when did you first find yourself saying "yes" to life?'

'Well, I'd always had a feeling for freedom and enjoyed doing what others were afraid to do, but the big moment, the symbolic moment, if you will, came when I invented the brassiere. That was the perfect enactment of breaking out of that life, which had been fairly strict and restrictive. I'd wanted to wear a low-cut dress to a dance and didn't like how it looked with my corset, so had my maid quickly sew two handkerchiefs together and attach some ribbons. That was all there was to it. Of course, all my friends were dying to see how it worked and begged me to make them one too, and soon I had a little business going. As it happens, I sold the patent for a hundred dollars to a very nice gentleman at Warner Brothers and thought myself the cleverest little thing. I realise now how meagre my first portion of profit was (they went on to make over fifteen million dollars with that patent), but there you go. I never was motivated by money and never have been. It's the creative spirit that interests me, and that has never been dimmed or diminished in any way. If anything, it gets stronger with time . . .'

'And you are well known for your own creative spirit. I believe I'm right in thinking that you caused something of a scandal in puritanical New England society when you left your husband and small child before setting off for Paris . . .'

'I did not leave my child.' Her eyes locked onto his.

'Oh. I'm sorry, it says here . . .' Martin glanced down at his notes.

'I did not leave my child.'

Martin scratched a line through something and then looked up, smiling. 'I'm very glad we've set the record straight on that. Do please tell us about Paris.'

'Well,' she moved on, 'really those early years are a blur, but it seemed that it was where life was being kissed till it hurt and there was nowhere else we wanted to go. Always yes and never no was our answer to the twenties and it was from our first tiny apartment on the Île Saint-Louis that I'd paddle my husband to work wearing a swimsuit in our bright-red canoe, flowing with the current past the Île de la Cité, down by the

Conciergerie, then the Louvre and under the Pont Royal as far as the Place de la Concorde; then pulling upstream all the way back – marvellous for the breasts, you know.' Caresse smiled, remembering the shouting of the drunks, the jeers of the workmen and the shocked faces of the grey crowds streaming to work over the bridges. The sudden darkness as she went beneath them, and then the brilliant sun in her eyes, arms pulling hard against the flow of filthy water.

'I was happy as a clam there and loved to go marketing in the back streets of that small island, bringing delectable meals home to our tiny apartment on the Quai d'Orléans, whose windows were quite choked with wisteria.' She laughed. 'Eventually, however, we needed to find somewhere with more space, a place in which we could expand our minds a little more liberally. And it was thanks to Cousin Walter that we found our first home.'

'Do you mean Walter Berry, man of letters?'

'Yes, I do. Cousin Walter was slim as straw and as *sec*; he could have exhibited as a sculpture by Lipchitz. A wonderful correspondent, of course, and a great friend of Proust. Their letters were one of the first works we printed, in fact. He was also Edith's lover, though really that word feels a little voluptuous as a description.' (*Wharton*, Martin jotted in his notebook.) 'He was responsible for passing on the extraordinary library we inherited after his death. Thousands of books, precious editions that almost made one want to give up parties for good and simply spend your nights in bed devouring what was inside all that skin. It was Cousin Walter who introduced us to the owner of 19 Rue de Lille (a most extraordinary Russian princess who kept a bear in her garden and quite refused to get out of bed) and really, that is where it all began . . .'

'And it was from this address that you and many of your fellow artists and writers wrote *The Revolution of the Word*. Would you mind if I quoted it here?'

'Please.'

'Tired of the "hegemony of the banal word, monotonous syntax, naturalism, the tyranny of time", you proclaimed instead: "Imagination unconfined, metamorphosis of reality . . ."'

'Talking a lot of balls?' Diana suggested, walking in, still damp from her swim.

'We're in the middle of recording my interview.' Caresse looked her over coolly. 'Gentlemen, my daughter Diana.'

Diana extended a hand to both men and liking what she saw in their reflection, sat down. 'Perhaps I'll listen in.'

'Yes, but you mustn't interrupt. Now, Martin, where were we?'

'". . . Hallucination of the word. The writer expresses, he does not communicate. The plain reader be damned!"'

'Hear, hear,' Diana said, leaning forward to pluck a grape from the low table between them.

'I never did like that part about being damned.' Caresse frowned. 'You know, we started the Black Sun Press because we wanted to get our own work in print, we wanted to *write*. Our editions were all very beautiful, with great care taken in the lining, colour and type. They were new thoughts in a classic binding, like an angry boy in his grandfather's jacket. Wonderful objects that transcended anything "modern".'

'Didn't Wilde say that nothing ages so fast as the modern?' Diana said.

'Well, quite. That hits the nail right on its behind.' Caresse nodded and Diana felt a little kick of pride that gave birth to a pleased smile, which she hid by bending down to adjust her ankle tie.

'And so Mary Peabody metamorphosed through the caritas of caring and the innocence of yes into Caresse Crosby, poetess and publisher.' Martin's honeyed voice flowed into the microphone and Caresse's smile became rather fixed, refusing to look at Diana.

'We found our little printer on the Rue Cardinale soon after we'd arrived,' she broke in. 'And really, Mr Lescaret was the most wonderful thing in getting the project of the Black Sun Press off the ground. His typesetting was absolutely meticulous and he set to the projects with real gusto. It was the craziest operation, crammed with papers, funeral notices, pamphlets; that sort of thing. My daughter used to be frightened of coming there for fear of the press itself squatting in the corner like a great spider.'

Diana looked at her mother in surprise. She didn't remember that.

'We published not only our own work, wonderful volumes,' Caresse went on, 'but many other writers and artists.' Martin sat forward with his microphone and the cameraman leaned a little closer.

'T. E. Lawrence, D. H. Lawrence, Wilde, Proust. The matching of the artist to the writer was most important: Polia Chentoff, Max Ernst, Alastair – Alastair was the most extraordinary character, straight out of a work by Poe – T. S. Eliot, Hemingway, Fitzgerald ...'

'You published some of Mr Hemingway's earliest works, is that right?'

Diana had always liked that direct handsome man. Knew a good fight when he saw one too.

'I must make it clear that I did not, as some have said, invent Hemingway,' Caresse said. 'He was a friend. We met at a circus and both took a liking to the owner, a lion tamer who wore the most beautiful evening dress to perform with his beasts. But yes, I did publish him and others too, Hart Crane and Joyce . . .'

'Tell us about Hart Crane. I believe he came to stay with you while he finished writing *The Bridge*.'

'Well, Hart was—'

'A menace,' interrupted Diana. 'Always roaring from his turret for more booze and going off to the docks to bugger more sailors. He managed thirty in a weekend once.' The cameraman leaned out from behind his equipment with raised eyebrows. 'Exactly.' Diana nodded at him. 'I never forgave him after he brought a chimney sweep he'd found back to my nursery and . . .'

'Yes, that was rather a mess,' Caresse broke in. 'I'd just had the room repapered in a terribly pretty rose print. Hart *could* be something of a menace when he drank,' she conceded. 'Though I don't think we should cast too many stones in that direction.' She glanced at her daughter. 'Besides, the artist needs fuel, and the more incendiary the better.'

Diana crossed her arms and pulled her mouth to one side, picturing the dirty smudges left on her broderie anglaise pillow.

'Hart would get caught, quite caught in love affairs that caused him an awful lot of pain. His work caused him a lot of pain too. He couldn't write without the shadows getting

51

all stirred up. And of course he struggled with the idea of getting older, losing his vigour, that sort of thing. That fog-horn voice crying out against the threat of greyness ... He couldn't take it, in the end. So many ... couldn't.' Caresse's voice drifted to a stop.

'My old nanny used to say that if those writers left any more out of those books there'd be nothing left to read at all. According to her – No Bad Thing. Then they could all go and get on with something useful,' Diana said drily, lighting a cigarette.

'You can leave that illiterate crook out of it. Mette was hardly an aerial for receiving the message of the modernists.'

'Though she did always say that too much thinking would be the death of—'

'Oh, do leave her out of it,' Caresse interrupted Diana sharply. 'Diana's nanny was a reprobate,' she explained to a puzzled-looking Martin. 'It was the deal that, along with looking after the child, she would also place and collect my husband's bets on the races. Her salary was supplemented by 5 per cent of our winnings, but she also took a 5 per cent deduction of any losses; that was the agreement they came to, anyhow. But it emerged that poor Diana was left to spend half her childhood in a freak show in the Marais while the nanny listened to the track results coming in at a bar round the corner.'

Diana closed her eyes against the memory of the hot tent that smelled of mowed grass and sweat and the strange shapes of the 'exhibits'. She tried to arrange the thought into a sentence quick enough to throw back out to the room, but her mother's voice was already running on ...

'Diana began to look quite ill, like the child of a fishwife. Quiet as a mouse, weren't you, darling? No, not a mouse, what was your name? Rat.' She pounced on it, delighted. 'That was it. The Wretched Rat. Awful name really, and not a bit true.' She smiled at Diana and then turned back to Martin. 'But where was I?' Caresse's voice flowed on like a tide. 'Yes, Hart. His dedication was messy, brutal; unlike Joyce, who was terribly precise . . .'

'Yes, do tell us more about Joyce. It's so rare to hear these anecdotes.'

'Well, Joyce was an elegant figure, a patch on one eye and walking with a cane. Very straight, very angular. He lived near the Boulevard des Invalides. His home was tidy but somewhat unimaginative with an upright piano and a gold-fish bowl. But his family life was very touching and he spoke Italian with his children. He was just a great big brain eating everything up. He wanted to know how it all came to *be* . . . He used to come to the house to collect proof, though the first time he came to visit us at home he only got as far as our front door because, on hearing Narcisse's bark from within, he walked right home again. He was very afraid of small animals for his eyes were so bad. The next time he came, we hid the dog in the bathroom, so that he could read us part of his Work in Progress. "Now," he would say, in a soft Irish key, "I wonder if you understand why I made *that* change."

'"No, why?" we chorused, and there ensued one of the most intricate and erudite explanations that I've ever heard, though unfortunately I hardly understood a word, his references were so esoteric. My husband fared a bit better, but afterwards we regretted that we did not keep a Dictaphone behind the lamp so that later we could have studied all that had escaped us. That evening he stayed three hours – he didn't want a drink – and by eight he hadn't gotten through with a page and a half. It was illuminating. We agreed to publish only the first bits that were ready for the press and when he left we guided him down the stone stairs and then I mixed us some very dry martinis to restore us to a more familiar sanity.'

'And Henry Miller? I'm right in saying you were among the first to publish him?'

'Well, he came to me when he was very broke and living in Paris and needing to be published. He showed me *Tropic of Cancer* and I was horrified. I wouldn't publish that book then and I wouldn't publish it now either. I still think he's written things that are more valuable and more to my taste and belief.'

'Like the porn you and he wrote for that dirty old Texan?' Diana asked. Martin and Caresse looked at Diana in surprise.

'That was an experiment in erotica, Diana, more in the line of fun,' she said. 'Is there anyone else you'd care to cover, Martin? I'm beginning to feel a little tired.'

'Yes, what about Mr Lawrence?'

'Ah, Lawrence.' Caresse sat back. 'Well, Lawrence was unusual. He loved to explore, was interested in everybody, in everybody's reaction – a great observer, as you know, of human nature, particularly love. He got mad with his wife Frieda one night and smashed a jazz record – I think it was "The Empty Bed Blues" – right over her head because she kept playing it and playing it and he didn't like that at all.

'One day Lawrence said, "There is a book but no English publisher will handle it, I guess it's too hot for them." So of course we clamoured to know what it was and that evening he read to us around the fire from *The Escaped Cock*, about the wanderings of Jesus after his resurrection and how he met and fell in love with a priestess of Isis in a little temple off the coast of Phoenicia. Well, we were terribly excited by it and we offered to bring the book out through the press, though as we did so all the candles burned low and guttered and went out and it really felt like some kind of conspiracy.'

Caresse was silent for a moment.

'I remember Lawrence being terribly shocked by Harry giving a dissertation in favour of *la morsure* during love-making,' Diana put in. 'I'll never forget the look on his face.'

'He had a wonderful face,' Caresse said firmly. 'Those wide-set eyes that gave his rather grave look an innocent quality. Between his hat and beard they were the only part you could ever see ...'

'Sorry to interrupt, but can we just clarify that Harry is ...?'

Caresse opened her mouth to speak, but as she did so Diana stepped in.

'Harry was Harry Crosby.'

'Your second husband?' Martin looked to Caresse for confirmation.

'My mother and he were married for a time, yes,' Diana again cut in.

'Lawrence was a wonderful conversationalist, challenging and earthy.' Caresse spoke slowly, as though pushing something heavy before her. 'Quiet and kind. His talk was like the earth, carried inside him. He was of the earth somehow, with that mushroom mind and those soiled fingers ... Words flowed from him in a stream, muddy with complex thoughts and ideas ... We promised to pay him in gold coins for the first piece he wrote for us, real pieces of the sun, much better than that bland paper stuff. In fact, in Peru they believe that an important relationship exists between the substance of gold and that of the sun, and that in the nuggets of gold they dislodge from the mountainside one can see the sun's tears. A wonderful image.'

Martin nodded in agreement, glancing between mother and daughter.

'Of course, Lawrence didn't think for a minute that we were serious about the payment, but we had a friend smuggle twenty-dollar gold pieces from Boston to Paris in the tips of his riding boots, which we then put in a hollowed-out prayer book that had once belonged to the Queen of Naples. At the Gare de l'Est we took a chance on a handsome man we liked the look of who was travelling down to Florence on the Rome Express. "Is it a bomb?" he asked. "No," we cried, as the train began to move. "It's gold for a poet." So ... we got him his bag of sun,' she finished with a slow smile. Nodding at the nurse waiting discreetly by the door, Caresse slowly got to her feet. 'Now, gentlemen, I'm needed elsewhere, but please enjoy all there is. Ask Roberto for anything you need. We will continue later.'

Paris, 1923

'And so it's decided – I'm changing my name.'

Diana carried on drinking until she got down to the heavy dregs.

'Diana, did you hear me?'

Diana put the empty cup down, gasping, black cocoa round her mouth.

Her mother's hands stroked the hammered gold necklace that circled the dog's slender throat.

'Do you want to know what it is?'

Diana shook her head, scowling at the animal, who turned his head away as if in disgust.

'Are you punishing me for yesterday?'

Diana nodded.

'You mustn't build such a pyre out of these moments, Diana. This isn't easy for any of us.'

'He scolded me in front of your friends.'

'Well . . . Why?' her mother said impatiently.

'Because I was singing too loudly.'

'I'm sure he didn't mean it.'

'He means everything. He's not like you.'

'Well, that's not very nice of you, Diana.' She was silent. 'Now do you want to know my new name or not?'

'Why are you changing it?' Diana asked.

Her mother smiled and it was like the sun coming out. 'Because Mary sounds as though I have cobwebs in my drawers.'

Diana glanced around to see if anyone in the heaving café had heard.

'I'm changing my name to ... Caresse.'

Caresse. Diana held the name up next to her mother. It was as soft as the fur that had just slipped off the back of her chair onto the floor. A waiter scurried over to pick it up.

'Will I have to call you that?'

'Yes, why not.' She smiled brilliantly up at the waiter as he smoothed the coat over the back of her chair. 'But this has nothing to do with you, Diana, it's for me. I need a new name so that I can finally shake off all that Boston dust.'

Diana had to admit that she liked it. It was a beautiful name.

'It's an affirmation, isn't it? An invitation almost. It's a *welcome*. Your Boston aunts wrote me and said it was like undressing in public. I wrote back and told them that, if I did, what of it?' Her mother took her hand in hers and Diana looked at it caught between the grey suede gloves. 'Names are important, Diana; they tell us who we are. I've been Mary, Mrs Peabody, Mother, and each carries its own weight. I didn't choose any of those names for *myself*, do you see? They all belonged to other people. This is a name that *I'm* choosing, that Harry and I have chosen. It's about freedom, Diana. The freedom to choose.'

Diana looked at her. But Diana was not to jump on the bed, nor run her stick down the banisters, nor press the buzzers, nor sing with Mette … She thought things were much more complicated than her mother was making out. She frowned.

'Do I have to change my name too?'

'No. But you will one day, you mark my words,' her mother laughed.

Alderney, 1993

A thin cry sounded from the garden. From an upstairs window, Elena watched her children playing below. On one side of the garden, Bay was attempting to hide and craning her neck Elena saw the two boys counting beneath the large leaves of the fig tree (the only thing her mother had brought with her from Ibiza). She listened to the faint, steady climb to ten and then they shot out from the tree's cover and ran directly towards where the little girl was still trying to fit herself beneath a low-lying shrub.

Elena recalled the hard polished playroom floor beneath her own head, Leonie's weight pressing on her chest. Why should I? her sister had said, laughing as she pinched her. She bit her lip and pressed her hand to the window.

'Elena.' She heard a raspy voice and turned away from the landing window to stare at her mother's closed bedroom door.

'Elena,' the voice called again from inside. She took a deep breath and, squaring her shoulders, went towards it.

*

Opening his arms, her father took Bay in, laughing softly. 'You shouldn't play those rough games if you don't want to get hurt, we've told you that.' She stood between his knees as he untied the rope. Keeping her between his legs, James took a walnut from a bowl and with a special movement, cracked it in his hand. Bay watched, mesmerised, as he knew she would. Shaking the debris into a small pile on the table, he held out the brained nugget towards her.

'Eat.' He smiled.

She popped it into her mouth and chewed the oily nut. She disliked the taste but wanted her father to repeat the performance.

'Another,' she said.

'No,' he laughed, pulling the book he had been reading back towards him. 'One's enough.'

'Where's Mummy?' she asked, holding her rope-reddened wrists out towards him.

'Upstairs. She's with your grandmother.'

Bay looked up at the ceiling. Her grandmother was awake. She listened to see if she could hear anything, and could just make out the murmur of women's voices.

She looked mournfully at her father, but he continued to read, so Bay went to the foot of the stairs and seated herself to wait.

Rue de Lille, Paris, 1923

'What are you doing out on the stairs?'

'I'm taking my shoes off so I don't disturb you,' Diana said quietly, not looking in his eyes.

He stood back and smiled. 'You don't disturb me.'

'Mother said I did.'

He knelt down and with sure hands took over the unbuckling of her shoe. Diana leaned back, staring at the blond head bowed before her.

'You look like a wretched rat I once saw in a sodden trench.' He looked up and smiled; Diana stared into his bright blue eyes. 'It was a lovely little rat.'

Diana felt herself smile shyly in return.

'I had to kill it with a baseball bat.'

'Why?' Diana whispered.

'Couldn't sleep with it scampering about all night.' He pulled her second foot free. 'Let's hear you now.'

Diana skipped silently up and down the steps in her socks. 'Wonderful.'

Roccasinibalda, 1970

Diana lay on the tiled floor of her large room and bathed her naked body in the sun, a frown creasing the recently tightened skin of her forehead. After the initial hell, the sensation was not unpleasant, made one feel rather *alert*. Her hands were slowly turning the pages of the manuscript her mother had had Roberto bring to her room last night and she shifted her body so that she sat full in the hard glare and flicked another typed page.

The title was stamped across the top in bold letters. *Shadows of the Sun*. She frowned at it. She hadn't *asked* for these edited copies of uniform type. She wanted the originals.

But her mother was being evasive, as usual, and something told Diana that the little sun-stamped notebooks she was after, almost black with the scratch of his writing, had gone with all the rest. She took a drink and turned back to the manuscript, looking for the page she'd been on, her eyes scanning for a particular word . . .

Children have a very picturesque *façon-de-parler* – Rat says 'someotherbody' and 'What part of us goes to heaven? Is it our thinks?'

She read and re-read the sentence, trying to remember saying the words. But she couldn't. Her eyes moved quickly over the following pages, searching.

Sitting up in bed having dinner (C and I in our matching Egyptian robes) when some sinkstone Boston cousins appeared and I was bored by them and C was bored by them and the Rat said *Nausea* and then one of Schiap's mannequins arrived and talked about her breasts (good but C's still unrivalled).

Diana laughed. Had she said that? A rather excellent word, how clever she must have been. She turned back even further and examined the date: 1924. Egypt. Bokhara . . . (She raised her eyebrows in surprise, her mother had left him in.) Yes, the place where they found his sun ring and bought her back that turtle, sadly eaten the very next day by Narcisse.

Bokhara the Temple-Boy and I fall in love with him (to hell with women).

Diana narrowed her eyes. That boy. She looked up at the ceiling and tried to remember the maxim Harry had taught her when he'd returned from that trip. 'A woman for necessity,' she murmured, 'a boy for pleasure, and a goat for delight.' She laughed, remembering her mother's expression as she came into the room and heard the phrase. 'No, don't get up,' she'd said, looking at them both coolly over the pelt of silver fox wrapped round her throat. 'I'm going out again.' Diana turned back to the manuscript with raised eyebrows.

We were photographed sitting together on the steps of the temple and afterwards I explored the enormous substruction called Solomon's Stables a harmony of arches with sunlight pouring through then up and along the ramparts and across a garden with three beggars like the picture by Breughel following us until we arrived at the Pool of Bethesda into which I threw a coin instead of giving it to the beggars. This took strength but a prayer is more important than an act of charity and in the afternoon to Bethlehem ('has existed without change for thousands of years' – like the minds of the majority of Bostonians) and the place was swarming with automobiles and Cook's Tourists like so many maggots but these were forgotten among the stone-cold Coptic singing of the Greeks and Russians. When we got back to Jerusalem, the British Regiment Band was playing or rather trying to play (how the hell can the British with their temperament expect to play jazz?). C and I drank brandy in the Sun from my silver flask and we dropped walnuts on the passers-by below (I concentrating on Cook's Tourists) and at sunset I wandered off through queer streets and had my hair cut by a young Jew in a dark niche under an arch . . .

She turned back further . . . Seville, 1924:

65

On our way south we stopped and saw a cockfight, known here as a *pelea de gallos*. A good, rough place with a rabble peering in through a slit in the wall and *se prohíbe orinar* scrawled in black letters and I invited my cab driver to come inside with me.

Inside there was a balcony that looked down on a small ring and they weighed the birds on large scales suspended from the ceiling. A gong and the cocks were set down and the bookmakers shouted odds and there were tense faces and all the seriousness of a bullfight. There were no other women. For perhaps a minute the combatants eyed each other, wings widespread, bodies elongated, and their heads not much more than an inch apart and one could see that they had gone through a long training for the momentous occasion. One white the other black, and it was not difficult to wager a peseta with my cab driver and another with a morose individual who had been a stoker on a tramp steamer. Chose black. And there was a *peck peck peck a peck a peck a peck* like the tapping of a woodpecker ever searching for throat and eye. Courage and speed (like my theory of attack – surprise, rapidity, consistency) and no more crowing at the sun, no more covering some squawking hen but attacking *peck a peck peck* and pinching of throat and coxcomb *peck peck* and a man garbed in black who seemed to have high authority and whose duty lay in regarding the tall sand-glass fastened to the iron rail of the ring and the fight was to last twenty minutes (about the time of a bullfight) and when one thinks of prizefighters and their intermissions every two or three minutes, one wonders at the endurance and pluck of these birds who go at it from the beginning hammer and tongs *peck a peck peck*.

But as the fight neared the finish it became sad and they began to tire and instead of darting at each other they waddled like ducks to the charge and then the cruelty of the sport revealed itself with the almost blindness of the birds, strutting past each other, pecking at space, searching with bloody unseeing eyes. Finally black (a white feather stuck in his eye) sought the other out, and the sand in the hourglass was almost out and white was groggy and sought shelter under black's wing, until black, his mouth full of white feathers, attacked throat and head, coxcomb and neck until white finally sank to the mat.

Seville rather bleak apart from that.

Good Lord! She remembered reading a letter from him about that. She'd hadn't slept for weeks.

Her hand turned a few more pages. Étretat, 1924. Their first holiday 'en famille'. Another of her mother's attempts to remould a family from clay already kilned.

She held a hand up to the window to shade her face, and recalled the sun glowing red through the back of the chauffeur's ears as he drove the Daimler up out of Paris towards the Normandy coast. Her mother's voice talking talking always talking and Harry silent, watching the fields with eyes half-closed against the heavy evening light, before suddenly sitting forward and asking the chauffeur about the prizefight he'd won the night before. The little house – an old machine-gun escarpment that her mother said hardly had enough room for two people, let alone three – squatting on a hill overlooking the chalk cliffs and far below the pebbled beach that dug into your back and the grey endless crash of the waves and a naked body running into the sea, a white parasol on the beach.

Nubile. Diana raised her eyebrows again as she shifted onto her side; her mother had also left that one *in*.

Simone, the rather simple daughter of a local farmer (she was meant to teach Diana how to swim) who had breasts too heavy for her age, and who smoked cigarettes on the beach, letting small stones fall from inside her closed fist onto her nipple so that it hardened as Diana watched, fascinated.

And the little bed made up for Diana in the dark outhouse so that Harry didn't feel *crowded*, even though the sea wind rattled the shutters right into Diana's bones. (What a lucky little girl! Most six-year-olds don't get to have their own house!) Diana took a sip of her drink and laughed, a hollow sound, as she pictured herself lying in the dark, listening to the moaning of the wind and the moaning of her mother, glumly stroking her own flat chest, a little comforted by the soft hiss of the gas heater a friend of her mother's had insisted she install to keep the poor child from freezing half to death. And then there was Harry – the morning sun himself – laughing by the open door of that shed holding a big glass of pale yellow milk, telling her that this wonderful girl child whom he had named Nubile thought Rimbaud was a scientist. And then her mother and Harry had gone off somewhere, leaving Diana standing in the cold sea with the chauffeur's freckled arms tight round her middle, his neck red, the light dancing on the water like her mother's evening laughter.

'Now kick, Diana,' he'd told her in his funny accent. 'Kick and use your arms. Don't be scared, the water's your friend.'

'Liar!' she'd shouted, laughing, as the unfriendly water licked her chest, far too cold so that she could only cling and shiver as the strong arms swayed her left and right, left and right, letting her swim without having to swim.

'Have faith, believe you can do it. The water will help you, if you let it. The water is your friend.' And his strong arms lifted her up and sped her along until she was moving through the water, kicking her legs again and again and again. Diana felt a rush of warmth towards that sweet midget of a man, wondering briefly what had become of him.

She flicked back further, right back to the beginning. Paris, 1923. And so it began ...

A mess moving into Rue de Lille.

Crates, trunks, impedimenta of every description (including the child).

There had been the large dark hallway with a stone staircase going up and up into blackness, every step a scuffed echo. An open door leading into the bare first-floor rooms that were full of new servants smoking and talking and unpacking their meagre things into thin chests (the thankful comfort of Mette's fat arms) and a nursery that was like a packing box: bare and brown and all the wrong size.

But upstairs ... oh upstairs!

It was like being transported into a dream. A marble bathtub big enough to float in without touching the sides, a hole in the wall surrounded by a jade slit for peeping, a bed that was pulled up through the window by ropes, its frightening headboard leaning against the wall covered in carved people doing cruel things (they agreed eventually and it was ceremoniously drowned in the Seine), and room enough for lots of people. (Diana was allowed to jump up and down on it once a week while Hélène changed the sheets, her face coming and going in the large mirror on the wall.) Soft grey carpets and rose-papered walls, Harry rushing past the workmen, getting it all done quicker, better, faster; on his hands and knees hammering tacks into carpets *rat-a-tat-tat*, raking leaves in the garden, lighting fires in all the grates and unloading the books into the bookshelves. Her mother whirling through the rooms, placing a vast orchid on this table, instructing the raising of a heavy gold chandelier in that hallway, having the door to the drawing room covered with a thick grey silk curtain that moved as though there were someone hiding behind it . . . and down at the end of the hall the staircase to his study, she behind him, watching as the picture of the dead soldier was nailed to the door.

'We who have known war must never forget war.'

'We must never forget war,' her mother had repeated, holding him tight, her cheek pressed to his back.

And Diana, eyes closed in prayer, sitting alone at the little desk in her nursery eating biscuits and trying to drink her watery milk. 'We must *never* forget war.'

And then more men came with tools and fed wires into holes that disappeared into the walls, and came back out on the floor below. One buzz for the maids. Two for the cook. Three for the chauffeur. Four for Diana.

God how she'd longed for that buzz. She lifted her chin defiantly and drank.

And then all the animals appeared: two love birds, Tristan and Isolde; two white kittens, Sagesse and Promesse; two terrapins, Cloaca and Sloth; and four goldfish – Sunwarm, Sunnygolden, Sunbeam and Sunbow.

But one by one the animals had to go until only the goldfish remained swimming round and round and round, no company at all; and the days slowed to her and Mette and the cook Louise and the maid Hélène (who slept in a bed together and made soft sounds all night) locked in domestic boredom. Auguste the chauffeur and his fights. Otherwise ... silence in the empty nursery as she listened to the footsteps that ran day and night up and down and up and down.

But sometimes ... sometimes ... those four buzzes and then piling into the car and the mad joy of running Narcisse and Clytoris in the Bois, screaming, lungs empty, being timed to run there and back, there and back, there and ... where did they go? And the finding of a great iron gate and inside a forgotten cemetery enclosed by blank trees. The muttering of the aged keeper in her black dress as she pointed quiveringly to forgotten names on forgotten stones thick with moss, limping through the overgrown grass, her sleeves becoming snagged on brambles. The air was cold and dank, a red-gold winter sun lowering itself to sleep, and they walked in silence among the dark lines of trees, Harry and her mother, hand in hand; Diana behind, kicking leaves with a vengeance.

Then beneath a broken wall Harry stopped and stared at something only he could see.

'I could die here.'

Her mother wound herself closer to him, staring up at his profile. 'If you die, I die,' she said, as Diana's blood, hot from running, cooled into something as thick and dreadful as the contents of the pot Louise had been stirring for the *boudin noir* they were going to eat for dinner that evening . . .

Those dinners.

The pink evenings darkening to a bruise as the endless mob moved up and down the stairs, walking all over one another, up the walls and through the roof. Poets and painters and pederasts and lesbians and divorcees and Christ knows who, all sitting in the garden on great piles of cushions that were always soaked in the morning, drinking champagne from bottles bigger than babies and, much more important, talking for hours, devouring the silence. Then the exodus as they climbed into cars to find more, more of everything, their laughter tearing the darkness into shreds to be swept up by the maids.

But there was always someone who'd gone to the john.

Been left behind.

Forgotten something.

The dreaded, awaited knock on her nursery door.

There was a sharp knock on the door and Diana opened her eyes wide. She glanced towards it, debating quickly whether to pull a sheet over herself. But with a shake of her head she pulled her shoulders back, and called out, 'Yes?'

Paris, 1924

'Where's the child?'

'Don't worry about *that*. Get back in the car, my love, let's drive all night. I could do with a big drink of dark air. With the bear on our knees we'll be warm.'

'No, I need to return home.'

Caresse looked at him searchingly.

'Well, I need a drink!' someone else shouted.

'Caresse, are you coming?' a man asked, his hand extended.

'Let Tourbin look after you, Caresse.' Harry smiled. 'He's terribly capable.'

'Mama?' Diana leaned forward on her bed, hearing quick steps on the stairs.

The steps stopped outside her room.

The door opened.

'Your mama's gone to Deauville with a count.'

Diana looked at him and hung her head.

'Don't be down. Your face looks like a friendly little moon

when it's up. Yes, like that. Now, let's go. I want to go and see a tragic lady, but would like some company for the drive.'

'Shall I bring my dressing gown?'

'No time.'

'Shall I bring my slippers?'

'They're only good for one thing.' He held open the door. 'Come.'

Along the gutters two rivers of piss were lit lurid green by the lights of the Marais as the huge black car crawled down the street. People moved out of its way, and on the open-topped back seat, miles away from the back of the chauffeur's head, they lay covered by the dark weight of the bearskin rug.

'Now sit up, Rat,' he told her, pulling her onto his lap. 'These people are your subjects.' He handed her a soft bag. 'And you are Selket, daughter of Ra.' Diana looked out at the smeared faces with a regal stare. 'Now throw them their pieces of sun!' he ordered, and she began to pull out the heavy pieces of gold and throw them one by one out of the car, like feeding the ducks in the park with Mette. Faces turned, leered, cursed, but as people saw what was happening a thick crowd gathered, running and yelling as Diana, frightened, threw the pieces faster at the grabbing hands.

'Look how they want you, little one. Look how they love you!' he shouted, and as the car picked up speed he grabbed the empty bag and tossed it into the crowd, throwing back his head, laughing. Turning in her seat, she watched the crowd becoming smaller and smaller while the car accelerated into the night.

Alderney, 1993

'So.'

'So.'

'You made it.'

'Yes.' Elena nodded, trying not to stare at her mother's face beneath the short sandy wig. She'd had even more work done, and it was hard not to search the sinking contours for evidence. 'We made it.'

'And you're all here?' Diana asked.

'All here. And one still underground.' Elena indicated her stomach.

'An invasion.' Diana sank back on the pillows.

'A holiday.'

Diana was silent, and Elena could tell her mother was waiting for her to say it.

'You look well,' she finally said.

'Well,' her mother said with distaste, as though holding the dead word up by its tail. 'Well, *you* look exhausted.'

'I am,' Elena said simply, forcing herself not to turn towards the mirror for confirmation. She was unable to master the movement of her neck, however, but, turning, saw that a scarf had been clumsily hung over the mirror of the dressing table. 'I can't get my head quiet. It's like trying to sleep in a zoo.'

'Ah yes.' Diana smiled. Insomnia was one of her pet subjects. 'You should take some of these.' She picked up her pills and gave them a happy rattle. 'Work wonders with some Amontillado.'

'You and your pills. They'll be the death of you.'

'Correction, Elena: *life* will be the death of me.'

'It took me months to wean myself off them.'

'Don't ever stop, that's my motto.'

Elena stood up to go. 'I need to help James unpack the children's things.'

'Is he paying penance?' Diana smiled knowingly.

'What do you mean?' Elena stopped.

'Has the golden boy been spreading his light a little too freely?'

'Not in any way.' Elena spoke with great precision, looking her mother straight in the eye.

'So sure.' Diana shook her head, smiling ruefully. 'I do wonder, darling, when you will cease to be a wilful innocent.'

'I'm flattered you think of me in that way. I feel as though I was born cynical. Now, I'm going to unpack.' She stood and stretched, aware of her mother's gaze on her body. She lowered her arms.

'How long are you staying?'

'A month.'

There was a shout from the garden, shortly followed by the thin wail of a child.

Diana pressed her hands against her temples.

'I'll tell them to keep it down,' Elena said. 'And I've already made the beds up. Besides, the boys want to sleep in the garden, so they won't disturb you too much.'

'No nanny?'

'I've got you, haven't I?' Elena said lightly.

Diana paused for a moment and then laughed, followed by a sharp intake of breath.

'What is it?' Elena frowned in concern.

'Nothing.' Her mother shook her head. 'My conscience, probably.'

Against her will, Elena smiled.

'And now you're bringing me another.' Diana glanced down and Elena held her arms out so that she could see.

'You and James *have* been busy.'

Elena replaced her arms. 'Please . . . don't.'

Her mother laughed. 'You can't do it and not talk about it, Elena. That's called cheating.'

'It's the way you say it,' Elena said quietly.

'I'll say nothing at all then.'

Elena looked at the empty space next to her mother and suddenly longed to lie down and go to sleep. But her mother's sheets had come loose at the corner and piles of books and clothes took up the other half of the bed. A used plate was tucked beneath a blanket and as Elena looked around the room she tried not to grimace at the mess of clothes strewn over chairs and the incongruous size of the silk four-poster dwarfing the space. 'Wouldn't you be more comfortable with a smaller bed?'

'Elena, if you are going to try and get me into some sort of commode I shall stage a violent revolution. I care nothing for this bed. Nor this room. Nor this horrid little island I've been wrecked on.' She stared out the window. 'Even the windows are ghastly.'

'Why don't we open them, at least.' Elena moved towards them.

'I will not have you shifting things about, Elena. Let it all be.' Diana dragged the covers over herself and angled away from the window.

'Just . . . please . . .' Elena gently pulled her mother forward and banked up the pillows behind.

'Ivan Denning is coming for lunch this weekend.'

Elena sat down on the bed and blinked in surprise.

'I didn't realise that was still . . .'

'Of course.' Diana smiled. 'He's sailing from Jersey.'

'I haven't seen you smile like that since you met David.'

The smile faded and Diana looked at her daughter for a long moment. 'Trust you to pierce the ballooning moment.' Elena looked away. 'Apart from being a good friend, Ivan is an excellent lawyer. Though I lay the fact that I'm living in this godforsaken place at his door.'

'Oh, Mum,' Elena said.

'Please don't call me Mum, it's so fucking awful.'

'I can call you Diana again, if you want,' Elena said, her cheeks colouring a delicate red.

'Call me Mummy, if you must.'

Elena shook her head.

'What?' Her mother stared at her, preparing for outrage.

'I'm not calling you Mummy. It's absurd.'

'Why?'

'Because you're not that kind of mother. Anyway, you called your mother Caresse . . .'

'I wasn't allowed to call her anything else!'

'. . . and Leonie and I always called you Diana when we were children.'

'Well, I regret that. I want it to be Mummy now.'

'You're being ridiculous. But I'll go back to calling you Diana if you really want.'

Her mother stared at her. 'Very gutsy, Elena. All that expensive therapy is clearly paying off,' she sighed. 'What with your sister in a convent, and you on the couch – talk about a rock and a hard place.'

Elena stared at her mother as she spoke. Her gaze moved over the familiar face with the hard clarity of morning light. She took in the deep-set eyes so like her own, the skin pulled tight and secured somewhere beneath that dreadful wig. The still-ripe mouth. Elena watched it moving, occasionally glimpsing a flash of her mother's teeth. The sound of her voice began to shape itself around her, and she forced herself to listen to the words.

'. . . I'm all for everyone having a good time. But why that means everything has to become so depressing . . . Spain's appalling now. Everyone staring at motorways from concrete balconies like overripe fruits on plastic chairs.' Sensing she'd lost her audience, Diana slowed to a stop. 'I suppose I might as well surrender to the rest.'

'But you're not unhappy here?' Elena said hesitantly, not entirely sure what they were talking about.

'That comment is so thin I can hardly spread myself an answer.'

'But I thought you liked being on an island again.'

'I loathe it,' Diana said bitterly. 'Two thousand drunks clinging to a rock.'

'Two thousand and one,' Elena said.

Diana threw her head back and laughed. 'Touché, Elena. I'm glad to see you haven't entirely lost your sense of humour.'

Elena leaned down to pick up a book that was lying spreadeagled on the floor, trying to conceal her pleased smile.

Diana turned her body slightly towards her daughter, seeming to relax. It was a movement of friendly invitation and Elena felt a familiar panic rush into the unexpected opening. Her head emptied of all thought, and she frowned as she tried to think of words that wouldn't murder the moment.

'Do you miss it?' she eventually asked.

'Miss what?'

'Spain.'

'I miss nothing,' Diana said with disdain, turning away again.

Elena smoothed her dress over her bump, and was silent.

'You know I can't stand your silences, Elena,' Diana said in a single aggrieved tone.

Elena looked at her mother without speaking.

'I recognise that dress you're wearing. Where's it from?' The voice was sharp, suspicious.

'It was Inés's,' Elena said levelly.

'It's falling to pieces.'

'So are you,' Elena shot back, and her mother smiled.

'My shoulder's been hurting again.' The voice became petulant.

'Have you been doing your exercises?'

'Of course not.'

Elena stood and took a brown glass bottle from the top of a dresser whose surface was strewn with packets of pills and other bottles of medicine. She wiped the dust from the top of it.

'What is that?' Diana peered at the bottle, frowning.

'It's thyme oil. The kind we used to make in Ibiza. I brought it for you last time I came.' Elena slipped her mother's nightdress from her shoulders.

'Lean forward, Mum,' she said quietly.

'It's Mummy.'

Elena poured some oil onto her cold hands and pressed her palms together. She waited a moment and then placed them gently on Diana's bare freckled back, just able to feel, beneath the slackened skin and curve of bone, the movement of her mother's heart.

Rue de Lille, 1924

'What did you do in the war?'

'Where did you learn that polite little phrase?' he asked hoarsely, putting down the cage of pigeons he was carrying.

'I heard someone ask it,' Diana said, eyes wide.

'Don't parrot those people.'

'But what's war like?' she said, trying not to look down as they walked along the edge of the roof.

'A mess. A great bloody mess full of rats big as little girls and mutilated things that were once men.'

'What did you do in it?' She peered over the edge at the street way below.

'I drove screaming ambulances. Tried to pick up some of the broken pieces.'

'Did you almost die?'

'I did die.'

Diana watched him, sunk now on his haunches, undoing the string that kept the cage closed.

'Ready?' he asked, and she nodded. And with a single

movement he opened the door and the birds shook the cage as they flew free of it, disappearing from the rooftop into the grey of the sky.

'Never let a moment slip, Rat.' He turned suddenly to look her in the eye. 'That's the sin. Always act.'

Roccasinibalda, 1970

'Are you ready to continue, Principessa?' Martin asked with a neat smile.

'Yes, I feel wonderful today. When these rooms are flooded with sun like this, one's mood seems to climb out of one's head and be among the angels.'

Martin waited just enough time before asking, 'If it's all right with you, I'd like us to dive straight in where we left off.'

'You'll have to remind me where we were, my mind's been roaming. All of these names lined up together – it feels like some sort of shooting range. All my dear friends in a row, bang bang bang. It's most unnatural.'

Martin laughed. 'Your note this morning suggested that we pick up with Ezra Pound in 1930?'

'Wonderful. Ezra is a very dear friend and my meeting him marked the beginning of a new stage of my life. A gentle expansion that would take me further into the world of art. There was one rather memorable night around the time we met, when I took him to the Boule Blanche where I knew a band of Martinique players would be beating out some hot music. We had a ringside table and Ezra was enthralled by the way they played, less so by the uninspiring dancers. I was in mourning at that time so wasn't entirely in the mood for dancing, but Ezra was desperate to get on the floor and let them know a thing or two. So as we sat and drank he began a sort of tattoo with his feet that grew in complexity until eventually he leapt onto the floor and, seizing a tiny Martiniquaise vendor of cigarettes, started a voodoo prance with packets flying, the girl quite glued against him. Well, as the music grew hotter, Ezra grew hotter, and one by one the uninspired dancers melted from the floor and formed a ring to watch that Anglo-Savage ecstasy – until with a final crash of cymbals the music came to an end, and Ezra opened his eyes, flicked the poor cigarette girl aside and collapsed into the chair beside me so that the whole room seemed to breathe a collective orgasmic sigh.'

'Extraordinary to see such unconstrained freedom in those times,' Martin said earnestly. Caresse gave a bland smile and then, deciding to humour him, nodded.

'Well, that was the thing about the Surrealists. The broken bonds of society had been talked about by the Modernists, living in the shattered aftermath of that war. But there were still lingering constraints, and the need to cut ourselves loose from all that really was a pressing *need*. Revolution of the spirit demands a certain severing action. A willingness to leave behind what has been and give rise to the new. I understand the conservative fear of change, but if people only surrendered a little more and stiffened a little less they would see that everything we accept as normal now was avant-garde once.

People seem to forget that. Max Ernst was wonderful in that way. He understood, and was terribly serious about the need for absolute freedom in order for the creative spirit to bloom. He did a portrait of me once during the time of my gatherings at our country house, Le Moulin, just outside Ermenonville. It was a lovely house, an old water mill – Rousseau died there, you know.' Martin shook his head, and made a note. 'And it was there, week after week, that the Surrealists used to gather around the pool and invent things that hadn't yet been invented, that most importantly weren't *needed* but that we felt should be invented. It was a time that was almost . . . electric with rebellion.'

'Do expand.'

'Le Moulin du Soleil was an extraordinary place set in the middle of a forest filled with deer and wild boar. It was a close friend of mine, Maxime du Tourbin – in fact, he later married my daughter – who introduced us to the mill. It was while walking on his estate that we came across it, then in a state of complete dilapidation. He agreed to rent us the place, and so we wrote him the cheque there and then, on the cuff of my white silk shirt. I think he liked the idea of being in such close proximity to all our goings on and was happy to have the chance to come and slum it and let chaos loose. So it was that we created a home where we could be amongst trees and water, and away from the madness of Paris. The plan only half worked, of course, because as soon as we left Paris, Paris came with us. You've never seen so many cars choking that poor forest road. There were two houses, fourteen rooms, five staircases and an enormous garden that tangled into a forest and a cannon on the roof which we would fire ceremonially for various people's arrivals, and occasionally departures too.' She smiled. 'And my, we had a lot of animals. Five donkeys – wonderful for racing – three dogs, a parrot, a slinky little ferret, a rather unpredictable leopard, and the ten or more guests who would arrive unannounced every Friday. It was such fun. Stretching up the stairs was a long whitewashed wall, under which we set up a number of pots of paint. Everyone who came to visit was made to sign and soon it was a living testament to that time ... And then the many people, that wealth of people – Dalí, Ernst ...' Caresse continued, swaying slightly left and right with the rhythm of the names '... Breton, Cocteau, Cartier-Bresson (I taught him how to use a camera, you know) ... I love to entertain, and there I was Queen Mistress of my own small realm.'

'And now you're Queen Mistress of a new realm: Roccasinibalda.' Martin smiled. The cameraman winced.

'Roccasinibalda. Yes,' Caresse echoed. 'Now I've fixed the roof there really does seem a possibility of turning this place into a world territory. The seed of that idea was given to me by Socrates, you know, when he said, "If they ask you what city you come from, do not answer that you are Athenian or Corinthian, but answer: I am a citizen of the world."' She smiled and shrugged lightly.

'A very admirable idea,' said Martin.

'When I was first here I was engaged in my campaign for Women Against War and so I asked the women and the citizens of the commune of Roccasinibalda to vote whether they would like me to come and make this place known as the Città della Pace. We put together a manifesto stating *Le guerre non fanno la pace, i popoli fanno la pace* – War does not make peace, people make peace,' she said. 'So they all voted and it was an overwhelming majority, and we decided to call it the Città della Pace, without laws and police, just human nature. A place of peace.'

'And is that the flag that we saw flying above the castle?'

'Yes, my idea was to create an atmosphere where the poet, the philosopher and the artist might really explore ideas that can lead the world to peace and sanity. I believe the national model is outmoded and that the politicians can lead us nowhere. We need men of vision, men of ideas and compassion.' She gave a shrug that would have let a silken dressing gown slip from one shoulder. 'It's a very big idea, but this is a very *big* place. With three hundred and fifty-two rooms there's plenty of space and I hope that others will come forward and help keep this idea in motion.'

'Some might say there's an innocence, a *naïveté*, to this whole scheme.' Martin sat forward and laced his fingers round a sharp knee. Caresse listened with something like a frown. 'But if anyone has proven a flair for discovering the new and an ability to reflect their times, it's you.'

Caresse smiled, mollified, and spread her hands. 'I've never understood people who get caught in the past. Times change, that should be obvious enough, but people do seem to get stuck. I haven't read the Bible for quite some time, but I've always remembered the story of Lot's wife fleeing Sodom and Gomorrah. They were told never to look back, and my but she paid for that glance.'

Rue de Lille, 1924

'The art is knowing when to let go.'

'When?' Her hands and voice shook as she held the pendulous, beer-filled balloon out of his top-floor study window. The woman below was approaching, her dog waving a nosy line as it trotted in front of her.

'You have to decide that for yourself.'

'Will it be now?' she cried, her voice rising in an anxious curve.

'You tell me, Rat.'

There was a scream from way down below in the street, and then bark bark bark, bark bark bark.

Alderney, 1993

'Let go, Bay.'

Her fingers were prised from the sides. Water entered her ears, a thick feeling that went in too fast, and her body rolled with a shudder as she was brought up again, hair lying flat and shiny against her scalp. She could feel the gritty under-side of the bath's rim. It was different from their bath at home which was surrounded by pale tiles edged in thick glue that meant no water could escape. Here it slopped over the sides and made the ceiling of the kitchen go a sickly brown. She looked about at the mirrored tiles that ran round the room, her face given back to her too many times to count. Gloved with soap, she saw her father's hands coming for her and she squinted as they rubbed quickly, first this way, then that.

'Found what you're looking for?' She saw her father's eyes smiling behind her.

'Am I a beauty?' she asked hopefully.

'You're perfect. Now, back you go.'

'But am I a beauty like Mummy?' Gripping either side of the bath, neck rigid, she held herself upright against his tipping motion.

Her father smiled down at her. 'You look more like your grandmother, funnily enough. Now back you go, my baby Narcissus.' His face swam over hers, hair falling over his eyes. 'Your face isn't as symmetrical, so perhaps not classically beautiful. More interesting. I think you're going to be what's called *jolie-laide*.'

'What does that mean?' Bay asked.

'It means you are beautiful and not-beautiful all at once. The most beautiful women always have something imperfect about them.'

Jolie-laide. She was set right and caught her image again in the mirrored tiles.

'Come on,' he said gently. And she was helped from the bath into the warm towel.

'Make me like Aunt Leo,' she whispered and her father draped a small towel over the back of her head and then quickly twisted and turned it back on itself. Bay carefully stood straight, and holding herself like a full glass turned to face the mirror, her hair hidden inside the white towel.

She half closed her eyes and pressed her hands together.

'Do I look holy?' she asked.

'Wholly,' he replied. 'And your neck is a thing of almost unbearable tenderness.'

Bay smiled and looked up at the picture that hung on the black wall. The steam from the bath had misted the glass inside the frame, but slowly it began to clear, revealing a black-and-white photo of a castle that seemed to grow out of the mountain it stood on. Its name was written beneath it in white stamped letters.

'Roc-Ca-Si-Ni-Bal-Da,' she spelled it out. Pulling her onto his lap, her father repeated the word properly so that it rolled like the hills behind it.

Bay leaned back against him and they regarded the picture in silence.

'Your silly grandmother sold it for nothing.'

'Why?' said Bay.

'Why indeed, Bay.'

'Is Mummy sad we can't live there?'

'No, she's not.'

She searched the photo. 'I would have liked to live there.'

'Yes,' her father said, in his thinking voice. 'I would have too.'

Rue de Lille, 1924

'You wanted to see me, Caresse?' Diana squinted through the steam.

'Yes, I did.'

She tried not to stare at her mother where she lay in the enormous tub. The water was as creamy as milk and her mother's breasts rose from it, nipples like dark islands, and appearing occasionally was the darkness between her legs. The dove-grey bathroom was hot, and though it was midday a fire burned in the grate. Diana sat on a footstool by the sofa on which her mother's dressing gown was strewn. She no longer wore the flower-sprigged white cotton one that Diana liked. This one was made of a rough gold material that crunched underneath her hand.

'I've had to tell you once already, and you know how I hate doing the same thing twice: Harry is terribly sensitive to sound, he's already struggling with Mette's incessant droning, and the way you run up and down those stairs makes a racket that simply can't be borne.'

93

'It's not running, it's skipping. And Mette's not droning, she's singing.'

'Well, skipping is fine and dandy in the garden of life, but those stairs are an echo chamber.'

'I know. I hear you going up and down all night.'

'Then you quite understand.' Her mother disappeared under the water and stayed down for a long time. Diana stood up, hardly breathing. She was about to reach her hand in when Caresse sat up and took a deep breath, pushing the water from her face. 'Well!' She smiled at her daughter, water in her eyelashes. 'A minute! Practically a Nereid.'

Diana was impressed, but said nothing.

Caresse shrugged and took hold of an enormous square of soap. She smelled it until her lungs were full. 'My God I could *consume* jasmine. Oh to be a bee and actually get inside it.' She began to lather the soap between her hands. 'So it's shoes off, dearest. You must learn to get about like a samurai. Silent and deadly.' She paused. 'Now tell me what you and Harry have been up to? I'm glad you're becoming pals.'

Diana fixed her eyes on the soap, now swimming scummily in the dish.

Her mother watched her. 'You know he and I will be gone to Egypt for a month or so.'

Diana nodded, still staring at the soap.

'Would you like to get in?'

Diana looked up in surprise and then uncertainly at the door.

'We've the house to ourselves.' She gave Diana a long look. 'Anyway, I'm getting out now.' Caresse stood, water streaming from her body, and wrapped a fine Turkish towel round her waist. She put out a hand. 'In you get.'

'Can I keep my clothes on?'

'Modesty is not a virtue, Diana, but yes ... why not.'

Alderney, 1993

'Are the children okay?' Elena turned towards James. 'What did you tell them?'

'That you were resting.'

Elena nodded and pressed her hands in between her legs where she sat on the bed.

'Elena, I think this might have been a mistake ...'

'In what way?'

'Let me count the ways ...'

'It can be what we make it ...'

'Previous experience would suggest it will be what *she* makes of you.' James looked at his wife, his eyes lingering where her short hair revealed the length of her neck.

Elena looked up and, seeing his gentle gaze, ducked her head. She could still feel her conversation with her mother drumming through her head, and even though she'd just washed them, there was a residue of oil on her hands that made her feel queasy. She stood up to wash them again, turning her body away from James as she went past into the bathroom.

'If it's too much, Ele, we can leave, like we planned,' he said as she went past.

She turned on the taps and watched the water pour over her outstretched hands. She clenched them into two fists and in the mirror behind her saw the bath that she'd washed that morning. A dark snarl of hair pulled from the plughole and then flushed quickly away. She went closer and, peering at the smooth white enamel, saw that a single dark hair remained curled on the side of the tub. She fished it out and flicked it into the bin.

As she came back into the bedroom, James said, 'You only ever agree with me that easily when you've decided to do the opposite.' He looked at her seriously. 'I just don't want you getting . . . overtired.' The word swam flimsily between them. 'Not after last time.'

She stretched out on the bed with a sigh, closed her eyes and her mother's words came back to her. 'If you're going to be sick, Elena, then at least give it a name.' And her grandmother had interjected from beneath her parasol, her wide red mouth spreading around the words. 'Oh, Diana, you're obsessed with knowing the *name* of everything. *Nessuno sa niente, e niente è reale*, and that is the only truth worth parking your car by.'

She smiled at the memory of that drawling voice, and seeing the change in her expression James smiled too.

'What is it?' he asked.

But she shook her head, unwilling to share, and the image dispersed.

'Have you eaten properly today?'

She said nothing.

She closed her eyes again, picturing her grandmother in her large wicker chair, a blouse cut arrestingly across her chest.

'Elena.'

She opened her eyes and looked at him. 'Of course I've eaten.' But seeing his hurt expression, she immediately sat up and put her arms round his neck. 'I'm sorry,' she said quietly into his neck. 'I'm sorry.'

'Just remember we've escaped all that, Elena.' He looked down at her, pushing back her hair from her forehead. 'You've escaped,' he said, gripping her tightly. 'You're a woman now, with your own family. Don't let her in.'

But as he held her to him she met her reflection in the glass of the window behind him, and her eyes seemed like two dark holes out of which anything could climb.

Rue de Lille, 1925

'Books books books.'

'Why are there so many?'

The solid men in overalls kept rolling the bookcases into the nursery so that they began to form a kind of maze.

'Because Cousin Walter didn't know when to stop.' Harry sat down on the edge of the bed and she felt the mattress shake with the excited tremor of his legs. 'There are eight thousand of them.'

'Where will they all go?'

'Into our heads to feed our guts.' He stood and took one from the shelf. 'Bound in the skin of an eighteenth-century courtesan.'

As Diana reached up to touch he snapped it shut, crocodile quick, and began shouting at the men where to put the next ones.

'But how will I get to my desk? Or my window?'

He looked around and smiled at the darkening room.

'I like it here now with these trenches made of words. And you little rat, scurrying back and forth in the in-between.'

Roccasinibalda, 1970

'Let me, Mr Porto. You're making a mess of that beautiful ham.'

Diana moved into the bright light falling from the open refrigerator and took the knife from the poet's hand. He threw a trailing strip of fat into his mouth and smiled.

'The most delicious ham in the world. When I think of the shit I eat in America. Did you know you can buy ham there that is formed in the shape of Mickey Mouse's head? A pig turned into a mouse – food to make kids feel safe. A fairy tale of the darkest order.' He ate another piece. 'The process for making this is very elaborate. A real craft. More than seven stages, over a year. I would not have the patience.'

'What about your poems?' Diana said, concentrating on the smooth cut of the knife. 'Isn't that a similarly arduous process?' She set a plate down and then eyed the remaining contents of the fridge. 'I'm ravenous.'

Ellis flicked his eyes over the body bent before him. She was wearing a dress that tucked in at her waist and those tied-on shoes – there was something about her that made him nostalgic. She stood up straight holding a plate of meat and a lettuce and threw him a smile.

'Would you like me to cook you something? I like to eat late at night.'

'Are you sure that meat's all right? It's been there for some time.'

She laughed. 'I like my meat hung until the first maggot falls to the floor. Brings the flavour to life.'

'You really are lost to your country. America wouldn't know what to do with you.'

'Now *that's* a compliment.' She turned away and, placing the bloody meat on a large slab of marble, began to twist a pepper mill over it.

'You never go back?' he asked.

'Occasionally. My money's held hostage by the draconian Bostonians.'

'And you're still welcome? Despite your mother breaking ranks?'

'Oh, she was never *out.*' She reached over and took a pinch of salt. 'There's no such thing when the blood's that blue. They all loved having someone to be scandalised by. She was doing them a favour. Probably made them all feel wonderfully *together.* There's nothing quite so unifying as having a common enemy, is there?'

He smiled and filled her glass.

'My mother did go back though, in the forties. For quite some time. Not to Boston, of course, but still . . .'

'Yes, she mentioned a haunted plantation in Virginia.'

Diana raised her eyes to the heavens. 'Hell.'

'An interesting choice, I must say.'

'She had a new husband, a college football player, and she let him choose where they were going to live. I think he wanted to be a corn farmer, little realising that where my mother goes, a scourge follows. By that time she was entirely caught up with that Surrealist psychopath Dalí and his band of exhausting hangers-on. He "enchanted" Mother's pond, which involved cutting my new bicycle in half and throwing it in the middle.'

'And where is the young husband now?'

'In a bar somewhere? Dead? Who knows. He turned out to be a nasty drunk. He would disappear for months, then come back when he needed some more money. He was only twenty-six when they got together and she was well into her fifties. I never understood what she saw in him, daylight-wise. I'm sure he was a riot in the feathers.'

'My old man was a mean drunk. I wouldn't wish it on anybody. Let alone a woman worthy of worship like your mother.'

Diana was silent as she crushed a white bud of garlic with the flat of a knife.

'Been working up an appetite?' He leaned back and crossed his arms.

'I always have an appetite.'

'I noticed you and the lawyer having a little quarrel at dinner. You don't like him.'

Diana looked at him as she poured vinegar into a jar. 'You're very observant, Mr Porto. I forget that about having writers around. And no, I don't like him. He's far too dependent, it's unattractive. A personally unsuccessful lawyer should set off alarm bells, don't you think?'

102

'I have no interest in them.'

'My lawyers are always the kind of men you can put your trust in. I met my most recent while sailing. He lives on one of those funny little Channel islands that were occupied in the war. If you're going to employ someone to keep your affairs in order then you might as well choose someone you want to have an affair with while they're at it.'

Ellis smiled obligingly. 'Where is he now?'

'Oh, he's around, but his wife keeps him on a tight leash.' There was a hiss of hot fat as she laid the meat in the pan.

'I didn't think you were the type of woman who would know how to cook.'

'Why?'

'Because.' He spread his hands.

'You only need to be able to do a few things well. Meat – rare. Eggs, obviously. A good green salad – only the tender leaves. A very tight dressing.' Diana shrugged. 'I like taking care of my friends.'

Ellis was careful not to register his pleasure at being counted as such.

'I was taught the basics by a wonderful woman when I was growing up in Paris. A lesbian called Louise, built like a longshoreman. She cooked good French food, though working for my mother meant she also had to learn how Americans ate. She became quite expert at frying chicken and making creamed cod for Mother's endless dinner parties. Nowadays, of course, a good cook is as hard to find as an albino alligator, though I was lucky with my housekeeper Inés. Loyal and lacking in self-esteem. Those are the qualities to look for.'

103

'Don't you think the days of servant and master are done? Why should some poor old broad have to pick up your panties just because you can pay her?'

'Because she needs a job?' Diana said, sounding bored. 'Mr Porto, my mother and I don't see eye to eye on many things, but we are in complete agreement when it comes to wealth not proportionate to personal need. I should also remind you that we're having this conversation in the kitchens of a castle.' She forked the chops from the pan onto a plate.

'You haven't cooked those for very long.'

'They're practically charred. Now salad.' She poured the dressing over the leaves lying curled in the wooden bowl and then undid the small buttons that ran up the length of her sleeves and pushed them up. '*La salade doit être retournée comme une femme.*'

'*Bien sûr, jusqu'à ce qu'elle soit bien mouillée.*'

Diana frowned. 'You speak French.'

'You're surprised.'

'Yes.' She nodded, her face softening. 'But pleasantly.'

'The Navy. I spent a lot of time in a French whorehouse in Okinawa. A lotta bangs all round. You?'

'I was taken to Paris when I was six and stayed there right through the war until I joined the Red Cross.'

Ellis raised his eyebrows.

'Yes.' Diana straightened her shoulders. 'I drove ambulances.'

'Very impressive.'

'I might look like I sit around all day, Mr Porto, but I've lived my life.'

'I believe it.'

'So,' she asked, smiling, 'did you ever go to France?'

'I'm an American poet.' He spread his hands. 'But it's like a broad that's had too many men. It's Greece that blew my mind.'

Diana laughed, a raucous sound, and they stood at the counter and ate, blood leaching across the shared plate.

'Everybody raves about Paris in the twenties, but I think the later times were more interesting in France. Life under occupation was grim in many ways, of course, but I'd be lying if I denied that I found it fascinating. One night I crashed a German nightclub by following two officers inside and my God it was a tawdry evening. The Nazis were treating the girls roughly and there was an air of absolute desperation about the whole scene. The evening was redeemed by a single moment of victory when I saw a pink-haired blonde retaliate with a resounding smack across the flabby face of the Prussian who was mauling her.'

'Why did you stay? You could have gone anywhere.'

'I was loyal to the place. My mother had returned to the States, enraptured by her surrealism. Her contribution to the war effort was to open a gallery of Modern Art in Washington.'

'Truth is needed more than ever in times of war.'

'Not more than bandages.' Her eyes flashed. Ellis continued to eat, and said nothing. 'I wrote a book about the war actually.' Diana spoke in a quieter voice. 'It sold very well.'

'What was it called?'

'*Through Occupied Territory.*'

'Your mother wrote one too, didn't she? *The Passionate Years?*' he hazarded.

Laying down her knife and fork, Diana crossed her arms. 'It's out of print.'

'So both you and your mother have written books about yourselves.'

'Well, some lives are worth recording,' Diana said with a lift of her chin. 'Why do you write?' she asked after a pause, wiping a lettuce leaf in the bloody juices collected on the plate.

'Because I don't know how else to fight the days.' He chewed thoughtfully. 'This meat is raw.'

Diana smiled.

'I read up about your stepfather while I was back in New York. Harry Crosby – the WASP war hero.'

Diana was still. Ellis noted this and the sound of his chewing suddenly became very loud in his ears.

'War is no laughing matter. I'm surprised you mock it so readily.'

'I don't mock war, I mock heroic labels.'

'We can't help where we're born.' She flicked her eyes over him. 'I've often thought that those who try to change that little twist of fate are reserved for some special punishment.'

They were silent for a moment.

'You know,' Diana began to speak again. 'Verdun devastated him, whatever my mother might say. He used to tell me about it late at night as the moon spilled over us. He would read aloud from his endless books.' She poured herself a glass of wine and then pushed the bottle towards Ellis. 'Occasionally he'd describe the bodies, horrible and broken, clawing at their mouths. The water alive with red slugs. Rats that invaded the dugouts and ran all over the bodies of the sleeping boys.' Her body was tensed. 'It was the end of his childhood. All the genteel manners he'd been guided by just . . . died. And he almost died, you know. He should have died.' She spoke earnestly. 'His friend was talking to him as they both cleaned their ambulance when a shell fell right where they were standing. Ambulance gone. Friend gone. Only Harry lived.' She fell silent and Ellis saw that her blue eyes had darkened as though a cloud were moving through her.

'The end of God,' he said, rubbing his thumb across his lip.

'How could anyone go on believing in the same God being prayed to by boys soiling two different uniforms?'

'And so he worshipped the sun . . . Gaze blank and pitiless . . .'

'Yes.'

'Some of Crosby's ideas about the sun are interesting. But a lot is derivative. Most of it seems like superstitious baloney.'

'Isn't that religion in a nutshell?' She raised her eyebrows. 'Anyway, isn't all this interest in another writer rather putting to bed the idea of the self-obsessed artist?'

'I like to know who I'm sharing a roof with.'

'But you're not sharing a roof with my stepfather.' Diana waved her hair back from her head and turned away.

'So, ambulances,' he said softly. 'Making the old man proud.'

'Old man?' she repeated, turning back towards him. She shook her head. 'He didn't let that happen to him.'

Rue de Lille, 1924

Mette was waiting to take her up.

'They've been home for a few hours. Can't think what they've brought back in all those boxes.' She breathed heavily as she heaved her body up the stairs. 'Even more dusty nonsense to keep clean, I'll bet.'

'They went to the desert,' Diana explained, her voice echoing on the shadowy stone staircase. 'And to see the tombs. They buried people with their pets still alive there.'

'Waste of time,' Mette muttered darkly.

There were many people upstairs, sitting around and standing in the hallway, talking in groups. Diana was led past Harry and she heard him describing 'a scorpion, that if it is cut in two, will begin a battle between the head and the tail ...' There was the pop of a champagne cork and through the chatter Diana could hear her mother's voice rising and falling above all the others, already telling her tales, as Mette's chafed red hand led her into the drawing room and then left her by a table. On it was the huge carved head she'd always admired, its eyes closed in sleep. She touched it and it was smooth under her hand. She drew it towards her, wanting to feel if she could lift it a little. She just needed to get a better angle so that she could . . .

'Diana?'

She looked up and her mother was looking at her. So was everybody else.

'She's making love to the Brâncuşi,' her mother laughed. 'Three months and she hardly seems to have noticed I've been gone.'

Diana stared hard at the floor, trying not to see the three blackened hands her mother was unpacking onto the table.

'Look at Harry's ring. A sun ring.'

He held his hand up to show the room the heavy gold ring on his finger.

'He will never take it off.' Her mother stood behind him, holding herself tight against him.

'I will never take it off.' He stared up at it, his arm held high.

'Come and get your present, Diana,' Caresse turned and called to her. 'Harry picked it out especially.'

Roccasinibalda, 1970

'Diana, you must meet Heike ...'

'Must I?' Diana came over reluctantly, holding a loaded straw basket.

'Where *have* you been? What bounty!'

'To the market in Rieti. Just look at these persimmon.' She put down the basket and pulled open a paper bag full of soft-skinned orange fruit. 'They're perfect.' She smiled down at them, but as she glanced up at the two women, her face closed again.

'Heike is here from Berlin and has been telling me all about a journey she's just made to the Australian outback. It sounds absolutely breathtaking. Apparently, there's a very important art movement starting there with the indigenous people beginning to share their paintings of the ... what did you say it was called, Heike?'

'Their dreaming,' the girl said.

'Yes. The dream time. It's quite wonderful, Diana. They each have their own song and the song gives them a map of the land and . . . well, it's fantastically complex and just *riveting*. I am going to write to a young artist I know from Sydney and ask him to begin organising something for next summer. I'd like to invite the aborigines here for an exposition, and perhaps a painting on the walls of the castle or a series of rooms . . . I'm so glad you've shared this with me, Heike. Don't you think it's fascinating, Diana?'

'Yes, I do.' She spat a shining brown pip into her cupped hand.

'And what do you do, Diana?' The young German woman turned to her.

'Diana drifts about,' Caresse interjected. 'Heike makes conceptual pieces, darling. It's an important new direction. You know, Heike, I must introduce you to a woman I know in Buenos Aires who runs a ranch that grows the hemp you were talking about. Perhaps you could go and spend some time there and make some of your work in the Argentine.'

'Yes.' Heike nodded, smiling. 'That would be very nice.'

'My mother is as good at fixing people up as she is bad at letting them finish their sentences. But you must make use of it, Heike.' Diana smiled at her as she stood to go, trying to ignore the little ache that was spreading up through her chest, threatening to pull the corners of her mouth down. She focused now on the girl; there was something pliable about her that she warmed to. 'I'm going to swim later, you should come with me. I've found a terribly good little trattoria in a village I pass through. We can have some dinner together.' She deliberately kept her gaze away from her mother.

'Thank you, I would like that.'

'Heike was telling me about the man she's fallen in love with, Diana,' Caresse said in an informative tone. 'He sounds like a perfect brute. Absolutely ravishing.'

Diana looked at the girl and raised her eyebrows. 'Is he here?'

She shook her head. 'No.'

'And what's the problem?'

'He can be rough with me. And he doesn't want just one woman.'

'Well, darling, the second part is no great shakes,' Diana began. 'Men are men and frankly, the more you lean into it, women are men too.'

'But, Diana, it's sweet that she *doesn't* feel that way. It's quite all right to prefer to be two.' Caresse leaned back in her large wicker sun chair and closed her eyes.

'I'm *aware* of that, Caresse,' Diana said, sweeping her eyes over her as the recollection of the big black car entering the courtyard of Le Moulin crawled into her head. She'd run up to the sun tower, taking his quick methodical steps, and when she'd got to the top – to her shock – she found him there, wrapped in a big coat and holding a bottle. He continued to stare at the car below in the courtyard, waiting. She went to his side, and though he still did not move she felt her presence accepted and they watched together, the sharp night air keeping them alert. After some time the car door opened and her mother got out, but whatever was inside pulled her back in and her laughter travelled, clear in the still night. She re-emerged and closed the door with a flourish. The car started with a low rumble and set off across the gravel, its lights searching the silent buildings. As it left, her mother was covered by the night, but they both listened to the sound of her heels as she walked crisply towards the bedroom, stopped for a moment (and Diana had known she was gazing up at the moon) then continued inside . . .

Diana turned to Heike with a gentle smile. 'You just have to decide what you're comfortable with. Everybody else can go to hell.' Heike looked down at her bare feet and laughed.

'But the roughhousing, Heike. That's no dice. For me, anyway. I ended my last marriage because of it and I stand by that utterly.'

'Oh but I've had some very passionate clashes in my time,' Caresse said without sitting up. 'They can be the bitter skin that gives way to a very sweet fruit.'

Diana leaned against a stone table, and shook her head.

'One thing I will say,' Caresse spoke, her eyes still closed, 'is that the man you choose is the man you choose. I have no truck for this sadistic practice of "whipping a man into shape". You must marry a man because you like him as he is, not with the notion that you can force him into something a little more to your taste.'

'And the same the other way,' Diana said. 'It's as you are, or *dasvidanya*.'

'How did you become so experienced?' Heike asked, taking a persimmon from the bag Diana offered.

'I realised early on that being a femme did not immediately equate to being a fatale. It can take a little practice. So I started as soon as I could. And these days, between you and me, time isn't exactly on my side.'

'You were *funny*, the way you'd try and be alluring,' Caresse said. 'Leaning against doorways with that little pudding bowl

113

haircut and your scuffed shoes. She tried to imitate me then, I think.'

'Well, the hair grew and the shoes came off,' Diana said, scrunching the empty paper bag into a ball.

Caresse seemed not to hear and continued speaking, a smile in her voice.

'I was always a natural flirt myself. I mean, my nanny was practically in love with me – I simply couldn't help it.'

Diana was silent. Suddenly she stood, and ignoring Heike's uncertain gaze, she picked up her bag and walked across the courtyard towards her rooms, closing the door with a slam.

'A passionate temperament.' Caresse smiled indulgently at Heike. 'Now do tell me more about these fascinating larra . . . larra . . .'

'*Larrakitj*. Well, they take a dead eucalyptus and . . .' Heike dragged her eyes away from the closed door and leaned towards Caresse. 'They wait to find a tree that has already died, been eaten from the inside by termites. What they want is that the trunk remains intact but is internally hollow. This they then paint with a brush made from strands of the passed person's hair.'

Caresse listened, her eyes moving as though she saw the vast expanse of desert spiked with the dead trees.

'The patterns are unique to each person's dreaming. If you look here . . .' Heike opened a monograph and Caresse inspected an image made of many daubs of paint, and soon she was immersed in the complex patterns of another place. Oh, she must go, she must. How fascinating. She looked closely at the image Heike was explaining. Brilliant marks telling another story entirely. She leaned forward, nodding and smiling.

Rue de Lille, 1925

'But you're not a poet. You work in a bank.'

He turned and slapped her hard across her cheek. Diana stared at him.

'Getting away isn't always such a clean cut, Rat. You'll understand that one day.'

'You mean escaping.' She refused to touch her stinging cheek. 'Mother says that we escaped.'

'Yes, but your mother,' he held her gloved hand up by its wrist, gripping it tightly, and waved it slowly left and right, 'brought a little stowaway. She was able to shrug Boston off like a stole. For me it was more like this.' He pinched the spare suede at the tip of Diana's fingers. 'You have to tug it off one finger at a time.' He smiled down at her and took her now bare hand gently in his. 'Did I hurt you?'

She shook her head, denying the sting, and tried to smile back.

Roccasinibalda, 1970

Bored of waiting in the corner of the small wood-panelled saloon, Diana came up to where Roberto stood at the bar ordering their drinks.

'What are we discussing?' She extended her hand to the two local men standing there, who each shook it with reverence.

'I've changed my mind, Roberto. *Voglio un Torito.*'

'*Cos'è un Torito?*' the barman said. The men gathered by the bar listened intently.

'*Una bevanda spagnola. Gin e sherry con un sacco di ghiaccio.*'

The old barman nodded and began to open a bottle. '*Una bevanda con cui vincere le guerre.*'

Diana hid her surprise. When she'd last been here there had been a shocked silence at a woman ordering hard liquor. Roberto had had to lecture her on the different attitude rural Italians took to women drinking.

She gave a quick smile to an old man she'd seen a few nights before in an underground room beneath a roadside restaurant. 'Did you win your lira back?' she called.

'No,' he smiled, revealing missing bottom teeth. 'But neither did you.'

She laughed and then, seeing Roberto's quizzical look, said, 'We met at a *combattimento*.'

He looked at her quizzically. 'What kind of fight? Where?'

'Cock.' She smiled.

He glanced at the man and scowled. '*Quello non lo praticano qui*.'

'No, no, *certo*.' The old man held up his hands, and turned back towards the barman, whose eyes slid between Diana and Roberto.

As they settled themselves at their table, Roberto shook his head. 'I'm surprised you engage with such ugly practices.'

'Oh, I love all those tense underworld faces. It has all the seriousness of the bullfight and some of the excitement.'

'Hardly fit for a woman.'

'What a ghastly expression, Roberto,' Diana said. 'I find it enlightening. You can tell the training the birds have been through. They're terribly courageous.'

'You don't find it cruel?'

'I suppose towards the end when the birds are tired and almost blind, going at it like pick-hammers until one finally sinks like a rag on the mat. Rather reminds me of some of the men I've known,' she said, lowering her head to light a cigarette.

Roberto was silent.

'Anyway, I won my wager in the end.' As she sat up a man approached them, his cloth hat folded in his hands. Diana recognised him as one of the gardeners who carried Caresse in her sedan chair up and down the winding walkway of the castle.

'Signora, my name is Bruno.' The man spoke so quietly that both Diana and Roberto had to lean forward to hear.

'*Piacere*,' she held her hand out to him. 'Thank you for the work you do. My mother's heart is weak . . .'

'It is truly my honour. I love her very much.'

Diana smiled politely, her thighs tensing below the table. She didn't feel like having this conversation *again*. 'It is my belief,' the man blushed, 'that she has saved my life.'

Diana lowered her glass a fraction and looked into his watery eyes. 'Saved your *life*?'

'*Sì*, signora. I was very sick, it was all through my body, when I was visited by your mother in a dream. A kind of . . . vision.'

'A vision?'

'*Sì*, a vision. She was dressed in white and told me to come to Roccasinibalda and continue the work she is doing here. For the women and for the young. So I did. And I will. Without her, I am nothing. I will honour your mother's memory for the rest of my life.'

'How extraordinary,' she murmured, smiling up at him. 'I'm very happy for you, to have something to believe in.'

'*Grazie*, signora.' Bruno bent, kissed her hand and left them.

'Well, what did you make of Bruno?' Roberto looked amused. Diana shook her head.

'I think it's rather sad.'

'What's sad, his belief?'

'No. Like it or not, I too have my beliefs. It's that he thinks this will last. You and I both know there's not enough money to manage this place for much longer. Who does he think will continue to pay for this?'

Roberto cocked his head to one side. 'What are your beliefs, Diana?'

'I believe in loyalty.' She took a long drink and waited for her voice to steady itself. 'And in not being afraid to see things as they are. Now, listen,' she bit at the skin on the side of her thumb. 'The thing I want to ask you. It's a small thing really.'

Roberto waited.

'I want you to keep the diaries for me. The originals. She's got a thing about me having them and I couldn't bear for them to be lost.' Diana stared hard at him.

Roberto shook his head, avoiding her gaze. 'Your mother works from printed manuscripts . . .'

'Roberto, please.' She put her hand over his. 'You have influence with her.' She watched his pride swell at that and had to force her voice to remain soft. 'She won't give them to me. But I feel sure she still has them.'

'I don't know what you mean.'

'Yes, you do.' She let him go. 'And don't destroy any of her papers without asking me first. You know, when she . . .' She could not bring herself to say the word. Oh, she hated it when her body betrayed her. Roberto saw it too and, his own eyes glistening, now covered her hand with his.

The bar was now full of talk and drink and Diana sat back and surveyed the crowd. The girls wore lipstick (many the same shade as her mother) and sat at ease among the boys, hands resting freely. A group began to play music and a young boy, slim and tanned in his short-sleeved white shirt, took a girl and they danced close, faces together. A group came in from the castle and the music became more raucous, a girl got up on a table and began to gyrate, her feet blindly gripping the wood. Through rough cigarette smoke, the older men watched impassively from the edges of the room, surreptitiously eyeing the girl's bare legs as she moved. As Diana drank, she felt a familiar clinch of anger and with every tip of her glass she felt it grow. What had happened here? These people were good country Catholics, what were they doing drinking and making a show like this? Why hadn't her mother left these simple people alone in their ways?

She looked at a boy's hand moving inside the neck of a girl's cotton dress. She was sure that it was one of her mother's 'peasant' dresses. The bodies moved and heaved and she stared at a girl's face as she laughed and laughed, her face getting redder. She shook her head. These wide-faced country boys and girls shouldn't be doing this, they should be allowed to *keep* their morals.

'Where is Caresse?' A boy pushed through the crowd and stood in front of Diana, chest heaving.

'She's dying.' She was motionless in her chair.

'What?' He squeezed closer so that he could hear.

Diana reached up, placed a hand on the side of his face and pulled his ear close to her lips. She could see the dark hairs fading into his slender neck.

'She's lying down.'

He looked at her for a moment, their faces almost touching, and blushed. Then he pushed back through the crowd to his friends.

'Diana, I think we should go.' Roberto got to his feet with difficulty, motioning aside the group that had gathered round them.

She stood, but at that moment the two men from the BBC came into the bar. They saw Diana and threaded their way towards her, eyebrows raised in greeting. Diana signalled for more drinks and the men found chairs and sat next to her, so that Roberto was forced to reluctantly follow suit.

'Well, gentlemen, how was that?' Diana asked, leaning into the centre of the circle.

'It went very well.' They glanced at one another. 'Your mother's energy is remarkable.'

Diana smiled tightly. She'd always noticed the very same quality, but this outsider's observation was not welcome.

'Yes, she knows how to talk.' Diana bent her head to light another cigarette. 'Holds her audience absolutely captive.' She put her head back and exhaled a plume of smoke, eyebrows raised.

'You know, we'd love to hear your take on that time,' the cameraman said. He'd like to film that elusive face. It seemed to change as she moved, shifting from sensuous to sharp and back again.

Diana shrugged. 'I was a child. It's rather a blur. Like all the best parties, I suppose.'

But the table was hers now, a round of pricked ears. 'I'm sure she's told you all about Paris and Harry, so I won't go into that . . .'

'No, actually.' Martin sat forward. 'She focused more on the later years, for the most part. The Surrealists and all that emerged after 1930.'

'Probably for very good reason,' Roberto said. 'I'm sure Signora Crosby has said all that she wishes to.'

'Well, Harry wasn't someone you can exactly leave out of the story. Harry *was* Paris.'

'Diana,' Roberto warned.

'To be honest, we were told not to ask about that.' Martin spread his hands.

'And my nanny told me not to tell tales.' Diana smiled at his dull, bearded face. 'But we do, don't we?'

'Well, we tried . . .'

'Yes,' Diana sighed. 'She can be stubborn.'

'Mrs Crosby has every right to protect her privacy, should she so wish.'

'Oh, have another drink, Roberto. When we settled in Paris, my mother and Harry were able to begin building the life they wanted.'

'And what was Harry like, as a man?' Martin, who prided himself on his ability to carve interviews with the deftest of hands, cut in.

'What was he like?' Diana repeated in a faraway voice, then, deciding to let them have it, she stretched her arms across the table and leaned towards the two men; a sinewy cat-like movement. 'He was the most beautiful man I'd ever seen. No, scratch that. *Have* ever seen. There was something in the way he looked at you that made you stop what you were doing. He had a hypnotic light. Unexpected. Unsettling. And he was never banal, never. I don't think I ever heard him ask anyone a question unless he really wanted to know the answer. *Politesse* was a dirty idea. Talk was serious. And he liked people for what they were, not what they tried to be, so that you had the feeling of being liked by him in a way you'd never been liked before . . .' She shook her head suddenly, retreated, her words faltering. 'It's

122

not easy to talk about him. He was more movement and feeling than anything else. There's so little that can be said that does him justice. You always end up sounding rather banal.' She gave a wry laugh. 'Like trying to describe the sea.'

'I think you sound anything but banal.' Martin raised his glass of white wine. His flattery was a familiar hand moving up her spine and she leaned in again, biting her lip.

'He was . . . unencumbered. A combination of blithe freedom, hard athleticism and drink delirium. He soaked his soul in booze and set fire to it every night. The morning was for grey remorse and running until his sweat ran clean. He was methodical, thorough, appreciative of honesty. He didn't lie. He didn't hide. He took what he wanted and discarded what bored him. He was only barely constrained by time. Those times. Barely a man and yet older than everyone. Ceremony, his own ceremonies, were sacred and he followed the wild urges of his imagination with strict solemnity. Ritual was everything, routine forbidden. He loved graves, loved to walk among them. And he loved death, that was the true dance really. That's what interested him. The only worthy opponent. He would do anything and everything that entered his mind. He was . . . electric with rebellion.'

'"Electric with rebellion",' Martin repeated, smiling at the cameraman.

'What?' Diana crossed her arms, looking between them, a little scowl twisting her face.

'It's a wonderful expression, that's all. Your mother used it earlier.'

'It might be her *phrase*.' Diana coated the word with oily disdain. 'But it was his *life*.'

Alderney, 1993

Bay was the first to wake.

Through her bedroom window she had seen that the zips remained closed on her brothers' tent.

She was the absolute first.

'The first shall be last, and the last shall be first.' Her mother's words echoed through the hall of her mind as she walked the dark silent house in her dressing gown, its cord trailing loose, looking at the closed doors.

She pushed open the door to the upstairs sitting room and was bathed in morning light, as rich and yellow as the yolk of her breakfast egg.

She felt her heart moving. Oh! This was beautiful.

Bay leaned against the wall and looked at the sun-striped shelves of faded books, being careful not to let her eyes find the one about Egypt with its pictures of girls with the heads of cats and, even worse, one with the body of a scorpion. Her brothers had told her, wide-eyed, that there was a scorpion who could be chopped in half and its head would *still* eat its own tail . . . Yesterday her mother had firmly taken that book from her room and put it up on a shelf where even its edge was hidden, and as she lay down on the musty bearskin rug sprawled across the floor, Bay tried her best not to search for it. She ran her hand over the worn fur, many scorpions now scuttling back and forth across her mind, and she turned away from the books and stared at the ceiling, imagining her parents above her in their big bed.

Last night she'd tried to go into their bedroom. Usually, the door would open without her even knocking, and her mother would swoop down and carry her into the darkness towards where her father lay, pulling the covers over them all like a warm dark wave. Then she would find herself tucked in the dark channel between their bodies, rich with the smell of white waxy flowers on one side and grunting animals on the other (they were very different creatures at night). Her father was like a boulder that she could press her back against, her mother the portal through which she could enter sleep. But last night her mother did not appear, so that eventually she'd gone back to her own bed to lie very still as she watched the night turning black then blue with the mothering sound of a wood pigeon going on somewhere in the garden.

She would not have children.

The thought was as familiar as the pet dog she loved to pretend she had lost and she lay on the fur rug playing melancholy, pulling together a few of the other sad thoughts (boarding school, funerals) that she often comforted herself with.

'I won't have children,' she had told her mother, in great confidence, as they'd sat together on the beach.

'Why, Bay?' Her mother had looked down at her.

'Because they are ungrateful.'

'Have you been talking to your grandmother again?'

Bay shook her head. 'Also children grow up,' she protested. 'And then they're not children any more.'

'We're always children, Bay, especially with our mummies and daddies. You'll always be my baby.' And she had pressed Bay close to her and kissed the top of her head.

'But Grandma doesn't look after you.' Bay struggled free and stared up at her mother. 'She just lies in bed like she's a baby.'

'Your grandmother's not well, Bay. It's hard to understand, but she's . . . she's . . .'

Bay frowned, remembering her mother's voice trailing into the push and suck of the sea.

She thought of the way her father had spoken yesterday morning. He had said, 'She can get her own fucking breakfast.'

'James, she can't,' her mother had responded.

'Not *can't*, Elena, *won't*.' Then he was stamping up the stairs, the tray in his hands.

Sitting on the garden steps, Bay had carefully turned another page of the large art book on her lap. Her father had said 'fuck'. She waited a pause before blindly turning the next page. And what was her father doing up there? She thought of her grandmother's see-through nightie and her mind raced. She might not have pulled up the covers in time.

Remembering the feeling of embarrassment, Bay pressed her body into the fur of the dead bear and tried to squash what was moving her insides about.

She heard a sound, and stopped.

Listening again, she made out soft noises coming from the end of the corridor.

126

Her grandmother's room.

She sat up and craned her neck towards it. Perhaps she would go in there today when her mother had her rest to look at the photographs that were stuffed in the wooden chest whose drawers didn't like to be opened. Many of her grandmother's pictures had been cut with vicious snips so that heads were missing, leaving her grandmother smiling victoriously beside no one. One that Bay liked in particular was of her grandmother standing with her mother and aunt on the deck of a boat, their bikini-clad bodies all curving with the same lines; Aunt Leonie had lost her head but her mother remained intact. She thought of her grandmother in that picture, smiling like a cat, and then looked down the hall towards the closed door. Yesterday afternoon Bay had been surprised to hear her laughing out in the garden. And when she'd looked out of her bedroom window, she had seen her sitting up beneath the shade of the fig tree, a small table with a bottle and two glasses at her side, talking to a strange woman in a brightly patterned suit.

'Grandma's dressed today!' She ran down to tell her mother in the kitchen, who was standing at the sink, tearing lettuce leaves into a bowl. She was wearing a striped shirt, tied underneath her bump with a length of rope.

'Yes, Bay, she is.' Bay knelt down and examined her mother's bare feet. The heel of the foot was a dusty white compared to the gleam of her skin on top. She reached a hand out to touch her, but as she did so her mother jumped and the head of lettuce landed on the floor beside Bay with a soft sound.

'You scared me!' She bent to pick up the salad. Bay, heart pattering, circled her arms round her mother's smooth leg.

'Who's she with?' she asked, looking up at her.

'A friend,' her mother replied, as she again began to rinse the lettuce under a running tap.

'But she's young.'

Her mother had glanced out the window and then back down at the stream of water, peering closer at a lettuce leaf as she cleaned its curled insides. 'About the same age as me. She's called Heike, and is a very important artist. She's one of your grandmother's special friends. She paid for her to go to a very good art school.'

'I thought she didn't like paying for things.'

'She's always taken special care of her friends.'

'But why's she not in bed? I thought she was sick.'

'She's feeling a bit better today.'

In the garden, the two women were laughing, their glasses meeting with a friendly clink.

'Do you wish Grandma was your friend?' she asked, staring upwards.

'It might have been ... easier.' Her mother dried a glass carefully. 'But it doesn't matter,' she finally smiled down at Bay. 'I've got you, haven't I?'

The kitchen was cold and grey now as Bay came down the stairs, as empty as a stage when a play has finished. She began to push a chair towards the fridge and it groaned in protest across the mock-cork linoleum. She was going to prepare her grandmother's breakfast. She pushed the stubborn bulk with increased determination.

Milk and a banana.

She knew what she liked.

*

Diana lifted her head from the pillow to see the sun fighting past the edge of the curtains. Already day. She sank back, listening. What in God's name was that wailing? A child crying about spilt milk. Christ. Groaning, she pressed her face to the cool side of the pillow and tried to ignore the drum-like ache in her head, *boom dada boom dada boom*. Why on *earth* were there so many children here? They never stopped crying. Inés should take them to the beach or something … Her wrist ached where she had fallen and now she remembered her daughter wrapping the gauze steadily round her wrist. It was uncomfortably tight. No, it wasn't Inés here, she pressed her eyes closed, *Elena* was here. These were Elena's children. And there had been many tears, though Diana couldn't remember *why*. Not here but out *there*, she narrowed her eyes at the door. The ceaseless shouting and squalor of children. Yesterday reasserted itself and she drew herself up with difficulty against the head of the bed. There had been a good Marqués de Riscal and Elena had made a fine *ajo blanco* for Heike, though the dishes were served and cleared in pensive silence. Really, she shouldn't offer to cook and clean if she was going to look so miserable while doing so.

'Is she going to be here every year?' she'd asked as she'd helped Diana dress.

'Yes, Elena, and I'm surprised at your lack of generosity. Heike doesn't have a family of her own and, besides, I like to have the occasional artist around. I can hardly count on you for stimulation. All you do is grow children and swim.'

'The swimming's a necessity.'

'A woman for necessity, a boy for pleasure, a goat for delight.' Diana laughed as she remembered the phrase.

129

Her daughter stared at her. 'What?'

'Anyway, Elena, it's exhausting the way you gripe about guests.'

There was stamping on the ceiling – someone was running about on the floor above – screaming as though being chased. Quick light steps going round and round and round. Diana widened her eyes and lay back. She'd used to do that around the edge of his study, running her fingertips over the leather-backs, young skin smooth against the hard skin. Round she went, past the skeleton (Who was she? Who was she? Princess or harlot, actress or nun, pretty and passionate or ugly and dumb?) once, twice, a third time – until he got her – caught! – and pulled her hands high above her head, so that she hung like a trussed bird and his laughter shook her body as though it were her own.

Rue de Lille, 1925

'Where have you been?'

'Down in the catacombs.'

Diana nodded and picked up the skull on his desk that he'd taken last week, her fingers worming through the holes where the eyes had been.

'Did you touch all the smooth heads with not a thought in them?'

He grinned, enjoying his words in her mouth.

'Do you miss Boston?' she asked in a voice that attempted nonchalance, trailing her hand along the back of the chair he sat in.

'No. Boston is a dreadful city full of nothing. All the men are as tall and organised as their brownstone houses, and the women are sad drab virgins. Don't ever be a virgin, Rat; it eats you up.' He looked back down at the letter in his hand as he spoke. 'Bostonian women are brought up among sexless surroundings, wear canvas drawers and flat-heeled shoes and, once they are married, breed for five or

131

six years and then retire to end their days at the Chilton Club.'

'Mother only ... Caresse only had me.'

'I didn't save her in time. Thank God we got out. Christ, what a narrow escape!' He ran a hand over his face. 'Far narrower than escaping the shells at Verdun.'

He folded the letter he'd been reading.

'Your mother writes from Boston that she is desperately bored and that her mother objects to her letting the hair grow under her arms. Ye gods!'

'When is she coming back?'

'Soon.'

Roccasinibalda, 1970

'Tell us about your interview, Caresse.' Diana leaned forward and addressed her mother at the head of the long dining table placed at the centre of a large hall whose walls bore the pale half-shapes of the frescoes being gradually revealed beneath layers of milky plaster.

Caresse gave her daughter a mild look, carefully concealing her alarm at Diana's light-hearted tone. She was aware of the guests gathered round her, their faces moving in the uncertain candlelight.

'Well, we couldn't cover everything.' With slow movements she pressed her napkin to her mouth and then placed it to the side of her plate. 'A life in half an hour is a somewhat Herculean task.' She smiled blandly at a young writer from Istanbul.

'What did you choose to talk about today?' Diana pressed on, undeterred.

'That would be telling.'

'I don't suppose Harry came up?'

133

Caresse declined with a small motion of her head and picked up her spoon.

'Who was Harry?' a moon-faced girl asked.

'My husband,' Caresse said.

'A poet,' said Diana.

'A true original.' Caresse spoke and it was a command for attention. 'A prophet, as all poets are.'

'Who was it that said that?' asked Diana lightly.

'Lawrence.' Caresse deflected her gaze. 'He used to call artists "the life-givers of the Universe", in that insect hum of his.'

Diana smiled at that, picturing the people swarming across the rugs in the garden as someone swam back and forth in the algae-filled pool (full of life, her mother always said) singing a song with only two words. How had it gone? She hummed it quietly to herself.

'Wasn't Harry Crosby the nephew of J. P. Morgan?' a bespectacled young man asked, settling his elbows on the table. 'I remember meeting a Crosby at a gallery opening in New York a few years ago and being told about a black sheep cousin that had gone mad in Paris during the twenties.'

'And what, in your opinion,' Caresse laced her fingers together, 'does "going mad" mean?'

'Losing one's mind, I suppose,' the man said. 'Being unable to take part in the shared narrative.'

Diana tried to place the young man, and then remembered Ellis telling her that he'd been overheard in the village asking for nut milk. That was right. He was writing a symphony of silence. She looked at him with amused interest.

'If you are given a mind shaped only to a broken purpose, then it might be best to lose it. Then you can grow a new one instead. A fresh head of lettuce rather than the rotten bag of mould we were all handed and asked to asphyxiate ourselves inside. After all, that's the entire point of this place. A nursery of new thought, each and every one of you seedlings.'

'There's plenty of manure,' murmured Diana, turning her glass in her hand, causing Ellis, who was sitting beside her, to snort with laughter.

'And we need new narratives, my dear.' Caresse smiled coolly at the man. 'The more insane the better. Insanity is not the problem, inhumanity is. My husband – whom you did not have the fortune to meet – had one of the finest minds I've ever known, and I've known a few.' She nodded briskly to the young man, ready to close the subject.

Diana stopped turning her glass.

'And he fought in France?' Ellis asked. He glanced at Diana as he spoke, but she was staring ahead of her as though lost in thought.

'Yes, he did,' Caresse replied, masking her impatience. 'That terrible war. By all accounts, it was a miracle he survived.'

'And you're currently editing his diaries?' someone asked. 'What a beautiful task for a wife.'

'I think so, yes.' Caresse smiled.

Diana stared at her plate as though she might break it.

'But the war must have affected your husband?' Nut Milk returned to his point, blinking a little behind his large glasses. Diana looked at him in surprise. He was entirely undeterred.

'Of course it did. How could it not?' Caresse glanced at him. 'But it didn't *define* him.'

Diana's eyes flicked between the two of them. Her mother hated this kind of talk.

'I think,' he leaned forward eagerly, 'that we are all at war. Either with ourselves or our past.'

'We're hardly qualified to delve into our psyche, my dear, collective or otherwise. What a bore. And if the psyche will reveal anything, let it be freed from the unconscious in all its uninterpreted Surrealist glory.' Caresse turned firmly back to the man on her right.

'But don't they fascinate you, Mrs Crosby,' Nut Milk interrupted again, 'the small details that make up our lives, the little scars that become the map of who we are?'

Diana crossed her arms and leaned back, delighted.

'No.' Caresse shook her head, eyes flashing. 'I can't bear details. Never could. They're for school teachers and secretaries. Endless dates, facts and schedules – death to life! People wrap themselves up in detail as some kind of protection. In my opinion, the only good thing about details is the devil inside them.'

Watched by Diana, the table laughed. Just as he had, she remembered, when he'd heard her say that all those years ago.

'You know, there are only two things that I hate: war, and tedious conversation.' Caresse's voice rose. 'I first tried to start our Città della Pace at Delphi in Greece on a little promontory of Mount Parnassus – the birthplace of democracy. The local people were all very excited about it and we had some wonderful meetings with the shepherds and their wives and children, sharing cheese and red wine and ideas under their lovely gnarled trees. Unfortunately, the government opposed what we were doing and threatened to expel us. Of course we stood our ground and things got a little heavy. But when the army came to move us out, there was a beautiful moment.' She paused and reached out to take a pink-flecked peony from the huge arrangement in front of her. 'Each of the men had stuck a flower into the end of the barrel of his gun as they came to escort us away.' She smiled and the guests smiled back. 'Now, here's to Life!' She raised her glass, her eyes slicing the young man out of the toast.

'To Life!' the table chorused.

'Well, he won't be coming again,' Diana murmured to Ellis. She could feel him breathing, a trembling aliveness that smelled of yesterday's booze. 'The mung bean shall sprout no more.'

'Your young friend tells me you went hunting for wild boar on Sunday with some of the local men.' He indicated to where David sat at the other end of the table. 'Apparently, you're a crack shot.'

She laughed, pleased. 'I should have taken aim at that one.' She nodded up to the head of the table, where Nut Milk was trying in vain to re-engage Caresse in conversation.

'Diana the Huntress. Where does the name come from?' Ellis asked.

'My mother, funnily enough.'

'But why Diana?'

'It was her middle name.'

'Caresse Diana . . .' He waited for the surname.

'She wasn't christened that. I don't know if you've ever been to Back Bay, Boston, but a name like Caresse was hardly topping the birth register in 1891. The family were collectively sick when she changed it. Running off to Paris with a second husband was one thing, renaming yourself in the name of tenderness, quite another. There is nothing more profane to the Bostonian than sex between man and wife. Let alone a woman and life. Now I think they rather like it. I suppose, given enough time, even the most violent rebellion becomes somewhat sentimentalised, which is a pity. It suggests a rather pathetic action of the heart, sort of like the tiresome way children always want to go home.'

'Well, we are all children yet.'

Diana looked up the table towards where Caresse was leaning into the glow of the candlelight, laughing in surprise at someone's remark.

'We should take some guns, go for a walk together,' Ellis suggested.

She laughed. 'Are you hiding weapons in the Città della Pace?'

'With people like you around, I'd be a fool not to.'

'Oh, I wouldn't use a gun for *that*. I have other means at my disposal.' She smiled, broad and unexpected.

He forked some food into his mouth but then paused and frowned.

'What's wrong?' Diana asked, laughing.

'What is this?'

Diana ate some. 'Tripe.'

He nodded and wiped his mouth with his napkin. 'Bad associations, that's all.'

Diana ate some more. 'I like this style of cooking. *La cucina povera*. Scraps from the big table transformed into something even more delicious. I admire it.'

'Your mother serves a lot of offal.'

'Were you hoping for lobster?'

He laughed. 'Ah, little girl, if you only knew what this meat is made of.' He patted his thick stomach. 'I'm like a pelican that lives on a dump.'

But Diana was not listening. She'd caught her reflection in the dimly lit mirror hanging on the opposite wall. She moved her head a little ... to make sure of ... With a slight inclination of her neck she met herself at her best. There. Those lovely planes and curves, the hollows of her cheeks (she sucked slightly and the shadow deepened), the turn of her brow (the recent tuck had neatened things up beautifully) and the wide, friendly expanse of her mouth. She smiled to herself and relaxed back into the conversation.

'So, you and the sculpting prodigy?' Ellis glanced back at David.

Diana's eyes flicked away. She disliked uninitiated intimacies. 'Why don't you tell me about your work.'

'The words were all right today.' He bent low over his plate and Diana could hear the food moving inside his mouth. 'But I'm no prophet.' He pulled a bit of gristle from his teeth and wiped it on the side of his plate.

She observed him, revolted. 'I don't know about all that prophet talk really.'

'More profit than prophet – J. P. Morgan's nephew.' He laughed. 'No disrespect intended. It's just that it's easy to play the artist with goose feathers in your pillow ...'

Diana dragged her eyes slowly over his plate, face and loaded fork.

'I'm a leech, I'll admit that.' He finished his mouthful. 'You don't need to insinuate. Your mother's got big generous white arms and she opens them to all of us.'

'It's not *her* money paying for this, Mr Porto; that's been bled dry. It's Morgan dollars putting the ink in your pen.'

Ellis laughed. 'I'm a hypocrite, *mon lecteur.*' He spread his hands.

'Everybody gets that line wrong,' Diana said with a sneer and turned away.

The girl on Ellis's left leaned across. 'Will you tell me what you've been working on, Mr Porto? I so love your work. When I heard you were here I was so excited. I said to my friend, I said, Ellis Porto!'

'You were excited, were you?'

'Yes, I love your poems.' The girl's lips were full and soft.

'What do you love about my poems?'

'I love their power,' she said shyly. 'They aren't afraid. You say what you think. What's that unforgettable line . . .?' She looked up at the ceiling as though it might appear in the vaulted shadows. Ellis stared at her from beneath his eyebrows, but the girl continued, oblivious. 'You just . . . go for it.'

'I go for it, do I?'

'Yes,' she breathed. 'Will you do one for us? Do a poem?'

Ellis looked at her and then, with a glance at Diana, who was talking to the man beside her, stood. 'Yeah. I'll do a poem for you.' He scraped his heavy chair back across the stone floor.

'A poem,' he shouted.

Caresse smiled broadly and leaned forward, so that the conversation around her subsided.

Ellis hoisted himself up onto the table, staggered for a moment and then stood bathed in candlelight from the enormous iron chandelier that hung above his head.

'I've been asked to do a poem,' he announced to the lifted faces. The girl below him clasped her hands in rapture.

'This doesn't have a title as yet.' He turned towards the girl, steadying himself on his feet. His hand unzipped his fly and with one movement he took his penis out of his trousers and began to rub himself, staring straight ahead.

There was silence, nobody moved.

The poet's shallow breathing got faster as his hand moved up and down, the unmistakable sound filling the cavernous space. One of the girls from the kitchen entered the doorway holding a large bowl, saw what was happening and disappeared back into darkness.

With a final weak movement, Ellis convulsed and grunted before letting go.

The girl before him was very still, a red rash creeping up her neck.

Each of the guests dragged their eyes towards Caresse at the head of the table. She pushed her chair back so that it groaned against the flagstones and stood, before walking with deliberate steps round the table, all eyes following her progress. When she reached Ellis's empty chair she stopped, and raised her white napkin up towards him.

'Thank you, Ellis, that was certainly something new.'

Le Moulin du Soleil, 1926

'What's your favourite letter, Rat?'

'Why?' she asked.

He lowered the shotgun that he was aiming through the bathroom window at a pheasant strutting on the lawn, and laughed.

'What's yours?' she asked, watching the bird's progress through his field glasses.

He lifted the gun again and squinted down the sight.

'I, of course.'

Alderney, 1993

'Are you ready to take it in?' Her mother held the tray out. Bay mournfully took in the grin of banana, folded napkin and glass of milk. She felt a lump in her throat at the missing little vase that normally held some wild flowers that her mother picked as she walked in the garden saying her prayers. Her father still needed to glue it back together.

'Come on, darling, take it.' Her mother held the tray out expectantly.

The door was pushed open, and Bay entered the dark of the bedroom. It was warm inside, the air heavy and sweet, and the body of her grandmother was just visible on the bed. Putting the tray down with shaky hands, she tiptoed lightly to the window and pulled the thin cord of the curtains as though hoisting a sail, so that light entered the room by degrees. She turned back and saw with surprise that her grandmother's head was invisible, wrapped in layers of material like a mummy. She peered at it, and then reared back when her grandmother sat up, her covered head looking blindly left and right. Thin arms raised themselves in a stretch and then, patting her head as though checking she was actually there, the hands began to slowly unwind the scarf from her head. Beneath it, her grandmother wore a mask over her eyes and between them a large sticker covered her forehead. These were pulled away in quick succession.

'It's you. How nice to have a maid again,' she said and leaned forward. 'Pillows.'

'Why are you wrapped up like that?' Bay asked, as she struggled with the pillows.

'It's my vanishing act.' She blinked a few times. 'What's your mother doing?'

'She's busy getting us ready for the beach,' Bay said quietly, not wanting to tell her grandmother that she'd asked to bring in the tray.

'Busy busy busy.' Bay did not like the way her grandmother said it. 'Your mother keeps herself so tightly wound,' she began to cough, 'she doesn't leave her hands free for much else.' Bay thought that her grandmother's face seemed crumpled, like her bed, and she wanted her mother to come in and pull it all smooth and tuck the corners tight.

'The perfect breakfast.' Diana gazed with satisfaction at the tray. 'The gallant banana, peeled thus. Perfectly ripe.' She took a bite. 'And then,' her voice was thick with the fruit, 'the cold milk. Keeps you strong.' She put the glass down and stared levelly at Bay. 'Aren't you going to ask me how I am?' There was milk round her mouth.

Bay shook her head and looked down.

'Well, I feel awful.'

Bay nodded. One of the photos on the bedside table was

an old man wearing a long coat, her very young grandmother beside him wearing a stiff white dress. Bay stared at it.

'What are you staring at?'

With a start, Bay indicated the picture.

'My first wedding. Look how sweet I was in my Schiaparelli. But I don't recommend marrying someone your father's age. No oomph.'

Bay put the picture down and took another.

'Now that one. That's more like it.'

'Who was he?' Bay asked, sitting half on, half off the bed, her thigh beginning to tremble.

Diana laughed, bitterly. 'He *was* my lover,' she said in a lowering tone. 'One of the greatest matadors in Spain. Could kill a bull with a single thrust. Best hands of any man I've been with.'

Bay stared at her grandmother.

'And what did he do?' She'd heard her parents ask that when there were silences.

'Do?' Her grandmother stretched the word into a world of possibility. She leaned back and smiled. 'He made love to me, Bay. Endlessly.'

Elena heard Bay slapping down the stairs, one two three, dragging the tray behind her. She turned away from the cupboard she was filling to look at her daughter. The child was thin, Elena thought. She looked like an old woman with that worried frown and hunched shoulders.

'Did Grandma like her breakfast?'

Bay nodded and went to the kitchen table. She put the tray down and climbed onto a chair, resting her head in the soft crook of her elbow.

'What is it, darling?' Elena asked as she took ham, tomatoes and lettuce from the fridge and laid them on a chopping board in front of Bay.

Bay shook her head.

'Are you sure?' Elena pulled a serrated knife from the rack and took a loaf of bread by its neck.

'Is there . . . something you want to say, Bay?'

'I . . .'

'Yes?' Elena looked at her encouragingly, knife poised.

'Will I *have* to have many lovers?'

'Lovers?' The knife bit into the soft brown bread.

'Grandma told me I'll have too many lovers to know what to do with.'

'She . . . she shouldn't have said that, Bay.' Elena's voice faltered.

'What do you *do* when you're lovers?' Bay darted a look at her mother.

'You . . . love each other,' Elena said carefully, as her mind scuttled down a darkened channel of thought. She was in her father's study, listening to him describe the new woman he'd met. 'She looked rather like this . . .' and she'd gone closer to look at the magazine he kept in the drawer of his desk.

'Can you do it in clothes, Mama?' Bay asked, but looking over she saw that her mother had gone very still. 'Mama?'

'You don't need to think about all that, Bay,' she said in a high, bright voice, and Bay felt a lurching in her stomach, as though they were walking down the steep cliff path to the beach, having to grip the tufts of grass sprouting from the rocks so as not to slip and fall.

Her mother came and knelt before Bay, her hand still clutching the knife, and now Bay became very still. 'You don't need to think about *any* of that, my love. You must just enjoy your lovely summer holiday. You must just enjoy.'

Bay nodded, once, and Elena slowly got to her feet. Turning back to the table, she took the bread in hand and, with some difficulty, continued cutting.

Rue de Lille, 1925

'I am unworthy.' He came in and lay down across her nursery bed.

'Why?' She put down her pencil and glanced at Mette, who crossed her arms and pulled her mouth to one side.

'It is disgusting to be so drunk,' he said with his face in her pillow. 'I will go running. I want clean lines and aching fresh lungs.'

'What happened?' Diana asked, getting up from her desk.

'*Pisse et fumier.* Most of the memories are still unconscious, thank God.'

'What's wrong with your wrist?'

'I fell off a table.'

'Mette hurt her back trying to lift me out of bed when I wouldn't get up.' Diana looked at Mette encouragingly, willing a show of empathy.

'Come on, Rat, enough of your copy book. You can take the morning off, Mette. I'll teach the Wretched Rat today.'

'We have not finished her lesson, monsieur.'

'Later.'

Mette stood and took down the small jacket from the hook. She helped Diana into it and then knelt to do up its buttons.

'Diana.' Mette looked into her eyes. 'I will wait here for you.'

Diana leaned briefly against the familiar, solid bosom and was held tight.

'Come on, Wretch. Caresse returns from Deauville today, let's have a breakfast of raspberries and bacon and eggs in the sunny golden garden of the Ritz. Luxury will purify, we'll make it our morning prayer for your mother's safe return.'

Roccasinibalda, 1970

Diana looked at her mother as she slept. Slackened by sleeping pills, chin tucked into chest, she was really rather ugly. She recalled her face in the garden of Le Moulin, then so gentle in sleep, completely abandoned. She'd always done that – slept like a milk-drowned baby – impervious to the loudest sound. Diana could scream at the top of her voice and she would not so much as stir. 'It's a skill, Diana, necessary for survival. When you've a husband who reads throughout the night with every lamp in the bedroom blazing, there's no other way to get the rest that beauty needs.'

But it wasn't just a skill for the bedroom. She had used it everywhere. Yes, her mother had been perfect lying asleep in the garden with a party going on around her, lips stretched into a satisfied smile as though she knew everyone was watching; her body in its yellow dress like a snake in the grass, stretched alongside another man.

She put the tray down. She could never sleep like that.

Bed was where her head came alive, thoughts pushing and shoving ... sweet mercy of Xanax.

Her mother moved slightly. Leaning forward, Diana saw that beneath the marbled lids the eyes were switching back and forth, her joints twitching, probably with the memory of some pleasure ...

Caresse felt herself pulled upward by the sly clink of ice in a glass.

Her eyes opened onto her daughter holding a tray and she frowned, squeezing her eyes closed, shutting her out, and pushed back through the fading movements of the night, searching. She had been at home on Singing Beach ... her father down by the shore. Yes, that was it, at the house made of shells, a scalp of seaweed heavy in her hand. But it was passing, she could feel the warm, sweat-soaked pillow beneath her head; and a small grieving sound escaped as she was returned to her body ... Her eyes opened again on the familiar bedroom and she felt the weight of herself beneath the covers. She grimaced as she tried to sit up, the papers she had been reading crunching around her.

She stared at the iced glass of apricot juice.

'There's no need to look like that. I didn't do it.' Diana glanced down at the tray and then deposited it on the bed.

'Well, who did? The girls are hardly prone to pretty gestures.' Caresse insisted on referring to the grey-haired women from the village who came every day to cook and clean as the girls.

'It was David's idea. He was going to bring it up, you asked to see him.'

'I stayed up late, working.' These days, Caresse did not

like to be caught sleeping. As she moved, the covers released a close smell, all too human, and she pressed them carefully back down, aware of her daughter's proximity.

'All the lights were on. The nurse should have turned them off.' Diana passed her the pills by her bed.

'I told you she was superfluous. The girls were doing absolutely fine. You can take her back to whichever asylum you found her in.' Caresse swallowed the pills. 'We've always had terrible luck with our staff, haven't we?'

'Roberto found her, actually.' Diana was not in the mood to play.

'Oh? Dear Roberto.'

'Yes, oh dear Roberto. I'll go and get her.'

'No, stay.' Something in her tone made Diana stop. 'I don't feel very well. I think yesterday tired me out a little.'

'Well, avoiding things is tiresome.'

'Oh, don't!' Caresse flapped her hand at her daughter. 'Don't start all that again.'

Diana retreated. 'I thought you would enjoy being interviewed.'

'Not particularly. They ask dull questions, I give interesting answers . . .'

'Yes, I've spent a bit of time with them,' Diana agreed. 'Not the sharpest blades on the rack. They wanted to know about my take on things too,' she added lightly.

'You are free to say what you will and do as you wish,' Caresse said, her voice low. 'If you've come here to look for ghosts, Diana, you'll find plenty. But I'll not help you grub about. It's the young who are important here. They mean something.' She pressed her hands to the sides of her face. 'Oh my head, you are hard to wake me up with this.'

'You are aware, Caresse, that the young grow old?'

'I don't like it when you're sardonic; you sound just like your father. Now, unless there's something you particularly wanted, I'd like to dress in peace.'

'You asked to see David. What did you want to talk to him about?'

'Did I?'

'Yes, you said you wanted to have a "little word".'

'Never mind. Let's look at the plan for today and see what's *happening*.'

'I do mind. What did you want to talk to him about?'

'Are you sitting for him?'

'No. He hasn't asked. Why? What the hell does that have to do with anything?'

'Well, don't sit around waiting to be *asked*, Diana. You should do one of him. I was always sculpting heads of the men I found interesting. There was once a very funny incident with a famous old artist who agreed to teach me to paint in his studio in Paris. He asked me to undress and I—'

'Caresse, *please*.'

After a moment's pause, Caresse spoke. 'I heard he was getting serious about you, that's all,' she said lightly.

'Yes, we've fallen in love rather.' Diana positioned herself on the pink silk chair. 'Well, he has, anyway.'

'You can't fight that.' Caresse shook her head. 'I've never battled my body on that count, and I think that's quite right. We are fools who don't listen to the wisdom of the corporeal. Mine's sending me rather bitter notes today, but I'm not fighting it.' She stopped and then went on: 'His little wife was terribly upset, you know.' Caresse glanced at Diana over the top of her glasses. 'She came to see me yesterday.'

'Oh really?'

'Yes. I gave her the money to fly home.'

'Economy, I hope.'

'Honestly, Diana, I dislike conversation without piquancy but sometimes you almost burn. The child looked about twelve, her mother's probably beside herself. Young heartbreak,' she sighed, 'so beautiful.'

Diana remained seated, waiting.

'Are you planning to take him back to Ibiza?' Caresse said after a pause.

'I'm working on it.'

'What does that mean?'

'He's still got some of his own ideas.'

'That's not like you.'

'He wants to go back to London for a while. His work . . .' She trailed off into thoughtful silence.

'And will Elena be in Ibiza when you arrive?'

'No.' Diana frowned, her voice hard. 'Why?'

'No reason in particular. I just know how important time alone is at the beginning.'

Diana sat back and looked at her mother. 'Shall we look at your list, Caresse?' she said, placing each word carefully between them.

Caresse opened the large diary. 'Yes, let's look at today.'

After Diana had gone, Caresse lay back and through the window saw cloud. It came quickly here in the mountains, a deft milky covering of green until the castle was submerged

154

in the drift of dense air. Caresse waited with one finger in the air until she heard the crack of thunder and then the wash of rain, tiny hands hitting everything. She loved it when it rained like this. It meant not feeling guilty at lying in bed like an old pillow – some kind of . . . matron. And it was a familiar sound, a grey sound, wrapped in warmth. Yes, rain was the Boston sky, home, her beginning . . . a heaped grey of boredom broken only by tears. That rain had fallen without stopping until everything was sodden and the streets were drenched almost black. Until he came. Caresse felt her heart move, and she shook her head as though refusing someone entry. Oh, it had been silent as she'd waited for him in that house full of clocks and whispered hallway conversations and cars driving past and never once stopping.

There was Diana, hidden away with the nanny in the barricaded nursery, and the stiff rustle of her mother-in-law drawing lines of duty around the house. 'I know it's not easy having your husband away, Mary dear, but you are a mother now and we must look on the bright side.' And the cosy little upward glance to the floor above. God, she'd sat for hours, like an abandoned fort, doing nothing, seeing no one. What a life. Waiting for visiting hours and the rounds of flowered hats and polite gossip stirred into Darjeeling with small silver spoons, the black tea turning milky with false kindness. The acid murmurs of the women, as gloved hands pulled the still-bloody scalps of those who had strayed from exquisite beaded bags to be compared, weighed, and then pinned to the noticeboard of the Chilton Country Club.

Then he'd come. Salvation in the wilderness.

Her mother-in-law at the breakfast table, looking up from a letter. 'Mary, would you like to chaperone a party going out for the day next week? You're twenty-seven now, that's quite proper. It's being organised by that Crosby boy. No, the blond one. Well, I don't know about that, I think he's rather strange-looking with those very intense eyes. His mother's in despair about him. Well yes, it's him.'

And there he'd been. The most beautiful man she'd ever seen.

The memory birthed and squirmed and beneath the blanket Caresse clenched her thighs – his uncovered head (house of those thoughts, all those thoughts) turning towards her and their eyes meeting as they each took off a glove to shake the other's hand. An electric connection. Taking each other in, giving themselves away.

And the torture, the *torture* of having to talk and look at all those people, braying about nothing but each other, unaware that she'd been cut, cut very deep, and was already drifting free above all of them. No more dates and diaries, just love and ideas and never having to stay. Never having to stay.

She tried to focus her eyes on the sky outside her window, wanting to hold on to the feeling of that first day, the certainty of his hands as he'd undone her ... But memory will not be dictated to – she knew that much – so here were the three of them at the funfair, Diana kneeling in the mud by the House of Horrors, given over to grief because she was too small to go in. And then it was goodbye to her husband's home, stuffed with fans and figurines, snuff boxes and lacquered screens. Then New York City Hall, long grey wedding gloves and a hotel bed full of pressed promises, the universe sought between their parted lips.

And here was the second blow of the huge ship's horn, causing Diana to grip her hand too tight where they waited on the dock, and here was the look on his face as he came towards them and saw the little hand that stopped her being able to fully raise her arm in greeting. Now the last warning blast of the horn that set the seabirds reeling, and she was alone with Diana on the top deck watching her old life recede.

But *he'd* brought something with him *too*. She felt a flare of rage that surprised her with its strength. He brought them *all*, the Boston Brahmins, with their hypocrisy and little ways – rebellion for six days and remorse on the seventh. They might have escaped but he never could stop taking their stale bread and sour wine. Measuring how far he'd come, but always by their rule.

But then – her heart changed direction and she felt about to cry – how do we *stop* believing in the very stuff we are made of? She just *had*, but that was *her*. Perhaps she'd never believed it, or perhaps it was that she believed everything all at once rather than one thing at a time.

And besides, where were these thoughts coming from? Where was this getting her? And how very far it all was from the way he'd looked at her as he came out of the sea, thighs straining against the tide, on the deserted beach in Étretat sunk between two abrupt cliffs.

Chest heaving, half-laughing, he lay down in the sand beside her, heedless of the red flag flapping crazily in the wind, or her panic at his having been gone for so long. That great, great gift of carelessness.

He'd looked up at her with those eyes, terribly blue, and said, 'You look like a saint.'

'I thought you were dead,' she'd replied laughing.

'Not without you.' He'd reached up and she'd pressed his hand against her heart.

Not without you.

She squeezed her eyes shut.

Not without you, Caresse.

Then why his naked feet dead and cold? Why those telegrams STOP. Death will be our marriage STOP. Those stockings like two shed snakeskins.

She pushed the image away, kicked it down like an intruder in her bed. But here it was, forcing its way in – the sound of the phone ringing and ringing as she stood in the New York Plaza tearoom with his mother's eyes watching her over the rim of her bone china teacup. And Hart's voice through the wire, pouring pain in her ear: 'Caresse, he isn't alone.'

He wasn't alone. Terrible comfort.

And then his mother's face collapsing inside her gloved hands. Having to share the grief with his mother, as though they were the same. She'd never made peace with that part.

'Roberto.' She slammed the memory shut as the lawyer walked in and stretched out her hands towards him. 'Come and sit. Come and sit over here.' She patted the bed while he carefully hung his jacket on the back of a chair and then came and sat down beside her. 'Now you must tell me what's been going on. How is everything downstairs? You must be exhausted. I'm *absolutely* exhausted.' Her voice was wheezing. 'And rather angry actually, with Diana, for being so . . . so . . . what was your word?'

158

'Ego-maniacal,' he said with satisfaction, feeling afresh the acuity of the observation.

'Oh, was that it?' Caresse said in a disappointed voice. 'It sounded rather better when you said it yesterday.'

'Diana has a narcissistic temperament.' He'd sat next to a young analyst from Copenhagen the evening before at dinner, and she had described the pathology in fascinating detail.

'That sounds rather simplistic, Roberto. You said something much more interesting last night.'

'She takes things too far,' he attempted, blindly.

Caresse stared at him levelly and then turned and gazed out the window. 'I wonder why she's compelled to continually dig things up? It's in her nature, I suppose. Though where she gets that from is anybody's guess.'

'She needs to take more care . . . she is not young any more,' Roberto said, trying to meet Caresse's eyes. 'Diana cannot continue cutting ties in this manner without ending up in a very lonely position.'

'Well, I don't know about all that. We're hardly in the spring of our existence, Roberto. Diana's life is her life. But she does seem rather hell-bent on getting *at* something. She can be such fun, you know, when she wants to be; it's a shame.'

'Fun is what you need, Principessa,' Roberto enunciated the nickname. 'Fun is who you are.'

She laughed and finally looked round. 'You are absurd. But it's true. I am fun. And it's been in rather low supply round here of late. Just look at me, spending an afternoon staring mournfully out of the window. You know, after Harry died I was in such pain that I threw a huge Surrealist party in Paris.

I placed a cow's carcass in the corner with a record player in its stomach, there were waiters wearing suits made of hair with cages of birds on their heads . . . It was vile! The perfect antidote to all . . . that.'

'Well, perhaps it's time?' He gave her one of the roguish smiles he knew delighted her.

'Time for a party?' She looked unsure for a moment but then laughed and it seemed as if there was something budding beneath her pale, veined cheeks. 'What reason have we?'

'As if you have ever needed a reason!'

'Ha! You know me too well.' She hit his leg happily with the back of her hand. 'Yes, let's organise a wonderful party.'

Paris, 1925

'How old is that child?'
   'Old enough to count to ten.'
   'She's far too young to be in the hotel bar.'
   'And you're far too old, madam.'
   'She's drunk.'
   'She's a little tight, I'll give you that.'
   'It's intolerable.'
   'Then do something to stop it,' he laughed.
   'She can hardly see straight.'
   'Yes, I can,' yelled Diana. 'I can see straight as a die.'

Alderney, 1993

'Slow down!' James called, and both he and Elena watched the small figures of their children dashing towards the abandoned road that stretched from the beach to the fort that stood on a small island a hundred metres from the shore.

'Shall we go across?' James asked. Elena nodded distractedly. 'Come back here,' he shouted, and the children changed direction and looped back towards them. Her conversation with her mother was turning itself over in her mind.

'What do they mean by "fight or flight"?' Diana had asked, looking at her as Elena retrieved the papers scattered around her mother's bed.

'Where did you hear that?'

'On the radio this morning. They were talking about soldiers, but I couldn't make the connection.'

'It's a mechanism of trauma,' Elena warily opened the subject. 'They were probably mentioning it in relation to PTSD.'

'Which is . . .?' Her mother listened keenly.

'Post-traumatic stress disorder.'

'Fight or flight? A rather limited menu of response.'

'There are others.'

'You neither fight nor fly. It was your sister who was the fighter.' She smiled approvingly. 'A tough little thing.'

Elena tensed her mouth.

'Whereas you, Elena . . .' Her mother dragged her eyes over her. 'You stick around. My dependable Elena.' She smiled into the mouth of her glass and drank.

'It's called freezing,' Elena said quietly. 'It's another response.'

'Hmm,' Diana said. 'Well, you have always been distinctly *froide*.'

'And the last is fawn. I believe that's what your friends are for.'

Diana ignored her.

'Besides, I do leave,' Elena said indignantly, already hating herself for being drawn in. 'I haven't been here for over two years.'

'You may leave,' her mother said. 'But you always come back.'

'I'm always asked to,' Elena said, exasperated.

'People can *ask* what they like. Some of the things I've been asked to do! My God, you'd lose your mind. You don't have to do them, Elena. You only have to *do* what you want. Your sister was always clear on that front. Always stood her ground. Solid, that's what she is. The fact that she spends most of her time kneeling these days, well . . .' She whisked her hand about.

'Didn't she always?' Elena said viciously, and Diana laughed, delighted.

Elena pressed her hands into her eyes. 'I don't mean that. Leonie's . . . amazing.'

Her mother looked at her for a moment. 'Hiding in a convent? What's amazing is that they let her in.'

'There's no hiding in a convent, Diana,' Elena said. 'She's chosen an arduous path.'

'Jealous?' her mother said, with a needling smile.

Elena shook her head. Her mother had the ability to locate the correct emotion in much the same way that she would immediately find the children on the rare occasions she was induced to join a game of hide and seek, without moving from the sofa or setting aside her magazine.

'Yes, I'm a little jealous. A life of silence is . . . tempting.'

'You do a bloody good job at trying . . .'

Now as Elena walked onto the short causeway that led to the gates of the abandoned fort, she saw the way the tide had pulled the sea back from the shore, revealing the rough rock formations usually concealed by the smooth sheet of water. The children peered left and right as they picked their way over them, occasionally kneeling down to put a tentative hand into the pools of warm water that lay in the lee of the rocks, daring themselves to touch what was inside them.

As Elena and James walked through the broken gates, the boys appeared at their sides. 'Can we go in there?' Jake asked, pointing to a dark doorway, surrounded by a tangle of nettles.

'Yes, but you must be careful,' Elena warned as she felt broken glass crunch under her battered plimsoll. 'Perhaps you should go with them, James?' And James let go of her arm and went towards the boys.

In the silence they could hear, from somewhere, a thundering sound.

'Why's the water in this hole black?' one of the boys shouted.

'It's not. It's clear as day,' James replied, disappearing behind them into the dark. 'A trick of the light.'

Through the doorway, Elena saw the beam of a torch moving over a concrete wall, marked as though it had been filled with dirty water that had slowly drained away over the years. She could hear James speaking to the boys.

'The Germans needed vast stocks of essentials in order to withstand a sustained assault. The beach we're on was in a vulnerable position and they laid a number of . . .'

'Bottles!' one of the boys exclaimed. There was a smash. 'Wait!' Elena heard James call. 'You mustn't smash a wine bottle until you're absolutely sure it's undrinkable.' There was silence. 'All right, you can break a few.' There were whoops as the smashing began. Elena followed through the doorway and felt herself swallowed up by the cool musty darkness. The sound of the sea beyond the fort's walls echoed in the abandoned space and somewhere there was the scurrying of tiny feet over broken glass. Elena felt a small hand steal into her own and she looked down to see Bay, backlit by the light from the doorway, staring into the dark at something only she could see. 'Have you had enough, Bay?' she said. 'Shall we go back?'

'Yes,' Bay said quietly, tightening her grip.

And turning round, they walked towards the square of light, leaving the noise of the smashing and whooping behind them.

Rue de Lille, 1926

'What is jazz?'

'An axe taken to a harpsichord.'

'How do you dance to it?'

'I don't.'

'Why?'

'I like to watch.'

'Well, I like to dance. I do shows for Auguste when he gets home after taking you and Caresse to the ends of the fucking earth.'

'Auguste is a very good chauffeur.'

'I'll go to jazz clubs when I'm older.'

'Jazz will be old when you're older.'

Diana was silent.

'I need to go and visit a man so that I can die tonight.' He closed his book and stood in a single movement.

'What will you die of?' Diana looked up at him.

'Colours. Too many colours. I feel I may crack open soon and what will come out will destroy the world.'

Alderney, 1993

Elena walked along the stretch of beach, arm in arm with the black-clad figure of her mother. She could see James in the distance by their red-and-yellow-striped windbreak. The long dress that she wore blew open as she walked, the pale grey cotton tangling round her and her mother's bare legs as they made their slow progress along the sand. Diana had insisted on wearing her heeled espadrilles. 'Can you walk in them?' Elena had asked as she knelt before her, winding the black ties round the ankles as smooth and age-spotted as polished walnut. And her mother had stared at her from beneath half-closed eyes. 'If I can walk the Hindu Kush in them, Elena, I can probably make my way to a beach blanket.' But now her mother gripped her arm tightly, and Elena had to bend towards her to keep them both from falling. She stopped briefly, pretending an interest in the horizon so as to give Diana a moment to breathe, and when she looked up saw James, standing now, watching them both.

It was strange, she reflected, that he had met her mother first.

She had heard many accounts of the meeting in Ibiza. The way her mother had pulled over in her dust-covered white Mercedes to pick him and his friend up from the side of the road in Es Canar – 'They looked like a couple of stray dogs, darling. Hungry as anything' – pushing her sunglasses on top of her head as she settled her blue eyes on them both. They parked in a thorny clifftop clearing and walked down a steep path to a cove where the boat was waiting, its sails slack in the afternoon heat. Elena remembered that she had been sitting with her sister Leonie on the sand, the two of them going round and round in one of their interminable arguments, while Elena stroked the neck of the frail hound she'd adopted. Diana had called loudly to her daughters, causing the people scattered on the small beach to turn towards her as she strode across the sand with the two young men behind her holding their tattered rucksacks. At the sound of their mother's voice, the girls had dropped whatever was between them and gone forward as one. Leonie, tall and confident, was the first to shake hands, so that Elena had time to watch the boys in silence as her sister spread her light, making everybody laugh. James had told her, many times since, that Elena had looked as shy of human touch as the lean dog she held, and that the way she had looked hard into his eyes as she took his hand in hers had shocked him. A look that neither he nor she, when they thought back to it, had ever been sure was a welcome or a warning.

'Diana!' James came forward. 'Good to see you up and about. What can I get you?'

The old woman slowly folded herself into a waiting beach chair and arranged her shoulders so that she was more comfortable. She arched her back and, indicating the bag now curled at her feet, gave him a smile. 'You can get me a drink.'

James leaned down and reached into the bag, pulling out a jar full of amber liquid. 'A Torito for the matador.' He smiled.

'I think we can make it a Toro today, if you'll join me.'

'You're always telling me I need to be more of a man,' James said. 'How can I possibly refuse.'

'Bravo, darling,' Diana laughed.

Bay came up and whispered in her mother's ear, telling her story in a stream of tears, turning and showing her marked legs.

'James?' Elena looked at him with troubled eyes. 'Have you ...?'

'Yes, he's over there.'

And down by the sea they could just see Tom sitting behind a large rock, his knees tucked to his chest.

Elena took a deep breath and pulling Bay towards her, whispered in her ear.

'Bay's going to bring you your drink,' Elena called, beginning to unload the food from the straw bags she'd packed.

'Ice. And a glass,' Diana commanded.

James handed Bay a stacked glass and she watched the ice crack and sigh as it was bathed in the warm liquid.

Her grandmother took the glass, her eyes not leaving Bay's as she drank.

'Equal quantities gin and sherry.' She held up a finger. 'Always Fino.'

Bay nodded solemnly. Always Fino.

'Bay, let me put some cream on you. I don't want you to burn,' Elena said, pulling the child between her legs.

'It's good to get a burn,' Diana said, watching them. 'A sun gift.'

'No.' Bay shook her head, looking over. 'My skin is too tight when it's burned.'

'Enjoy it while it lasts, Bay. You'll pay good money for that feeling one day.'

Elena gently pulled the straps of Bay's swimming costume off her shoulders. She stared at the golden down that ran from the nape of her daughter's neck into the low line of her costume. She ran a finger down it and saw a shiver roll through the small body.

'You know the Egyptians thought the Sun was actually the eye of a great cat opening in the morning and closing at night,' Diana said to Bay.

Bay turned her head sharply to look up at the burning whiteness, but her eyes were forced closed.

'Tell your grandmother what you did this morning,' her mother said steadily, shaking the blue plastic bottle in her hand so that it gave up its cream in a thin squirt that Bay felt, with another shiver, on the back of her neck. She twisted round to look up at her mother as the cream was rubbed in. She could see inside the curve of her slender nostrils to the dark space edged with very fine golden hairs. Her mother raised her eyebrows in question. Bay stared at her a second longer, and then closed her eyes. She did not want to turn her thoughts inside out today.

'Okay then, off you go. All done. Go and look at your rock pools.'

Bay nodded and dragged her bucket behind her until she got to a point where the sand became dark and mud-wet. Kneeling, she ran her fingers over its waved contours, feeling the warm water they held. She could just hear her mother's voice carried by the wind. But as she scooped up the sand, the sensation of its satisfying weight absorbed her thoughts.

'I've never liked those stories,' Elena said.

'What stories?' Diana said sharply.

'Those stories you tell about the sun. They give me the creeps. Always have.'

'Everything gives you the creeps,' Diana replied. 'You can hardly hear a dirty joke without entering a state of nervous collapse. Your sister's the same. I obviously failed to give either of you a sense of humour.'

Shielding her eyes, Elena watched as Bay made her way down towards where the boys were playing. 'You can hardly blame us. We had to swallow an awful lot of tawdry humour over the years.'

'Sex shouldn't be kept in the dark, Elena. That's where it becomes monstrous,' Diana said.

'Nor should it be draped across the hall, up the stairs, in the cupboards ...'

'Fabulous.'

'I don't want them to be ... exposed.'

'It happens sooner or later.'

'So let it be later. I don't want you putting ideas into their heads.'

'Balls. You just want to fill their heads with *your* ideas. Ideas are like the wind, Elena, they fly where they will.'

'I think it's understandable to want to change the narrative a little,' she murmured.

'Change is overrated. Nothing's ever that different. I once saw a church in Mexico City that the conquistadors built with the stones from an Aztec temple. One for another. All the same. Like men. One after another, one way or another.' Her rings clanked against the glass as she tipped its contents back into her throat. 'All the same,' she repeated. 'One way or another.'

'They're *not* all the same,' Elena said. 'We are not all the same.' The words were a flag, quietly unfurled.

'How so? How are you different?'

'I don't . . . you don't have to break things.'

'Don't be so sure.' Diana looked pointedly at her daughter's lap. 'Breaking things is how it all begins.'

Down by the shore, Bay watched her brothers at work, kneeling and patting wet sand into a wall that they had built and lined with rocks.

'Go away, Bay.'

'Why?' she asked, hands on hips.

'Because you told,' said Tom.

'But you hit me.' Indignant, she pointed out the mark, tears coming easily.

He refused to look at her, arms folded, his own mouth beginning to tremble.

'Drop it, you two,' Jake interrupted, tall and capable. 'Just ignore her, Tom.'

Bay felt tears begin to rise in earnest. 'But Daddy said . . .'

Her eldest brother turned to Bay. 'Just lie low, Bay,' he advised. 'You can watch for the waves.'

172

Shoulders slumped, she moved away to a safe distance. She always had to watch for the waves.

The wind was getting up. Trembling with cold, Bay picked her way along the tops of the sharp rocks, looking into the little mirrored bowls of sea. She crouched over and was about to mar the surface of one with her finger, when she saw her face reflected back at her, the sky above and behind, and she turned her head side to side, *jolie* and *laide*, *jolie* and *laide*, *jolie* and *laide*.

'Where is the photograph that was hanging in Bay's bedroom?'

Elena, who had been watching Bay by the rock pools at the water's edge, turned her attention reluctantly back towards her mother.

'I moved it.'

'Why?'

'I don't think it's . . . helpful.'

'*Helpful?*'

'It's a naked woman with her legs open.'

'Where exactly do you want those children to believe they came from?'

'A place of wholeness,' Elena said defiantly.

'Wholeness?' her mother laughed. 'That sounds like something from one of your self-help books.'

'Yes, wholeness,' Elena insisted. 'Rather than all that . . . muck.'

'Muck!' Diana laughed.

'There's a difference between biology and pornography, Diana.'

'It's art.'

173

'It's disturbing.'

'It's a fucking Man Ray.'

'I'll put it in your room as soon as I get home.'

'You'll put it back where you found it. I won't have all this prissiness. What is this sudden mania for innocence? Leonie was exactly the same. It's quite impossible to be around.'

'I don't see what trying to keep my children from harm has to do with any belief of mine.'

'Harm?' Diana raised her eyebrows. 'Harm, in a Man Ray. What next, demonic signals in Picasso?'

'I wouldn't know, you sold them all.'

'Your grandmother lost them all. Or, more precisely, her crooked fairy of a lawyer lost them all.'

'*I don't want to do this*,' Elena said in a single loud tone.

Diana brooded for a moment. 'Harm in a Man Ray.' She shook her head. 'Good *grief*.' She held out her glass and Elena refilled it with minimal grace. After a pause, Diana spoke: 'He was a character, I always liked him. Had those very sharp black eyes that seemed to cut you out so that he could stick you somewhere else in his mind.'

'I remember Caresse saying he was a bit dotty.'

'Dotty? Elena, what the hell has happened to your turn of phrase? He was crazy as a fucking quilt.'

Elena closed her eyes and pushed her toes blindly into the cold sand. She waited a few moments before opening them and avoided looking at her mother. Bay was walking slowly back towards them, shoulders hunched against the cold wind that had begun to blow the length of the long beach.

Diana swung her head round and observed the child. 'Like a little jazz girl with those small-boy buttocks.'

Elena looked over. Bay seemed terribly exposed on the wide stretch of beach. 'Please don't tell her that,' she said, almost to herself.

'Discovering your body can be an exciting time. All those feelings. It's most pleasing.'

Elena's eyes darted back and forth along the horizon. 'I'm taking her to have her hair cut tomorrow. I want it to be short like mine. So much easier.'

'You used to have very good hair. Why did you cut it off?'

Elena shrugged. She did not want to share with her mother the feeling of cutting through the thick dark hair until it sat just below her ears, revealing the length of her neck. She had turned her head left and right as she pulled the towel from her shoulders and then cautiously opened the door to show James.

'Well, you can just about carry it off. Gamine,' said Diana.

Reflexively, Elena clasped the back of her neck, waiting for the sting. But none came.

'I think it will suit Bay too.'

Diana dragged her eyes over. 'How old is she?'

'Six.'

Diana nodded. 'I had a little crop when I was six. I looked very sweet. Around the time I first fell in love.'

'Love?' Elena said.

'Yes,' her mother replied. 'Love at first sight.'

'That wasn't love.' She shook her head.

'It was my first great love.'

'You were too young to know any better.' Elena shielded her eyes as she looked at the approaching children. 'Hello, boys.' They pushed themselves into her and she received them

175

with open arms, gasping at the strength of their young thin bodies.

Jake pushed the hardest, and with a single arm holding Tom back, showed her the small fish held on the flat of his palm. The slender silvery body had stopped flipping this way and that, and now lay, barely quivering, its round gold eye staring up at the sky.

'We caught it,' he said breathlessly.

'It was my idea,' Tom called over his brother's shoulder, arms flailing, and then in a mutter that only Bay heard, 'and my net.'

'Aren't both of you clever. Now, I think you'd better put it back, don't you? There's no use keeping him, he's too small to eat.'

Jake gently prodded its pale belly with a single finger but, seeing the truth of her words, handed it to Tom.

Tom took the fish eagerly, but registering the ease with which his brother passed it to him and its consequent loss of value, tossed it into a bucket. 'Take it back.' He passed it clumsily to Bay. She took it, her heart full, and turned towards the sea, the bucket thumping against her legs.

'Go and get your father. It's time for lunch.' The two boys set off running, their shouts ringing out across the beach.

'Why don't you get a nanny?' Diana had taken in the entire scene without changing her slumped position. 'They're practically feral.'

'Because we can't afford one,' Elena said mildly. 'And, more to the point, I don't want them to be looked after by people that are going to cut in and out of their lives with no rhythm, no warning.'

'But you've always said that you would have *died* if it weren't for Inés.'

'Inés was more than a nanny,' Elena replied.

'You could afford one if James got a proper job. Your father made him a generous offer. And a little bookshop is hardly enough to keep Noah's Ark afloat.'

'I would only *need* a nanny if James had taken that job. As it is, we do it together.'

'Well, that's *abundantly* clear. Sorry, sorry.' Diana held up her hands. 'But in all seriousness, you can't find it attractive, Elena. Your man, knee-deep in nappies.'

'It means I see him,' Elena said. 'It rather helps with marriage, that.' She stood without waiting for her mother's reply. 'Now, I want to go and swim. The baby's getting so heavy.'

Diana ran her eyes over her daughter.

'Your arms are far too thin.'

Elena glanced down. 'Perhaps.'

Diana looked over to where her granddaughter was kneeling in the shallows, trying to make the fish swim again.

'I think Bay's more like me. She'll have my figure, I'm sure of it.'

Rue de Lille, 1926

'I visited a place last night called the House of All Nations.'

'What's it for?'

'Where people go to buy love. And pain, of course. There's a Persian room, a Russian room, Turkish, Japanese, Spanish – not to mention the room King Edward used to use, and a bathroom with mirrored walls and mirrored ceilings.'

'Why are they mirrored?'

'So you can keep an eye on things. I talked to the Madame and caught a glimpse of the thirty harlots waiting in the salon. There was a very lost-looking blonde hugging her knees. And there was a flogging post where men come to whip young girls . . .'

'Why?'

'Because love hurts.'

'Is the Madame married?'

'To half of Paris.'

'What questions did you ask her?'

'How many men a day? Average one hundred and fifty.'

'How much does it cost to love there?'

'Fifty francs for ten minutes, one hundred for an hour, three hundred for all night.'

'Do they really whip the girls, Harry?'

'Half to death, Rat.'

Roccasinibalda, 1970

'I'm thrilled you could all come. Thank you, Roberto, for organising this little get-together. Now I know we have some wonderful ideas beating about, and I can't wait to hear them all. Why don't we discuss what needs to be discussed and then let our imagination out the sack, how does that sound?'

The ten or so heads gathered on the terrace nodded seriously.

'Let's all have some wine. Maria, thank you.' The wine was poured and enormous platters of meat set down on the low table. A few cautious hands reached out and took a small slice or handful.

'Don't be shy.' Caresse, seated in a wicker chair whose back rose above her like a wing in flight, brought her hands together in a light clap. 'The joy of a party starts in its conception and should not finish until ... well, it should not finish at all, but live on in the mind's eye, to be returned to many times over the years.'

There was the sound of footsteps, slow and meandering,

and a voice singing a broken Flemish folk song and everybody turned to see Diana appear around the corner.

'Oh.' She stopped and raised her eyebrows. 'A committee. Saving the world or organising a tombola?'

'We're planning our party,' Caresse replied.

The company smiled shyly, they were all a little frightened of the daughter.

'Where have you been, darling?' Caresse said. 'You look very nice.'

Diana smoothed her emerald watered silk dress over her behind and sat down, brushing a curl off her forehead. 'I had an appointment in Rome with my new lawyer.' She grinned at Roberto as she took a piece of ham and wrapped it round a long grissino.

'Oh.' Caresse regarded her with interest. 'You must tell me about him.' She glanced at Roberto. 'Right, let's get back to business.'

'Caresse,' Roberto murmured stiffly, refusing to look at Diana. 'Alessandro had an idea that he wanted to discuss with you.'

'Wonderful, well do speak.' She addressed the whole group, uncertain who Alessandro was.

The boy who rose was about fourteen and only recently aware of his beauty. Diana watched him, recognising that budding awareness, and then glanced at her mother's rapt face as she listened to the boy whose slender neck rose tenderly from the collar of his borrowed shirt.

'. . . and so we thought,' the boy was still speaking. 'We thought that we might have this party to celebrate you.' He glanced up and then back down at his feet, surprisingly clean inside his brown leather sandals.

'For me?' Caresse's eyes shone brightly in her pale face.

'Yes, Caresse.' Diana's eyes flicked between them. 'He wants you to throw them a party in your honour.'

'Hush, Diana. Well, Alessandro, you know I love giving parties.' Something was stirred in Caresse and she sat forward. 'But I really don't think I can give one for myself.' Seeing their disappointed faces, she held out a hand. 'But if you like, you can prepare a little impromptu speech for after dinner. Make a note, will you, Roberto.'

'Signora, we also need to look at our finances.' A boy in a neatly ironed shirt spoke up.

'Well done, Michelangelo. How much have we got saved?'

The boy, whose name was Massimo, shifted in his seat. 'We have thirty thousand lira.'

'Such a lovely word, don't you think, "lira". So much nicer than that clumsy dollar or clunky pound.'

The assembled group nodded tentatively. She held her glass up to the light so that the sun warmed the pale wine a rich, clear yellow. 'Not until you feel the satisfying weight of a bag of gold do you understand the real cost of things.'

'What exactly is it you all like about parties?' Diana leaned back and lazily tossed another piece of ham into her mouth.

'Everybody likes parties,' Caresse said, also resting back. 'There's nothing quite so fun as supplying a group of people you really like with enough booze and food to keep you all together and in high spirits for a good few days. Oh, I love it!'

'And we like' – a girl with pale green eyes began moving her hands slowly – 'the music. Signora Crosby's bands stay all night so that we never have to stop dancing.'

'I like the girls looking so beautiful,' said Alessandro,

turning his head towards Diana, who was next to him. The scent coming from her hair was unlike any flower he'd smelled. 'Especially Signora Crosby.' Diana's smile faded.

'You absurd boy, I'm older than these hills.' But she laughed and it was so natural and full of joy that everyone laughed too.

Diana watched them all. Honestly, this place was turning into a fucking *cult*.

'I used to give so many parties. Do you remember, Diana? Well, you couldn't remember all of them, you were too young.'

'I remember.'

'Oh, do you?'

Diana looked at her mother, wondering how far she should go. She had never worked out the impulse that compelled her to open the floor like this. She knew by now the endless drive, the relentless push that never let thought act as a barrier – she was like him in that way. 'I grew up at my mother's parties,' she told the group.

Roberto's eyes moved between the two women. He did not like scenes.

'There were so many it couldn't really be helped, I suppose.' Her mother closed her heavy-lidded eyes. Roberto watched her closely. They remained closed for so long that he wondered if she'd gone to sleep. She opened them suddenly. 'I dream of that room in Le Moulin so often. Hardly even the room, just the colour of the walls, that deep violent violet. It was right at the top of the house . . .' She smiled dreamily. 'A large circular room with a fire at its centre. Zebra-skin shadows on the walls and everybody passed out in various dream piles on the floor. And that infernal cannon – it used to drive the animals quite wild.'

Diana nodded, despite herself. The needle scratching round

183

and round. Bodies pressing. The frenzied barking of the dogs. The desperate neighing of the donkeys. And occasionally, the roar of the leopard.

'But the best of all was the party known as the Beaux Arts Ball.'

Diana's gaze remained fixed as though still looking into the open fire in the centre of that room.

'My husband and I threw a drinks party every year for all the young artists studying around the corner from our house in Rue de Lille. Our poor chauffeur had to lift so many cases of champagne up to the library that it absolutely did for his back. He couldn't work again, poor man. So sweet – do you remember, Diana? He was about four foot high. It used to look as though the car was driving itself.'

'Of course I remember.' Diana dragged her gaze towards her mother. 'His bedroom was next to mine. He taught me to swim.'

Roberto raised his eyebrows in interest, but Caresse carried on.

'One year, the theme was "Inca".' She washed the image across the room with her hand. 'I was painted blue from top to toe and wore nothing but a long turquoise wig that came down to my waist.'

Diana closed her eyes. The noise of the graphophone being turned and then her door opening and a man making his way over to the bed, sitting down heavily, trapping her underneath his weight. She stayed very still . . .

'Do you remember, Diana?' She opened her eyes and her mother was looking at her expectantly, the gathered teenagers all watching wide-eyed.

'Yes.'

'We walked in procession down the Champs-Élysées,' Caresse continued. 'I sat astride a baby elephant with my back straight and my chest forward.' She demonstrated the pose and could feel her heart beginning to move with the memory, taking her up and down as she'd swayed along the light-strung street, the grey hide like a dry riverbed come to life between her legs . . .

Caresse smiled. 'It was a night I shall never forget.'

'It was also a night I shall never forget,' Diana said, drawing all the eyes in the room back towards her.

'Harry had a string of dead pigeons round his neck, didn't he?' Her voice became stronger as she finally looked over at her mother's pale face. 'He held a bag of snakes.'

'Yes, that's right. And he was painted ochre.' Caresse nodded, arms crossed over her chest. 'A Red Indian.'

'Yes,' Diana said. 'I remember finding a dead bird on the stairs. Its beak had been crushed into the stone and there was a stain beneath it.' Diana looked at her mother, who was frowning, shaking her head.

'You were quite furious with the maids for not being able to get the blood out of the stone.'

'Well, the entire house was practically destroyed.'

'And everything was stained ochre. It was all over my hair, my bed, my walls . . .'

'No, I don't remember that.' Caresse shook her head again, her face clouded.

'Oh, but I do.' Diana put down her glass and smiled, baring her teeth. 'It was the night you decided that Paris was no place for little girls.'

Switzerland, 1927

'What's your name?' Diana asked.

'Isobel.'

'How old are you?'

'Nine.'

'I'm ten.'

The blonde girl was quiet and Diana kept her eyes on her. She looked like a little rabbit. Closing one eye, she turned her fingers into a pistol and imagined the 'pop' and then hanging the limp furry thing up by its legs.

'Do you like this school?'

'Yes.' The girl nodded.

'Come and sit on my bed with me.'

The girl came over and sat down uncertainly.

'You don't need to be shy. That's just a convention. If we want to, we can communicate without words at all.'

'How?' the girl asked.

'Like this.' Diana took the girl's hand and looked into her eyes. There was a long pause. 'Now what was I saying?'

'I'm not sure.'

'I was saying that you look like a rabbit. Try with me.'

The girl looked into Diana's eyes, then shook her head. 'I don't think I'm allowed to.' She glanced at the door.

'Why?'

'It's not Christian.'

'Oh, don't worry about that.' Diana smiled. 'I don't tell tales.'

Alderney, 1993

'Where have you been?'

'Church.'

'I think you go to that grim little hut just to annoy me.'

'I go because I find it peaceful and a good kind of sad.'

'Sad it certainly is. Sexless puritans droning in a frigid room. Hell is organ music.'

'Perhaps it's best not to talk about it.'

'I think Inés is to blame,' Diana continued. 'That's where the rot set in.'

Elena thought of the simple white room of the roadside chapel in Ibiza, the sound of the occasional car passing in the midday heat, waiting outside with Leonie while Inés knelt to pray (for you, two *traviesas*) in the cool darkness.

Elena looked at her mother and then, remembering the words of the sermon, came and sat down beside her. She took her hand.

'Ivan is coming at eight and you haven't told me what we're eating.' Diana pulled her hand free.

'James has ignored my suggestion that we make a fish stew and has bought lobsters.'

'First sensible decision he's made. As long as he paid, that is.'

'Oh, he paid, Diana.'

'I don't want the children flying about.'

'They'll be in bed by the time Ivan arrives.'

'Good.'

Diana looked at Elena. 'Why do you insist on going to that church? I know you don't believe in all that really.'

Elena looked at her mother wearily. 'Why do you care? You hang your garland round every passing calf. The complexity and purposelessness of your rituals has never ceased to mystify me.'

'A sense of awe is exactly what they should instil.'

'I prefer something simpler.'

'I blame Inés. I should have been far more careful with that woman. If I'd known she was quietly converting my children I'd have got rid of her far sooner than I did.'

Elena stood abruptly, gathering up the folded clothes she held in her arms.

'Never trust a converted Catholic,' Diana murmured. 'Your father was right about that.' She glanced at Elena, but seeing that she had lost her, drained the remains of her glass and then dropped the empty tumbler onto the carpet with a thud.

'You look lovely, Diana,' James said, and Bay turned to watch her grandmother sway into the drawing room, a wide gold belt struggling against her waist, her eyelids swiped with bronze.

'Thank you, darling,' she said, smiling.

'Diana,' the white-haired man said, going forward to kiss her on each cheek. 'Wonderful to see you.'

'Ivan,' she laughed, pressing a hand lightly on his chest. 'It's been far too long since you paid me a visit.' She swooped the hand up in a gesture of mock outrage. 'You'll have to work hard to make it up to me.' The room seemed uncertain in shape and, making out the solid form of a chair, she set her path towards it, aware they were watching. She turned, her feet seemed to be caught in some kind of glue, and gratefully lowered herself into it, shaking her hair back to try to hide the effort the action had cost her. 'Now which one of you is going to bring me a drink.'

There was the sound of footsteps on the stairs and Elena rushed into the room.

'I'm so sorry I'm late, somebody rang,' she said breathlessly. 'Oh, you're already down.' She looked at Diana apologetically.

'Elena.' Ivan came forward. 'It's been some time.'

Elena smiled tightly as she received his greeting kiss and admiring stare, and then sat down in a straight-backed chair beside her mother, snatching up a handful of nuts from a bowl on the table.

From the drinks table Bay made her way towards her grandmother, carefully holding a glass stacked with ice, gin and sherry.

Frowning, Elena watched anxiously as she crossed the room unsteadily and handed the glass to Diana.

Diana took a long swig and then placed the glass beside her.

'Is that Seduction or Devil May Care?' Bay asked, looking at the imprint of her grandmother's lips on the glass. She'd been learning the names written on the bottom of each of the gold tubes of lipstick strewn across her grandmother's dressing table. Her mother rarely wore make-up but her grandmother dragged it across her mouth without even looking in the mirror.

'One shouldn't draw attention to these things, it negates the whole exercise. But if you must know, I call this one Laudanum Red.'

'Time for bed, Bay,' Elena said.

Elena pulled the covers back and Bay slipped between them. She stroked her mother's pale mouth and then wound her arms round her neck, drawing her towards her. She smelled of full-blooming white flowers and her hair was pinned away from her face. It seemed to Bay that her mother was somehow impermanent, as though she might not ever come back upstairs at the end of the evening, and Bay clung to her neck, unable to stop breathing in her scent.

'*La salade doit être retournée comme une femme,*' James muttered as he turned the leaves in a wooden bowl, his hands becoming coated with oily dressing.

'Tell me, Elena.' Ivan turned to her with a diplomat's smile. 'Where were you born?'

'I was born at sea,' Elena said reluctantly, unwilling to be drawn into a tête-à-tête. She could sense her mother observing Ivan closely. 'My father bought my mother a boat as a wedding gift. I suppose I was the bottle smashed across the prow.' She repeated the familiar line, loathing herself for it all over again.

'Do you still sail?'

'No. These days I associate boats with nausea.'

Ivan admired Elena's profile. There was something fine and distant about her, he thought. Quite different from her mother. None of that raw danger. Meeting Diana had been like watching a lion unscrewing a jar of honey. Now of course . . . He looked at her across the table for a moment. She was regaling James with a lively story.

'I used to see your father from time to time,' he said, turning his gaze back to Elena. 'We were both members of the same club.'

She inclined her head dutifully towards him.

'Very good oysters there.' To his surprise, she shuddered.

'I can't stand them,' she said, and then glanced at her mother. 'Unlike some, I don't like eating things alive.'

Ivan laughed, causing Diana to turn and look at Elena. 'Your father was known for being able to eat several dozen in a sitting.'

Elena wiped her mouth with her napkin.

That club. Those lunches.

She recalled the last time she'd seen her father, just after she had discovered she was pregnant with Jake.

She'd felt terribly sick on the tube as she was carried through the bowels of London towards St James's and had walked as slowly as possible towards the imposing stone building, had forced herself up the stone steps worn smooth by countless hard soles.

They ate the same meal every time. Oysters. Montrachet. A grilled sole meunière in front of each of them, her father neatly separating the flesh from her bones.

'Anthony?' she'd repeated. 'What do you think I should do?'

'I was thinking, Elena,' he said reprovingly, as he leaned across the table to fill her glass, ignoring the shake of her head. He'd always loved her name and he savoured it in his mouth like a good wine. She could just make out the faint lemon cologne he wore. Had noticed it when he'd bent to kiss her hello, his liver-spotted hand on her shoulder. 'Dealing with your mother takes a great deal of concentration, with the majority of the energy being completely wasted. Unless in bed, of course. There was no problem getting her to do as she was told there.'

Elena busied herself with her napkin and pretended not to have heard.

'Now, while I keep thinking about our little problem' (she hated it when he called her mother that) 'you must tell me a bit more about how you're getting on. I haven't seen you for quite some time . . .'

But as she'd sketched a bare outline of the life she'd excluded him from, she caught the claret-heavy gaze of one of the other members. The way the man had looked between Anthony and herself had caused her to lose her thread.

'So . . . What do you think?' She returned to her point, hands twisting her napkin beneath the table.

Anthony sat back and wiped his mouth slowly.

'Your mother is a complicated woman. I can't believe I lasted as long as I did. Surely it's up to that boy to look after her now.'

'The "boy" is why she wants to sell Ibiza, Anthony.'

'Really?' The still handsome face expressed some surprise. 'I thought he'd married her for it.'

'David's not interested in her money.'

'"David", eh?' He glanced at her over the rim of his glass.

'He's married to my mother; I think first-name terms is fairly common.' She shook her head. 'He's a good person. But it's falling apart. She's *mad* to sell her house and follow him to London. She'll be miserable there.'

'A "good person"? High praise from someone who follows the ten hard rules.' He looked at her levelly. 'So she's determined to sell?'

Elena nodded.

'And you want to stop her.'

'She said she would leave it to Leonie and me.' Elena blushed.

'What about doing away with all your worldly goods? Wasn't that why you refused my help?'

'It's not for me, it's for him.' She rested a hand on her stomach.

'You look very pretty with some colour in your cheeks. A smacked bottom always did the trick.'

Elena checked to see if anyone had heard.

'There is very little,' Anthony continued smoothly, 'you can do to influence a woman like your mother. She exists for no other reason than pleasure. It's all she knows how to do. Unfortunately, she also finds pleasure in destroying things, so that's what she'll go on doing. She's like some Hindi goddess of war. There's not a man on earth who could stop her. I certainly couldn't. The very sight of my name is enough to send her to whichever lawyer she's fucking now.' He spoke with the hardness of a man who knows the woman in question can no longer hurt him.

'She's not . . . like that now.'

'Don't bank on it. Never met a more sexual woman in my life. She made brushing her teeth a kind of dance.'

'Please, Dad.' For a moment she forgot that she no longer used that name.

'It's my belief,' Anthony leaned forward and the scent of lemons washed over her, 'that she was unduly influenced by that *woman*, that "mother" of hers. She hardly had a thought of her own for all the ideas she put into her head.' He sat back. 'She shouldn't have been a mother really,' he said.

'You don't think *any* woman should have been a mother.'

This time his eyes flicked over her. 'Not true.' He sipped his wine. 'I'm thrilled mine was.'

'Were you close to your father?' Ivan's voice broke into her thoughts and Elena jumped.

'No,' she said quickly.

'I was impressed by the defence he built against your mother when they divorced. Managed to discredit the majority of her case.'

'Yes.' Elena looked down at the table. 'He was good at that.'

'And remained married to his housekeeper?'

'Anita . . . yes.'

'Did they have any children?'

'No, thank God,' she said. Laughter from the other end of the table caused them both to look over, and Elena smiled absently at the increasingly raucous story her mother was telling James. Something about Hemingway and the *corrida*.

'Forgive me for saying so, Elena, but you seem rather tired.'

'Yes,' she said, willing James to meet her eye.

'Motherhood.' He smiled.

She shook her head. 'Children are exhausting, but in the best possible way. It's a gift to be so tired that one's body pulls you into sleep. Left on my own, I'd barely lie down.'

'A night bird,' he said.

'There's nothing romantic about insomnia.'

'You should try sailing again. Works wonders. You're welcome to use my boat any time you'd like.'

'That's very kind.' Elena looked down at her hands.

Her father's hands.

'What's wrong with you, Elena?' her mother said. 'You look sick as a dog.'

Elena tried to smile. 'Nothing. I'm fine.'

'I hope you're behaving, Ivan,' Diana admonished, slurring a little.

He laughed. 'Of course, Diana. Simply paying my respects to your beautiful daughter.'

Diana sat back and drank.

'And to this wonderful meal.'

'I agree,' said James. 'To Elena.'

'It's hardly cooking. Boiling some lobsters and putting leaves in a bowl.'

'Death and salad. The perfect meal,' Diana said, her glass at half-mast. 'I'm glad I taught you to cook. It's a wonderful gift to pass down the generations.'

Elena thought of Inés in her steam-filled kitchen, watching keenly as she lifted the casserole out of the oven. She would give a single, serious nod. But, looking at her mother in her *ibicenca* dress and straining gold belt, and the way Ivan's eyes only ever passed over her, Elena merely smiled.

Diana leaned over the table.

'I know what you two were discussing, Ivan,' she said. 'And spending a million dollars on a roof was an act of *insanity*, not philanthropy.'

'But it was in the service of art, Diana,' James said. Elena's shoulders tensed.

'What do you know about art?' Diana turned on him viciously.

'We were not actually discussing that, Diana.' Ivan pressed his napkin to his mouth and deftly changed the subject. 'James was telling me earlier that he's managed to locate some of the remaining Black Sun Press editions that went missing after your mother died. As you know, they're terribly hard to find these days.'

'Oh, I see, the bookseller is on the make.' Diana narrowed her eyes at James.

'Hardly,' he laughed, spreading his hands. 'Independent bookshops are no goldmine, Diana. But I'll always be fascinated by your mother's press. I think the books they made are rather wonderful.'

'I've heard enough about books for one lifetime. Writers are parasites.' She drained her glass. 'Children too.'

Elena stared at her mother across the table and then down at her plate. It was too late to do anything.

'Come, Diana, you love books,' Ivan said, smiling gently at her. 'Writers need support.'

'I like *some* books, Ivan.'

'Don't play the literary snob, Diana. There are more than a few Nevil Shutes knocking about in that library of yours,' James said playfully.

'A damned good writer. Much under-appreciated,' Diana laughed, squaring up to him for more.

'Well, I bow to your superior knowledge.' James smiled. 'Your library is still a thing of beauty and I'm grateful that you let me read what I do.'

'Those are the dregs of what it was. My God, I used to have some books. My stepfather gave me one that was bound in the skin of a courtesan. And you might make that face, Elena, but they meant something to me. It was most careless of my mother to buy that wretched place and spend such an insane—'

'Oh, I don't *care*,' Elena said. 'Treasure things if you like. But I have no interest in ruining yet another meal by sitting and counting the losses. I'd prefer if we spoke about how grateful we are for what we do have, rather than what we don't.' Elena realised that she was echoing the closing words of the morning's sermon.

Watching her, Ivan sat back and smiled. 'Hear, hear, Elena. I'm sure I could learn from that too.'

'Ugh,' said Diana, with a toss of her head. 'I *loathe* being grateful.'

Switzerland, 1927

Isobel and Diana lay in their slim dormitory beds. The huge moon shone in through the uncurtained window and if she lifted her head, Diana could just see their shoes, lined up neatly together in the corner of the room.

'Diana, what happens in Paris? When you're at home?' The quiet voice reached for Diana in the dark.

'I stay in my nursery mostly. Sometimes I go out on the town.'

'What's your mama like?'

'Like a crazed bird, always flapping about.'

'I saw her when she came to bring you. She had a beautiful black dog.'

'That dog's the devil. Mine's much sweeter.'

'Where is it?'

'Waiting for me in our country house.'

'I'd like a dog.'

'The thing about animals, Isobel, is that you have to show

them who's boss. Harry gave me a whip for my birthday to beat the donkeys with if they don't go. He uses a hammer, but I think that's too sharp.'

'But I don't think animals like to be whipped.'

'Nobody likes it, Isobel. But sometimes it's necessary.'

Roccasinibalda, 1970

The castle was swarming with people. From her window, Diana could hear the endless tooting of horns as delivery trucks clogged up the village square and wheelbarrows were trundled up and down the entrance to the castle. She put her pen down in frustration. She'd already had to banish David, was she going to have to ask *every* fucking person in this madhouse to keep quiet? She undid her dress and stood in her slip, fanning herself. This letter to her wretched husband was turning into something of a chore. She couldn't find the *words*. She groaned, pressing the heels of her hands against her eyes. Fine if he wanted the boat, but she was bloody well keeping that house. He hadn't even *heard* of Ibiza before she took him there. The audacity of the man, the sheer bloody-minded *frustration* of him. As the vitriol rose, so did something else and Diana felt a familiar longing begin to build between her legs. Oh, she *hated* him, she hated him, she hated him, hated . . .

The growing sound of raucous whoops and laughter sailed through the open window. Throwing her hands up, she went to the casement and stuck her head out. A troupe of men wearing offensively patterned clothing were hanging around in the walled garden below.

'Do you mind!' she shouted. 'I'm trying to *work* up here.'

A man in pantaloons ran beneath the window and began shouting up at her in Spanish, his hands pressed to his chest. She glanced down at her flimsy slip and back at the men gathered below.

'*¡No voy a jugar contigo! ¡Tú, sigue jugando con tus bolas a solas, payaso!*' she shouted, laughing.

There was a cacophony of words in an accent she couldn't place, but as she turned back to her desk, Diana was aware of something landing softly on the floor behind her. She whipped round, ready to pounce, and saw the flower on the rug, a red thread tied round its stem. An enormous blowsy rose, its petals loose and open, unable to contain its scent. She'd never much liked flowers, but there had always been something about the smell of roses that seemed to envelop her in a gentle embrace. She pressed her face into the blushing petals and breathed until her lungs began to ache. She felt a tug on the string and frowned for a moment but pulled back. A harder tug. Oh, she liked this game.

But really, she flung the flower back through the window, she didn't have time to play. She wasn't going to lose the battle this time. She was not going to let Elena's father lord it all over her again. She sat down at the desk and tapped a finger against her lips, bringing to mind things said in the tender moments. What was the point of all these memories if one didn't *use* them when they were needed most?

*

'Did you come here hoping to find me weak?' Caresse wheezed, sitting up in bed, her face quite grey. 'You know I don't go in for all that.'

Diana glanced at the nurse taking her mother's blood pressure; she couldn't remember if she spoke English or not.

'No, not weak.' She sat at the foot of the bed. 'A little meek, perhaps. And your heart *is* weak, you can't deny that.'

'Meek? No, Christ had that all wrong. Being meek is neither chic nor helpful. We have to move *with* life, not sit in the corner waiting for someone to bring us a highball so we can get up the courage to dance.'

'I've never waited for someone to bring me a drink in my life.'

'Yes, I've noticed.' Her mother looked at her over her glasses. 'If you're not careful, you could end up like your father.'

The nurse murmured to Caresse in Italian.

'Look, you're making my blood pressure go up. I think you'd better say whatever it is you wanted to and then leave me and the evening sun in peace with one another.'

They heard a shout from outside.

'As if there's any peace in this place,' Diana said, getting to her feet. 'You know there's a troupe of clowns living in the walled garden?'

Caresse nodded. 'They're from Peru. Real troubadours.' She smiled, though her breath shuddered in her chest. 'I'm making plans with Roberto to stage a Surrealist festival. Salvador and Gala have promised to come. Buñuel is going to film, and there's the ...'

'Mother,' Diana said.

'The young here have so much to learn. I just want them all to enjoy.' She coughed, one hand batting the air.

The nurse placed a tray with a folded white napkin and a bowl of steaming minestrone in front of Caresse.

'Yes, but be realistic.'

'Oh, Diana, you and your realism. We have to look forward—'

'Mother.' Her hands twisted the matter. 'You might not *be* here.'

Giulia tiptoed from the room and closed the door.

Her gaze locked on the view outside, Caresse nodded, once.

'Are you frightened?' Diana tried to take her mother's hand, but it moved blindly away. She continued to stare straight ahead, with a fierce, fixed gaze.

'No, not frightened,' she said after a pause, smoothing the blankets with a sweep. 'I don't think I ever have been, really. It's the people left behind whom I feel for. It hurts me,' she clenched her fist, 'that people don't realise that change is possible. That they can give birth to themselves. They think this is it,' she held out an empty hand, 'and lead sad, drab lives, freighted with whatever hell they've been lumped with. But anyone can escape, can make a different world. You see that, don't you?'

'Maybe they don't want to change everything, or even anything.'

'Of course they do.'

'Well, *I* don't want to.'

'That's because you've always been free, Diana.'

'I didn't have a choice.'

There were more shouts from outside and Caresse turned

back to the window with a look of longing. 'I just want them to enjoy,' she whispered. 'To know what it is to enjoy!'

Diana felt her cheeks burning.

'I think all these people have enjoyed enough. You're starting to sound ridiculous.'

'Ridiculous?'

'Yes. It's absurd to spend this much time and money on a party. You haven't finished paying for the roof!'

'Always so protective.' Her mother shook her head, picking up her spoon.

'Well, I'm sorry if I'm looking out for myself. And the girls.'

'You're never going to starve, Diana. You have your little trust from your father, you know that.'

'My little trust.'

'Which you can do what you like with.'

'There'll barely be enough for a packet of razors after the death duties. I might not be fine at all!'

Caresse looked at her in surprise and then took a sip of soup. 'I'm sorry you feel that way. There will be plenty left for the girls, I'd hardly forget them. But here, now, all I want is to enjoy, for us *all* to enjoy. The soup is delicious, you should have some.'

Unable to move, Diana remained very still, glaring at her mother. Waiting. She did not know what for.

'You know, you're not tied here.' Caresse moved her hand towards the door. 'Now, I need to call about the orchids, or they'll be delivered too late.' She drew the telephone topped with a bright red lobster to her chest. 'You needn't hang about. You can go and do whatever it is that you *do*.'

*

'You're upset.'

'Yes, perhaps a little.' She laughed gently, wiping away a tear. 'Talking seems to only get harder. I don't know why I thought she would soften with age; people aren't meat.'

'Do you like the people here at the moment?' With deliberate motions, David wiped his clay-whitened hands on a cloth and came towards her.

'I can't keep track, David. What with all these teenagers running about and that team of restorers covering everything in dust, and that ridiculous German ... what does he call himself ... bard? It's too much. It's making me long for something ... something a little simpler. My boat, my home, *my friends*.' She was quiet, gnawing at the inside of her cheek.

'You need to spend some time alone at sea. With me.' He held her and she allowed herself briefly to lean into him. 'And then ... London.'

'Ibiza.' She grabbed his shoulder firmly and shook it a little.

'Let's see.' He took her hand from his shoulder, kissed her palm, and then returned to his work.

'I think we'll sail well together, won't we?' she said, her head to one side. He looked levelly at her as he began to carve into the heavy clay. 'You know, the first time I went on a boat was when I crossed the Atlantic with my mother to get to Paris. I never wanted it to end. Everyone else was sick as hell, but I loved it. I liked being in transit, surrounded by all that blue. Playing alone in the shadow of those huge funnels, with the sound of the creaking lifeboats and the clouds moving silently over the smooth wooden boards. *That* really was freedom. Probably the last of it.'

'How old were you?' David asked.

'I was five.'

'Did you want to leave America?'

'No, I wanted my mother and father to remain together and for us all to be *terribly happy.*'

'Poor little Rat.'

She smiled. 'I forgot I told you that.'

'A very beautiful rat.'

She stared at him, her heart beating. She had him. 'Come to Ibiza.' She leaned back and touched the inside of his leg with the tip of her shoe. 'I know I said I'd come to London, but I've changed my mind.' She looked at his young, tanned face, the fine bones beneath the skin. 'Come with me.' Her voice trailed over him. 'I want you to say that you'll come with me.'

He didn't look up from his work. 'I've said I'll think about it, and I will.'

Diana felt panic begin to tread uncertainly inside her chest. She glanced at her reflection in the dirty mirror, hung by a nail to the wall. The north-facing room was filled with a harsh glare and her reflection was thrown back at her in an unforgiving light.

'I'm not going to make any promises I can't keep, that's all.' David's voice spoke to her turned back. 'I have my life too. That's a good thing. You've said so yourself. I've said I'll come to Ibiza for the time being. Let's start with that.'

Diana could not look at him.

He set down his tools and pressed her into his embrace. 'Diana,' he murmured. 'Don't turn away from me, please.'

Finding her face in the mirror again, her hands gripping the back of his shirt, Diana saw herself in a different light.

'Will your daughters be there?' he asked huskily, as their faces were about to meet.

'My daughters? Why?' she asked, her voice hard.

'Because,' he said in a measured tone, 'I'd rather there was nobody there but the two of us.'

She pulled back. 'Leonie still refuses to write, but I got a letter from Elena this morning. How strange that you should mention her now.'

'Diana, I didn't want to discuss them, I just wanted to know if they were—'

'She's found God,' Diana continued, moving away and sitting on a sheet-covered stool as she unbuttoned her dress. 'And she's getting married. I don't know which is worse.'

'Do you know the man?'

'Yes. *I* found him. He was hitchhiking. Deeply handsome, but hasn't got a pot to piss in.' She gave him an arch smile. 'All sounds rather familiar, doesn't it?'

'Vaguely.' David smiled, leaning down to tie up a bag of clay. 'Though, luckily for you, I have a pot. Small blessing that my father died before he pissed the whole lot up the wall.'

Diana laughed. 'Ha, echoes indeed. Anyway, Elena shouldn't get married yet. First marriages are always a disaster. Leonie has only just got out of hers.' Her dress slipped to the floor. 'Then again, maybe it's best to get it over with.'

'Perhaps it will last.'

Diana shot him a look. 'Like yours?'

'There was no God in my marriage.' He laughed, dusting his hands together. 'Anyone was welcome.'

'Well, *this* marriage is going to be in a church, where no

one is. Especially not me. Still, at least she's not threatening to become a nun like her sister.'

'Two God-fearing children? What *did* you do to them, Diana?' He came up to her and pulled the strap of her slip down. 'So you weren't one of those little girls who dreamt about getting married?'

She shivered, feeling his clay-roughened hand on her collarbone.

'No ... I never wanted anyone.' She began loosening his belt.

'I don't believe that,' he said, tracing the line of her shoulder.

'It's true. When my mother divorced, I decided never to get married. Not if you could undo it that easily.' She slipped her hand inside his trousers.

'But you did,' he murmured.

'Maxime was persistent,' she shrugged. 'And besides, I wanted to get away from ...' She moved her body very close to his.

'From what?'

'From all that.' She took him in her hand as she spoke, but felt something in him retreat. He was loyal to her still. She'd forgotten that.

Switzerland, 1927

Diana stood in the hallway, watched by a pale-faced nun who stood with eyes half-closed as the child listened to the voice worming through the black earpiece. The school was empty and quiet, the hallway filled with abundant, early summer light.

'It would have been wonderful, darling, but it's not to be. You must enjoy a summer in the mountains. All that fresh air and those sweet little goats. It's much the best place for you.'

'But everyone has gone home.'

'Remember what we said about "*home*", Diana ... You have the whole place to yourself! Make a game of it. I must go now, the train's going to leave. I'll see you when I return. Wish me bon voyage!'

The line went dead.

Unable to meet the nun's eyes, Diana stood on tiptoe to replace the receiver and, turning away, went down the sun-striped corridor towards the empty dormitory.

Alderney, 1993

Elena walked, her legs moving like two long switches as she made her way along the empty track, the baby slowing her down only a little. The sky was clear and blue with a cold wind pushing against her, so that her dress was blown like a sail against her body.

James had taken the children to the beach so that she could go out walking alone, and as she thought of them driving to the other side of the island her stomach was a churn of gladness and guilt.

She'd been pulling on her plimsolls, about to leave, when she'd heard her mother moving about upstairs.

She waited by the door, listening.

'Elena?' The voice dragged her up the stairs.

'Where are the beastly brood? They're being awfully quiet.' Her mother was propped up against the pillows, the sun streaming across the bed.

'At the beach,' Elena said breathlessly, sitting down on the mattress edge.

'We're alone?'

Elena nodded, pulling herself apart with quick fingers as she tried to decide whether to ask her mother to come and walk with her. 'They'll be back for lunch.'

'What are we having?'

'What would you like?'

'Some peace and quiet.'

'I'll have the boys bring it up.'

Diana laughed. 'I want minestrone. The soup you made yesterday was like gruel. Darling, you mustn't frown like that, you look a hundred years old.'

Elena pressed her hands to her eyes and, in the sudden darkness, saw an image of her mother doing the exact same thing. She dropped her hands and breathed, almost to herself, 'Oh, I'm so tired of you ...'

'I struggled to sleep when I was pregnant,' Diana said thoughtfully, seeming not to have heard properly. 'Are you *sure* you need another?'

'I'm six months pregnant.' Elena folded her arms protectively over her stomach.

'I had to get rid of several. Some quite late. It is possible, you know ...'

'Yes, you've told me that before,' Elena said quietly.

'David never knew about the last one.'

'Yes, you've told me that too.'

'A boy.'

Elena was silent.

'And there was another ...'

Elena glanced up uncertainly, unwilling to be drawn in. 'When?'

'In the war. But he was too small and it was too cold. I thought it was wise of him, really.' Her voice did not change as she spoke but Elena saw that her mother's mouth struggled to maintain its smirk.

'Oh, Mum,' she breathed out in a soft collapsing movement.

Diana was silent. 'Well, you're far from blooming,' she said, after a pause.

Elena's chest rose and fell as she stared at her mother.

'What's that shirt you're wearing?' Diana leaned forward and took a cuff between thumb and forefinger. 'That's one of your father's, isn't it?' She kept hold of it, looking at Elena.

'They're the only thing I can fit into at the moment.' Elena stood, pulling herself free. 'The silk's a godsend in this heat,' she continued. 'You know what my skin's like.'

'Thin. Like his.'

Elena's eyes met her mother's. She felt metal enter her gaze and her voice became cold. 'I'm going for a walk.'

'Before you go,' Diana said, 'I think you might apologise.'

'For what?' Elena stared at her, mystified.

'For trying to seduce Ivan last night. I know how hard it can be to feel that one is losing one's looks, but it was really rather embarrassing. For both me and James.'

Elena looked at her for a long moment. 'I'm terribly sorry,' she finally said.

'I forgive you, Elena.' She looked regally out of the window. 'I forgive you for it all.'

Her mother's words came back to her now as she walked and she shook them free from her head, spreading her arms out either side of her as though to catch the wind. She kept her eyes open and her pace up, opening her mouth so that it was washed with the salt that blew in from the sea. But as she made her way down the track, the shape and weight of her mother's presence grew. She stared at the sea in the distance, her chest heaving.

Breathe, Elena. The voice came to her with the wind and she did so, through clenched teeth, and then, keeping her eyes on the water, began to make her way towards it. Her bare legs kept getting snared in the brambles and dried bracken, so similar in feel to the parched ground of Ibiza, and she had to pull herself free with a yank as she finally stumbled onto grass that thinned into sand. Below her were the grey backs of the rocks and, beyond, the sea.

Her mind whirred onwards to a picture of her mother lying flat on her back on the deck of the boat, her hands lost in somebody's hair, laughing gently at the conversation around her as the boat moved up and down on the water, going nowhere. 'Get Elena to do it,' she'd said. 'She loves being told what to do.'

Elena quickly undid the buttons of her shirt and viciously pulled it loose.

She looked at her outstretched hands.

Her father's hands.

Jump. She dared herself, just as she used to.

But this time, she paused, her arms resting over the round of her stomach. It already swam. All it knew was water and the sounds that travelled in from other rooms. 'All right down there?' she murmured, stroking her tummy back and forth. She looked out and, finding a safe route, made her way carefully across the rocks until she reached one that slanted gently into the water and then, taking a deep breath, gasped as she submerged herself in the cold sacrament of the sea.

Bay sat on the closed loo, cradling her arm in the sling her mother had made as she watched the water thundering from the bathroom taps. As the water rose, she pulled her legs up to her chest, eyes wide. The terrible pounding noise squeaked to a stop and her mother put out her hand.

'In you get, Bay.'

Gingerly accepting her mother's hand in her good one she stepped into the tub and lay down in the warm water, her arms crossed over her chest. She closed her eyes and pictured the beach and the man who had pulled her out of the sea where she was being tossed like a matador on a bull's horns.

He had carried her from the sea, salt burning her eyes and nose, pressed hard against him as though she were his baby.

'Arm up.' Her mother's voice startled her.

She looked up. 'A man held me tight at the beach today.'

Her mother stopped lathering the soap between her hands.

'He pressed me to his ...' Bay looked up at her mother, but something in her face made her stop and she sank below the surface.

There was a sudden crash from her grandmother's bedroom and her father's voice began shouting. 'Elena! Elena!'

A low groan came from the floor above.

Hearing her name, her mother seemed to wake up.

She plunged her soapy hand into the water and pulled the plug out, her shirt-sleeved arm emerging dripping wet. She stood, suddenly very tall, the front of her shirt plastered against her round stomach, and then, hearing her name again, threw the door open and ran from the room. Feeling a gust of cold air from the hall, Bay pulled her knees up against her chest again. There was a cacophony of footsteps and then her mother's voice shouting for an ambulance. The groaning continued from the floor above and Bay clutched her wrist to her chest with wide eyes, staring at the ceiling.

With a sick gurgle, the water began to sink.

Revealing her knees . . .

Legs . . .

Feet.

She sat naked in the tub.

Stranded.

Switzerland, 1927

'And what's wrong with you this time, mademoiselle?' The doctor looked at her over his glasses.

Diana said nothing, staring up at the white wall of the school infirmary.

'Where is the pain located?'

Diana shrugged.

'Is it here?' She shook her head.

'Is it here?' She shook her head.

'Here?'

'I'm sick all over, Doctor.' She turned towards him and arched her back.

'Sick all over?' He sat back. Disbelieving.

'I need an aspirin for it.'

'Diana,' he chuckled, 'you've become a little too fond of aspirin.'

'Please, Doctor. I'm terribly sick.' She smiled. 'No, that tickles. Doctor, that tickles.'

Alderney, 1993

'So you're healed, are you?'

Her grandmother looked at Bay's arm in its loosely tied bandage.

'No,' she said with a little quaver in her voice, holding it tenderly. 'It still hurts.'

'You're a rotten liar. It's fine.'

'You're not ill either,' Bay whispered fiercely.

'I've fractured my *hip*.' She glared at the child, then seemed to lose all strength and sat back with her eyes closed. 'We're all sick, Bay. It's the ones who pretend to be well that you should worry about. The ones like your father.'

Bay stared at the waxy face with growing dislike. Her grandmother looked like a bird that had grown too fat and old for the nest.

'Anyway,' her grandmother sat forward, her voice hard again. '*I'm* leaving!'

'Well, I'm getting my *hair cut*,' Bay said, and they glared at each other.

'I'm not hungry. The smell.' Her grandmother waved at the tray. 'Take it away.'

As soon as the door closed, Diana poured a glass and drank, letting the gin send a charge of good through her body. There was no sound apart from the tick of the clock, her father's clock, pushing the minutes jerkily forward. Neat time washed nightways by the infernal wooing of that owl in the garden. She should never have let Anthony have her gun. She closed her eyes and the steady tick tick tick sank into the click click click of her mother's heels as she made her way down the long hallway, Narcisse at her side, hands swirling in the air as she spoke to the nun who glided silently beside her, telling her all about how *ghastly* America had become (infantilised . . . just infantilised, the whole place is just a great sugary billboard . . .).

And later in the small mountain tearoom . . .

219

Switzerland, 1928

'Look, Diana.' Her mother opened a grey suede-covered book to the first crimson page, and pointed with a gloved hand.

```
        C
        A
H A R R Y
        E
        S
        S
        E
```

'Clever, don't you think? I'm having it engraved on our gravestone as we speak.' She traced the names with her finger. 'Harry can't wait to tell the aunts about it when we go back next month.'

'Why do you always go back when you hate Boston so much?'

'Harry can't let it alone,' she sighed. 'His mother.' She bit her lip. 'The umbilicus has not been cut. He still receives some sort of vital nourishment from them all. Besides, I don't hate Boston. I don't hate anywhere really, it's just the boredom that I can't stand. But like them or not, Harry wants to go, and where Harry goes I go, so off we go together. Besides, it's always fun to give those old birds a good ruffling. They're so *shockable*.'

'And I can't come? In his letter, Harry said I could.'

Her mother's eyes darkened. 'Don't tell tales, Diana. You can go in your next holidays, if your father will have you. He's quite different now, apparently. All dried out. Practically a biscuit, no doubt.' Seeing Diana, she stopped. 'He sent Harry and me a very nice letter the other day.' She looked out towards the mountains in the distance. 'He just wants me to be happy, Diana. It's the most important thing, you know: understanding one's ability to make one-self happy. What else is all this about?' She waved vaguely at the nearly empty café and the waitress slumped against the counter.

'Harry says we are all sick and death is the only truth.'

'Well, there's truth in that too.'

'Is he still getting all those telegrams every day?'

Her mother continued to play with Narcisse's black silky ears, but her mouth had become unusually tense.

'You know. The ones he asks Henriette to keep in the kitchen.'

Her mother looked at her levelly and then pulled off her glove and leaned across the table to take Diana's chin in her hand. 'Harry has an unusual heart, Diana,' she said in a low tone. 'He likes to fill it with different people. Why he does that is difficult for you to grasp, and I wouldn't want to burden you with it. But remember this. There is a central chamber to which nobody else has access. Nobody. And that is where I live. Do you understand?'

Diana nodded, and pulled her chin free.

As Caresse was gathering herself to leave, she took a letter from her bag and held it across the table. 'Harry asked me to give this to you.'

Diana looked at the black-rimmed envelope in her hand. 'What does it say?'

'It's for you to open.'

Diana took it, but her mother did not quite let go.

'I'm pleased that you two get along now.' Diana pulled but her mother still held on. 'I knew he *would* come around, in time.' She let go. 'You are half me, after all.'

At nap time

> *Dearest Harry,*
>
> *I have just finished reading your letter so am answering it right away. I have not forgotten you at all. J'ai REVE of you again last night and in the dream you were mad at me for some reason or another. Perhaps you were still angry at me for beating you in the donkey race?*
>
> *Which will be the best address that will get the letters to you the quickest in America? The Hotel des Artistes?*
>
> *The doctor here is in love with me and says I am a friponne.*
>
> *I hope this letter won't bore you.*
>
> *Goodbye, I love you*

from
The Wretched Rat

PS Please send me more aspirin

PPS JE T'AIME DE TOUT MON COUER

Roccasinibalda, 1970

Diana knocked on the door of her mother's rooms.

'Mama? Are you there?' Over the noise of the band downstairs she heard what sounded like an answer and pushing open the door saw her mother sprawled in an armchair, her breath coming heavily, so that her silver lamé dress rippled across her body with the effort.

'Are you all right?' She shut the door and the music was muted. 'Shall I get the nurse?'

'No.' Caresse put out her hand with difficulty. 'I just ... need to be still.'

'Can I pour you a drink?'

Her mother shook her head, keeping her eyes closed. Diana poured herself one and then came and sat beside her.

'You look wonderful,' Caresse said with some effort, smiling.

Diana ran her hands over her severe black dress, a high black mantilla draped over her hair and shoulders. 'I don't normally care for fancy dress, but I feel good in this get-up.

A lapsed Catholic.' She raised her eyes to the ceiling. 'All full of sorrow and prayer.'

'How do I look?' Caresse asked, her eyes shining. Diana had never heard her mother ask that question before, she'd never needed to, and she took a moment to answer.

'You look wonderful.'

Her mother's grateful smile was so unfamiliar that both were silent, save for the sound of Caresse's laboured breath.

'It reminds me of that gold suit you used to wear,' Diana said, sweeping her hand down the molten run of silver.

Caresse nodded, her eyes closed.

'That caused a stir.' She opened one eye and half-raised a smile. 'Though I remember you saying I looked like a clown.'

'Did I?' Diana blushed and looked away. 'I was probably jealous. You should get into bed.' The way her mother was breathing was making her nervous. 'You're not well enough to come downstairs.'

'I don't want to miss it.'

'Come on, let's not argue. You know what the nurse will say.'

'I'll only stay a short while.'

'You shouldn't.'

'I'll sit on the balcony, so I can look down at the dancing. They'll be terribly disappointed if I don't make an appearance.'

'They'll be much too busy to notice anything. It's not your duty.'

'No, it's my joy.'

Diana remembered her mother's words on the morning of her first wedding.

'We follow desire, Diana,' she'd said.

225

'And what about duty?' Diana had asked, looking at her mother in the dressing table mirror as she fastened heavy diamond clips into her hair.

Her mother had thought for a moment and then set her words down decisively. 'We choose yes, duty is no.'

'What about love?' Diana bit her lip. 'Doesn't that become duty?'

'Choose desire and you can't help but *be* love. I always have been, and I've always been loved.' And she was gone. Up and out, Narcisse trotting after her, like nails drummed impatiently on a polished table, so that Diana had walked down the dark stone staircase to the car alone.

'How are you feeling now?' Diana brought herself back to her mother.

'Do you really want to know? For God's sake, don't ask to be polite.'

'When have I ever been polite?'

'In truth, I feel a little unwell, but I don't enjoy being forced into bed, Diana, not alone anyway. I will go when I'm ready.'

The nurse came in and both women looked up gratefully. 'Oh good, you're here.' Diana jumped up.

'Go downstairs, Diana. You'll have to be the hostess.'

Diana took a deep breath. 'Yes, all right,' she said falteringly and met her mother's anxious gaze. 'I'd like that.' She stood. 'I'll go down and explain.'

'Don't explain anything,' Caresse said sharply. 'The last thing people want to think about at a party is sickness.'

Diana nodded, surprised at her mother's choice of words.

As the door closed behind her and the nurse began to undo the small covered buttons that ran up Caresse's sleeve, Caresse

226

laid her head back and thought of the way that gold suit had shone under the lights on the staircase of the Bal Nègre, setting green eyes flashing, and later, the way he'd picked the spill of it up from the floor and held it to his face so that he could inhale the smell of her in its creases. Yes, people had always been a little envious of her, there was nothing she could do about that.

It was lucky, she reflected, that it had never been something she suffered with.

Jealousy was really for those who didn't have enough – it was a lack of imagination about one's own abundance.

The nurse began to take her blood pressure.

'You know,' she looked at the blonde woman bending before her, her hair threaded with silver, 'Edith was jealous of me too. She couldn't *bear* it when I was the hostess.' Caresse paused to catch her breath. 'Uncle Walter *loved* Harry and loved me. And oh we both loved Uncle Walter.' She smiled at the nurse. 'Walter Berry, do you know of him?'

'No, signora,' the nurse murmured, shaking her head and smiling apologetically.

'As Harry's wife, it was right that I should act as hostess at his parties, do the menu, make it swing, that sort of thing. We were new in Paris ... Harry was terribly young, only twenty-two, and though I was a bit older and already a mother, Edith felt we were quite unable to manage the grand social event of a formal dinner.' The nurse put her hand on Caresse's forehead and frowned. 'But Walter and I had great fun choosing the guests for those meals; a perfect purée of wit, beauty and bitchery. I think he just liked the way I made a party go ...' The room was silent save for her laboured breath. 'Edith would often refuse to come . . . which I thought,' Caresse lowered her voice conspiratorially, 'was a bit *wet*. After all, Giulia, it's how we behave in defeat that is the measure of the man. Or indeed woman. After Walter's death, she tried her best to make off with most of the library that he left Harry. It was all very awkward and bitter. I don't doubt she loved Walter – called him the love of her life – but they were so formal with one another. He described her as "his good friend" in his will – can you *imagine*?'

The nurse was busy with her instruments.

'Though,' Caresse looked down at the sheets, 'I suppose that's better than nothing . . . People can be so careless with what they leave behind. Perhaps they forget that it can be the one thing that threatens to wipe all the other memories clean away.

'It was the times, of course, Edith and Walter were of a quite different generation. Jazz didn't touch them. But I often wondered, as I would look at her across Walter's beautiful table, what she would look like with her hair let down across the sheets, naked and laughing. I was *very* sexual then, though I wouldn't have called it that. In those times it was simply love. An expression of desire. The body's dance. But love always, even the parts that hurt terribly.'

Her voice was quiet and sad. 'Harry adored making love to me, of course – all my husbands did – but I liked making love with Harry the most. It always felt as though we were getting somewhere, as though each climax was the beginning of the next part of the journey towards the place we return to. Perhaps where I am heading next.' She laughed, her eyes brightening. '*La petite mort*, Roland called it. Well, there

228

was never anything petite about it, in my experience. It was everything. More and more. A glimpse of the cosmos.

'I never did understand my girlfriends in Boston. They were so strange about all that, could hardly bear to touch it, as a topic. But I loved it. Even as a girl I would often feel things there, sitting on a tree or riding my horse. That lovely feeling that made me so happy that I was a girl. It was all the greatest fun. What do you think?' She looked at the nurse with interest.

'Signora, my husband left me a year after we were married. I'd saved myself for him. I can't say I cared for it. Not his way, anyway.'

'And no one else?'

'No.' She smiled shyly. 'No one else.'

'How interesting. Do you miss him?'

'No.' She shook her head. 'He was *uno stronzo*. I only married him to keep my mother happy and I only saved myself because no one else asked.'

Caresse was thoughtful. 'We must find you a lover. It is important to explore that side of life, Giulia. There's a whole world in there.'

'Oh no, signora. There's a whole world up here too.' She pressed her heart. 'And I feel happy alone.'

Caresse gripped her hand. 'What wonderful words. Thank you! I do that too. I also travel in here.' She pressed her fist to her own heart. 'Where I'm going is a mystery, but I also travel happily alone.' She closed her eyes for a moment, suddenly very tired. 'Yes, love is wonderful, but it's . . . not easy.' Caresse allowed the nurse to slip the dress from her shoulders and lead her towards the bed. 'I've never been jealous myself, not of

229

anybody. Well, that's not quite true. I *was* a little jealous of the others . . .' Her voice was slowing, becoming thicker. 'We had so many *others* and I didn't always want to share . . . and of course there was that . . . woman . . . and Diana . . . was trying . . . It was all a little trying . . . having to protect and defend all at once . . . it was all a little . . .'

The nurse waited a few moments to see that she was asleep. And with a click turned out the light and tiptoed from the room.

Switzerland, 1928

'Diana, you shouldn't have those aspirin. You're going to get in trouble if they find out.' Isobel stood by the bed, wearing her coat.

'Well, they won't find out, will they?' she said, staring at Isobel. 'Not unless somebody tells.'

'I'm sorry my parents won't let you come and stay this time.'

Diana shrugged and rolled over in bed. She waited a beat, then, sensing her friend coming close, turned and saw Isobel's concerned face above hers. Snaking her arm round Isobel's neck, she pulled the head towards her and kissed the half-parted lips.

'I love you, Isobel.'

Isobel's breath was shuddery and strange and Diana kissed with more force, trying to push open the clenched teeth with her tongue.

Roccasinibalda, 1970

'Yes, yes, I'm coming back for the speeches, just give me one moment,' Diana called behind her, walking briskly down the hallway away from the shrieking noise of the party. She passed a group of masked youths and then two women carrying an enormous platter on which lay the plump golden bodies of at least twenty roasted doves.

Pushing at the first door she came to, she closed it behind her, her breath the only life in the darkness. Feeling blindly with her hand over the wall she caught the switch – nothing happened. So stretching her arms straight she made her way slowly into the dark, grimacing in preparation for the inevitable bump, but then stopped in surprise as her hands met something curved and familiar.

She ran her fingers gently along their spines.

Books.

She was in a room full of books. Moving along the shelves, she inhaled the rich dusty musk of them. Her hands reached the slats of the shutters and she levered them open, so that a rectangle of moonlight stretched across the floor and from somewhere out in the garden the music of the band floated in. She ran her eyes over the titles nearest to her, pulled *The Count of Monte Cristo* from the shelf and turned the familiar blue cloth cover over in her hands. It was one of the first she'd ever read (hidden inside the cover of *Ulysses*) on those afternoons in the empty gymnasium while that little friend of hers ... Isobel? ... prayed for her in the chapel with all the other girls. She had liked those quiet hours, sitting at the solitary desk as she watched the sun move across the floor, knowing that back in Paris he too was sitting at his desk. Some ideas were easier than others to take in. Dantès struck a little deeper than dead-weight Dedalus wandering about like a lost smell on a windy afternoon in Dublin. She walked her fingers along the titles her mother had kept. This was the family her mother had drawn around her, Hemingway, Crevel, Boyle, Jolas, Eliot, Lawrence, Joyce ... all bound together and stamped with suns of gold. Diana looked at their stiff spines and familiar names, wondering where they were now. *For Whom the Bell Tolls*, *Mr Knife Miss Fork*, *The Pleasure Garden*, *The Rubaiyat* ... The great gift of Cousin Walter. She remembered the men in overalls rolling the endless bookcases into her nursery.

'Books book books,' he'd shouted. 'Into our heads to feed our guts.'

She continued to trace along the rows of familiar titles, and stopped when she saw her mother's name on a series of pale grey volumes. She removed a slender book and opened it past the rich crimson frontispiece. She read a verse, mouth moving in whispers around her mother's words.

Life is a picture-puzzle
Of a thousand silly bits
Of every shape and colour;
Yet how lovely, when it fits!

If there had been someone there with her she would have mocked, but alone in the darkness she did nothing more than finish the poem and place the book carefully back among the other titles.

Perhaps, she shook her hair back, she *should* try to write another book. Something a little more experimental.

Set it all down. The story of her childhood.

There was plenty to say. Too much, perhaps. Where would one start? So much of her childhood was covered in a kind of mould that made her feel grim to even think of it. She could have been a great writer, if she'd had any kind of an education. The repressed ramblings of a bunch of nuns was hardly a foundation for great literature . . .

A shout disturbed the familiar line of thought and she went over to the window. Lights had been strung across the courtyard and beneath them a couple was coming to rest on a large bed that had been dragged outside. Well, that's the natural play of a party, she thought. Everybody up up up and then drifting down. Hadn't it always been like that, all those bodies standing about and she like a little ball, bowling them all over. Her and Clytoris, lying on the bed listening to the stream of guests at Le Moulin, the gurgle of laughter and tangled words below her window, music slowing to a scratch and then the rising screams and shouts of the guests who never stopped coming. Her and Madame Henri killing themselves to get all the food and rooms ready. Diana had helped – no one could say she'd never worked – cleaning out the animals (that unhinged leopard), taking water to all the rooms and watching the couples heaving on the beds or smashing things and each other because they could not make the words go. René Crevel screaming from the tower: 'Do not succumb to domestic fires. They are death, they will eat you!' She laughed softly, that must have been rather a rub to Madame Henri, busting a gut to prepare dinner for twenty cooked on a fucking candle.

Below her, a woman with a white halo of frizzed hair entered the courtyard and staggered along a wall, staring at the couple on the bed. Diana drew back into the dark room, aware that she needed to return to the guests. As she retraced her steps through the now silvery dark of the library she pictured everybody spread around that violet firelit room, eyes half closed after the heavy blessing of the pipe, as easy in their drugged sleep as the discarded clothes on the floor. And a strange woman, hair blonde, tight and curled – terribly ugly – eyes smeared with black, saying, 'Is she yours, Harry? I didn't know you had a little girl.' And then catching her foot on a body so that she stumbled into the two of them. 'Isn't it time she was in bed?' the woman had laughed and her teeth were yellow inside her red lips. 'Time is the disease, madam,' he'd replied. 'And it's rotting your soul quicker than your face.' Diana ran her tongue over her own teeth. She must go to see the dentist when she was next in Rome. Drinking all this red wine.

She heard car horns down in the village. People were leaving, she noted in surprise.

Well, *she* wasn't ready for bed. Didn't she still have a life ahead of her ... there was so much to do ... her body still firm ... she'd go back and indulge that man a little longer and then she and David could go to bed. She hoped David was tired. She wasn't *that* young any more. Still, she straightened her black lace dress on her shoulders, a get-up like this shouldn't be wasted in a library.

'A toast, a toast!'

'Not another performance, Ellis,' someone said.

'Worry not,' he laughed. 'A simple toast to the wonderful Caresse.'

Glasses were raised, and there were shouts and whoops and a smash as someone threw theirs from the window.

'What about Diana?' David asked Ellis with a smile as people relaxed into small groups. 'Would you dare leave her out if she were here?'

'She deserves her own toast,' Ellis said, sitting down on the chair next to him in the light-strung courtyard, his eyes watching the couple moving on the bed. 'Probably a few. That woman's got more twists than a length of rope.'

David nodded. 'There's a lot to unravel.'

'Apparently, around occupied Paris she was known as *la débrouillarde* – Diana the resourceful.' Ellis took the joint handed to him by David and took a long pull. 'A compliment paid by Marshal Pétain, no less.'

'She's an impressive person.'

'A handful, I imagine,' Ellis said.

'A little untamed,' David laughed.

'That's often used as a euphemism.'

'I'm no walk in the park, myself. Perhaps that's why we like each other.'

'She was taught well, I suppose.' Ellis coughed. 'From the way she speaks, it sounds as if Crosby dug a deep groove.'

'The prophet poet.'

'A minor poet, if that.' Ellis swigged from a bottle of Cutty Sark and David raised his eyebrows briefly, deftly rolling and sealing another joint.

'But dedicated?'

'Oh, by all accounts, lived and breathed it. That "frail and glittering literary interlude of inter-war Paris" or whatever schmaltz is now being applied. "A lost generation." Too much money and too much gin – shit will happen. It's the same now in Brooklyn, although there it's too little money and too many bennies. But before you cut me off,' he laughed, holding up his hand, 'I do not downplay the horror of the war that led to that time, nor the quality of the work that sprouted from it, only the lumping together of so many stories in a single silk stocking. Some of those people were truly lost. Some just wanted a little vacation.'

'You think Crosby was a rich kid playing at being an artist?' David asked. 'Is it impossible to be both?'

'No, I think he was a broken boy trying to get fixed with all the glue he could get his hands on. And I don't have any answers, David. I'm just talking.'

'You seem very well informed.' David inhaled deeply and leaned his head back, staring up at the sky.

'Well informed ... I spent the day lying on a sofa in the library instructing a young man from Istanbul on the art of fellatio,' he giggled.

'And what do you make of Crosby's end?' David looked up. 'A dramatic way to go.'

'"Of all deaths, the violent death is best",' Ellis declaimed. '"For from ourselves it steals ourselves so fast / The pain, once apprehended, is quite past."

'Crosby was enamoured of the act itself, and there's a purity in that,' he went on. '"Die at the right time".' He waved his hand.

'And bravery, I suppose, in a way,' David mused.

'It's getting old that's brave, young one, not cutting the line,' Ellis said. 'Sudden death has a transformative power, it preserves with its severity. Old age is life's flabby joke.'

'He certainly seems to have inspired devotion in his women.' David cast his eyes up to the open window of Caresse's rooms way above them.

'We all need heroes. After my father turned out to be the nasty shit he was, I made my hero me. Keeps the cycle of devotion nice and clean.'

'I find it hard to paint Crosby as a hero,' David said. 'Sounds like he gave them a rough time.'

'A paradox of the highest order. Wants his women both free and enslaved. But women want that too. Not easy in today's world, by any stretch. Broads have broad minds these days. Which can both serve and complicate the pursuit of a good fu—'

'Diana.' David stood as she entered the courtyard and Ellis clumsily followed his lead. Both men took in her body wrapped in black lace, her eyes that were very dark.

'What an unexpected pairing. Is it a success?' She looked them both over as David came forward to kiss her and she

238

laced her fingers through his, enjoying the look on Ellis's face.

'Join us.' Ellis spread his arms.

'Yes, all right, for a moment. But there's a man I want to say goodbye to, so only a quick drink.'

A waiter in a collarless black suit, his bare feet in moccasins, came over and filled her glass.

'So what have you been discussing?' she said, giving them both a smile that suggested she knew the answer.

'Your stepfather, actually.'

Her face did not move, but David could tell that she was holding her smile in place.

'And where did you get to?'

'Women and writing,' Ellis said, feeling a stirring in his groin as he remembered the look the waiter had just given him. He was on a slick streak this summer. He glanced down at his stomach. Why, he could not think; he felt like an aged pork chop.

'Well, he was enamoured by both,' Diana continued. 'Though show me a writer who isn't. He'd often read to me from the dictionary – great lists of words: mysterious, macabre, merciless, massacre, morbid, nostalgia, noon, nakedness, obsolete, orchid . . .' She counted the words off on her fingers with a laugh that did not carry her usual enthusiasm.

'Words can be a life raft,' David suggested, his hand flat against Diana's back.

'A cruel trick.' Ellis smiled. 'They only ever approach, never arrive.'

Diana looked at him without smiling. David kept his hand on her back.

'And what else did you glean from your stepfather's study floor?' Ellis asked her.

She turned her head to the side with a barely visible wrinkle of her nose. 'Perhaps it's time you focused on your own work, Mr Porto.'

'Perhaps you could show me how, Diana, given all you've achieved.'

'I wasn't educated enough to write properly. Besides, when you've lived with a real writer, it can seem like everything else is just making notes.'

'You rate his work?' Ellis asked.

'You don't?' she returned.

'Flashes of insight. But he was messy.'

'You didn't know him. He *was* his work. He lived what he wanted to see on the page, there was no separation *there*.' She flicked her eyes over him.

Ellis was quiet.

'May I look in your notebook?' Diana leaned over and touched it.

'No, you may not.' He swept her hand away.

Her face was a challenge and he laughed it off as he got to his feet, tucking the book inside his jacket.

'Smeared thoughts, not suitable for eyes of such patrician blue.'

'You don't know what my thoughts are like.'

'Never been less sure of anything in my life,' he replied. 'But comparison is death.' He picked up his glass and drained it. 'Good night, young lovers.' He turned, singing a low broken chord, as his form was swallowed into the dark mouth of a hallway.

*

Lying in the almost dark of Diana's bedroom, David watched her hand tracing a crack in the wall.

'Do you ever think about when you'll die, David?'

'No, not really. My thoughts are taken up by life.'

She was silent for a while.

'My mother took me to see a clairvoyant once. He was a baker and lived above his boulangerie in the Latin Quarter. We sat in a room covered in flour as he told her, without asking any questions, that she had been born in 1891, had a daughter of eight, had been married twice, that her husband was a genius but very difficult to live with, and that she would die when she was seventy-eight.'

'How old is she now?'

She rolled over on the bed and looked at him. 'She's seventy-eight.'

He was silent for a moment.

'I wonder if she remembers?'

'If it's something she liked, then she will.'

'It must have been painful for her when your stepfather left her like that.'

'Yes, it was hard.' She seemed to be treading a careful line with her words.

'Did you know the . . . other woman?'

'No.'

'But he still loved your mother?'

'Yes,' she said quietly, turning away from him. 'They were wholly in love.'

'Have you had a love like that?' David had not noticed the sarcasm in her voice.

She shifted onto her back. In the candlelight her expression

241

was rich and confusing, refusing to stay still. 'Yes. He loved her enough not to give her children.'

'What do you mean?' He frowned.

'He loved her so much he didn't want her to have children. He wanted her alone, perfect, her womb a vessel that could contain all of his desire, unspilt.'

'Would you like to be loved like that?'

Diana turned her face to him and smiled. 'Darling, I think that's a must.'

She looked away at the wall again. 'I had a fight once with my mother's dog. He would sit on a sofa and refuse to look at me. One day I got a rope and whipped it round his neck before he knew what was happening. I pulled him forward and he pulled back with all his might. The muscles of his thin neck were surprisingly strong. He leaned his whole weight back and I heaved with all of mine. Thankfully, the shiny lacquer floor worked in my favour and his feet couldn't get any purchase. My little leather shoes worked hard and I dragged his stiff body towards the garden. I had to break him. Just like a horse.'

'A lot of your stories are about animals that end up dead or lost,' David said.

'They were the ones I liked the most.' She turned to him suddenly. 'Hold me,' she said.

He pulled her close.

'Tighter.'

He laughed and did so.

She shook her hair back and laughed too, like someone who has got out of cold water and feels the enclosing comfort of a towel.

He looked down at her face, pale in the moonlight, her eyes wide open and very still now.

'You won't leave, will you?' she asked.

'No,' he said, frowning, feeling with dismay a part of himself retreating.

'But I want you to know that you're free, David. Keep it neat, but I have no expectations in that regard.'

He looked away, confused. 'I don't need you to say that.'

'I'm not saying it for you. It's for us. And trust me, it's for the best.'

Rue de Lille, 1928

'The doctor thinks you're going to die.'

Harry stood at the end of Diana's bed, a bottle of champagne in his hand.

'What?' She tried to lift her head.

He sat on the edge of the bed and she laid her head on his lap, feeling the rough cloth of his suit against her cheek.

'You took too many of those aspirin, greedy Rat. The doctor thinks you could die.'

'Will I have to go back to school?' she asked, feeling weak.

'I don't know.'

'I don't remember arriving.' She frowned, confused. 'I don't remember anything.'

'The doctor's very cross with your mother. Thinks it's all her fault. Now here . . .' He poured two glasses of champagne and passed her one. 'Here's to a lovely little life.' He emptied his glass. 'Your mother and I are going to dinner.'

Alderney, 1993

'Your mother asked to see you,' James said as Elena and Bay came into the kitchen holding two straw bags full of vegetables. 'She's being even more maddening than usual.'

Elena put the bags down on the table and immediately went towards the stairs.

'Do I not get a kiss?' James called, and then, 'No, Bay, you wait down here with me.'

Bay went to sit on the stairs, dangling her legs through the banisters, waiting.

'Come here.' Her mother reached forward.

Elena went towards her uncertainly. There was a strange light in Diana's eyes, the sickly movement of the moon over an unsettled sea. A sickness washed over Elena and she reached out for the bed before she sat on it heavily. Her mother put both her hands over Elena's stomach.

'Let me feel it,' she slurred, and Elena leaned back, not breathing.

'Sweet little thing,' Diana crowed. 'All curled up like a rat in its den.' She smiled and stared at Elena, who looked away.

'No, Elena, no, show that pretty face.' Her mother put a hand under her chin and tilted it upward. 'The one that all the boys liked. Yes, yes,' she ignored the shake of her daughter's head, the rearing away from her grasp. 'It's the one everybody liked the best. Even your father couldn't resist. My worthy successor . . .'

Tired of counting the fine golden hairs on her thighs, Bay felt that she had waited long enough. Standing up, she crept to where her grandmother's door stood just ajar. She put her head around it and saw that her mother was sitting on the side of the bed, her back rigid, staring fixedly out of the window as her grandmother rocked backward and forward stroking the round of Elena's stomach and crooning a strange song in a language Bay did not understand.

Rue de Lille, 1929

'I don't remember anything more after that.' In the court-yard, Diana leaned against the solid curves of the Daimler that Auguste was washing with long soapy strokes, his sleeves rolled to the elbow.

'But you could have died, could you?' he said, a cigarette clamped in his mouth, the front of his shirt wet.

'The doctor said it was the *worst* case he'd ever—'

A noise from above and both Diana and the chauffeur stopped and looked up.

On the top floor of the building a bedroom window had been thrown open with force and shouting could be heard from within.

Auguste immediately turned and began attentively wash-ing the car again, but Diana remained fixed, staring upward.

Her mother appeared in the window and without think-ing Diana's hand raised itself in greeting. But as she did so, half-expecting her mother to shout down a greeting as she normally would, Caresse raised her arms like an emperor at a circus and threw a great pile of paper from the window, the torn pieces scurrying on the wind. She disappeared inside again and there was more shouting, hoarse and wild, from within.

Diana picked a piece of the paper up from where they were scattered around her like enormous confetti.

```
I want to devour you STOP Will eat nothing until
you arrive New York STOP
```

A movement above caused her to look up and she saw her mother lean right out of the window and put a leg over the railing, the long silk ribbon of her dressing gown streaming out in the wind, her face just … anguish. But two arms circled her waist and dragged her back inside, and the window closed with a slam.

Diana looked at Auguste, but he was peering intently at a wing mirror, polishing a stubborn spot.

She turned her gaze down at another piece of blue paper soaked grey on the wet stone.

```
Death will be our marriage STOP
```

Roccasinibalda, 1970

The bells were ringing in the town. The round iron clang echoed across the valley and entered the windows of the castle. Down in the village, the streets were deserted to the midday heat as everyone gathered round the small chapel awaiting the bride and groom.

Diana turned over in bed and swept her arm over the empty space beside her. David was already awake. She thought briefly of her mother's face creased in sleep, and wondered if she'd been in a similar position when he'd got up. She'd tried to teach herself to sleep on her back ('It will save you,' one of her mother's friends said, her gloved hands cupping Diana's small face), but her body always folded itself closed in the night. She pushed the thought off, deciding not to care, and, easing herself from the bed, walked to the windows to open the shutters. The sky was a clear blue, the hills green and bright. She breathed deeply, listening to the bells going on and on and on. She rolled her neck on her shoulders. A wedding day. Hip hip hooray. But as she stretched her arms above her head she recalled Anthony's face as he had watched her walk towards him and she smiled sadly to herself. He had never looked at her like that again. She pressed the tips of her fingers against her eyes and, on hearing a knock, immediately swept her hands up and back through her hair, as though refreshed. 'Yes?' she called and one of the girls entered with a tray holding a glass of milk and a banana.

'Oh, you're wonderful, thank you.' She went back to the bed and lay down with a smile of satisfaction. She would eat this and then have a bath before going up to see her mother. She squared her shoulders; perhaps a little glass of wine.

'Have you heard the bells?' Caresse asked as she sat down opposite her by the wide open windows.

'Hard not to.'

'Aren't they wonderful?' Caresse breathed, and Diana could hear the wheeze behind it. 'I lay in bed and listened all morning. Such a sweet couple. They came to see me when they got engaged.' Her mother shook a handful of pills into her hand.

'Did you give them your benediction?' Diana handed her a glass of apricot juice.

Caresse held it up to the sunlight that played across the peeling plaster walls. 'Look at that colour . . . Of course I did, I adore weddings. Not the church and all that mess, but the union of it. The cosmic balance.'

'I'm rather off them myself,' Diana said.

'Oh, Diana. Your first wedding was lovely.'

'All I remember is my hair pinching and Maxime being blind drunk by ten in the morning.'

'Darling, if you marry the heir to a champagne dynasty it's hardly surprising that people get a little tight.'

'Tight! I had to untie his shoes.'

'Yes, men can be rather a bore when they drink too much. Although I could have told you that about Maxime.'

Diana's nose wrinkled. She did not appreciate her mother pointing out any of their shared interests. 'Your father and Burt were absolutely blotto during both ceremonies. It's often a problem with men ...' Caresse's voice drifted. 'Harry was the only one who was really there ...'

Diana looked down at her hands. Her mother had worn long grey gloves and a dress the colour of wet sidewalk to the register office in New York. Nothing white. No bridesmaids. Diana had cried bitterly at that. She'd thought it no wedding at all.

'I'm done with marriage,' she said decisively. 'The whole thing's a circus. I should have been put off by my first, but I was somehow duped into the whole thing again with Anthony.'

'What did you wear to marry Anthony? It was a shame that I missed that.'

'I thought about it this morning, actually.' Diana smiled sadly. 'I was remembering the way he ...' But as she spoke, her mother's telephone began to ring.

Caresse waved a hand as she answered and Diana crossed her arms and pulled her mouth to one side, aware that she had allowed herself to drift into an open current. She could hear Roberto's voice melting through the earpiece. 'Absolutely not, *abbiamo fettuccine ... a posto ... abbacchio e cicoria. Sì, veramente ...* ' Caresse paused. 'Do use your imagination,

251

Roberto, it's lunch, not the Geneva Convention.' She replaced the handset and looked at Diana expectantly. 'Where were we? Yes, you and Anthony. You were saying?'

Diana shook her head. 'Nothing. It was a mistake, that's all. I knew it from the moment I said "I do" in that ghastly Caribbean heat.'

'St Lucia, wasn't it? What happened to that little island he gave you?'

'I didn't like the sailing so gave it back.'

'Well, you got Ibiza anyway,' Caresse said comfortingly.

'I don't own it, Caresse, I built a house there. There'll be no buying of islands now we've got this bag of rocks slung about our necks.'

Caresse shook her head sadly. 'You take a very negative position, Diana. Roccasinibalda will begin to pay for itself as the movement grows. You'll see.'

Diana was silent.

'Do you think you'll finally settle there now? In Ibiza?' Caresse decided to keep the mood light.

'Yes. Provided Anthony signs the papers Ivan has drawn up. The whole thing's going to cost much more than I thought.'

'But he won't take the house?'

'No. Elena tells me he's dragging his little wife back to the family pile in Kent, so he'll have his hands full for quite some time. I remember when he took me there to stay with his parents. It's the only time I've ever had to wear clothes in bed. Those awful English country houses.' She shivered. 'Though this tomb's not much better when the temperature dips.'

'Big places are where big things happen.'

'Big mistakes, certainly. Ivan says most big houses are good for tax and nothing else, and I agree with him.'

'Who is this Ivan?'

'My marvellous new lawyer. Knows tax law inside out.'

Caresse laughed. 'You've always been very clever with all that. I just pay.'

'Your pot's rather deeper than mine.'

'You will say if you need money, won't you? You can always write to the relations in Boston.'

Diana shifted uncomfortably. 'Yes, perhaps.'

'Are the goblins guarding the vault? Lord, they get wild about being overdrawn. Permanent terror of the well running dry.'

'I think mine actually might have.'

'Oh. Well, you'll have to go and see them.'

Diana bit her lip.

'I think they're a little more forgiving of all that now. When I was young, becoming overdrawn was a more grievous Bostonian sin than being homosexual.'

'Yes, you've said,' Diana replied.

'I do think you might have kept the place in St Lucia anyway,' Caresse said thoughtfully. 'For the girls or something.'

'I should have kept it so I could sell it. I could do with the cash now. But anyway,' Diana said with a proud shake of her head, 'I prefer not to have anything of Anthony's. A child is quite enough.'

'Yes, I understand that. You can't put a price on being able to start over.'

Diana nodded and looked out the window and they sat

in silence. 'Do you remember when I was sent home from school because I ate all those aspirin?' Caresse looked at her in surprise. Diana rarely did this before lunch. 'It was just before you both sailed to New York—'

'Is there a point to this one, Diana?'

'I remember woozing down that wide corridor beneath the heavy gold chandelier, the mirror below it stained in one corner with a spray of black.' Caresse nodded and gathered her wrap a little tighter. 'And you and Harry were inside your bedroom and he was sitting on the bed drinking out of an enormous vase.'

Caresse didn't take the bait and remained looking at her levelly, only her chest rising and falling.

'You were crying, but you didn't shout at me to go downstairs. You just stared at us both and said, "I want this one *out*, Harry. She's hurting us . . ." And he said nothing at all, just went on watching you. And then you told me to come to you, even though he was in the room . . .'

Caresse was silent for a moment and then spoke with purpose. 'He was drinking a gimlet out of that vase. We both thought we'd hit on the perfect "one-drink-a-day" solution.' She laughed and then stopped as though she'd just seen the joke die.

'Who were you talking about?' Diana said.

'You know who we were talking about.' Caresse looked at Diana from beneath heavy lids. 'She was quite insane.' Caresse pricked the words with precision. 'And, from start to finish, refused to understand the game.'

'Was it very hard to read what he wrote about her at the end?'

'Not at all.' Caresse picked up some of her papers and put them on the table beside her. 'She was just like all the others. No substance to any of them. There were always others, Diana, it was accepted.' Caresse's expression was calm. 'That *was* the game.'

Diana returned her mother's gaze, waiting.

'But that woman was just determined ... Oh, I won't bring her in here.' She raised her hands. 'She doesn't have a place.'

'Is that why you cut so much out at the end?'

'I cut nothing. I *edited* the diaries as I've edited all the books I've published. He only left a very rough copy for me to work with.'

'But it ends as you sail for New York. The last month is missing.'

'It was a mess. He was a mess. He would never have wanted his words to be published like that.'

'You didn't include the last time we all went away together. The weekend when I had to sit up front beside him in the car and all the rest of you were behind. You didn't include what he said about that.'

'There was nothing of interest.' Caresse smiled. 'A few general remarks. Nothing of any lasting interest. I know you like to scour every page and photograph for your reflection, Diana – yes, I've noticed – but this is one you'll have to let go of.'

'Why can't I see the originals? It ... it would help me. Being here's churning it all up for some reason and I think it would help me to lay it down somehow. I thought I might write about it so that I—'

'Diana.' Caresse did not open her eyes. 'I have told you already. There is nothing here.'

'Then where are they? Did you burn *everything*?'

'Of course I didn't. If you must know, I sold them.'

'You what?' Diana stared at her mother.

'I sold his papers and books.' Caresse shrugged. 'A great clearing out of all that has been. You can go and see them in the University Library of Southern Illinois.'

'Southern *Illinois*?'

Caresse shifted in her seat. 'It's a very progressive university. And something had to pay for the roof. So now you know. Whatever it is that you might want is available for all to read in the new Crosby Archive in their university library. I agree that it's in the public's interest to have these things, and they will remain there for posterity. So now you can stop digging about, put those claws away.' She folded Diana's outstretched hands.

'But some of it's ... private.'

'That, my dear, is an opinion.'

'You sold his books.'

'Not all.'

'For this roof?'

'Yes.'

Diana stood up.

'You didn't love him enough.'

'Diana. We will not do this again.'

'You left him.'

'Left *him*? He left *me*. He left us!'

'No.' Diana shook her head. 'You left him with no choice. You knew what he was like. Why didn't you do what you

256

were supposed to? You'd planned it. All those walks in the *cimetière*, choosing the right spot, that awful crone mumbling. Your *real* burying place. What was all that? Talk? Was it all just talk?'

'Mothers don't leave.' The unexpected vehemence of Caresse's voice silenced Diana for a moment.

But then Diana spoke, her voice very low. 'That's *not* why you stayed.'

'Always so certain. Always so sure. It might do you good, Diana, to admit that there are some things it is impossible to know.'

'I'd give my right eye *not* to know half the things I know.'

'But you don't have to believe in any of them! That's the whole point. Freedom! That's what you've been given.'

'But what about sticking to your guns? What about your beloved *word*?'

'If you want to traipse about feeling like hell wearing concrete boots of morality then be my guest. Although you probably wouldn't be my guest, as people like that tend to be continually morose and steeped in regret.'

'All I know is that you had the chance to do something . . . something true, and you . . . clung.' Diana gave her mother back her own phrase triumphantly. 'Yes, you clung!'

'I did not cling,' Caresse said, drawing back. 'What good would it have done, Diana?' She leaned forward now, on the attack. 'Hmm? Tell me that. More ugliness, more pain. More war.' She thrust her arms out. '*This* would never have happened.' They stared at each other. 'I wasn't ready, Diana. I had too much to give. Too much to *live*. I wanted to get ready and go to the party Hart was throwing for us to celebrate finishing

257

his poem. I wanted to eat a vast meal and then come home and be undressed and made love to, and then do it again and again and again for the rest of my life. Yes, to life, yes to life! I followed him as far as I could go. As far as I wanted to go. And that was our deal. Each to his own. You don't force your desire on anyone else.'

Diana was silent and then said, 'Didn't you?'

They were both silent for a moment.

'Don't hate me for it,' her mother said quietly. 'But I was also your mother. I couldn't do *that*.'

'But you didn't do it for me. None of it was for me. Don't try and make me grateful for it. It was your life you loved, Caresse, not mine.'

'They were the same thing!' Caresse held her hands out. 'Haven't you seen that by now?'

Diana shook her head. 'Elena and Leonie are entirely different to me.'

'It's not difference, Diana. It's distance. We *have* to keep our children close, at least at first. I went, you went; it was as simple as that.'

'And now?'

'Now.' Caresse looked away, and her eyes shone. 'Now is a different story.'

Diana was quiet and then moved a little closer. 'I suppose we were in it together.' She picked up her mother's hand and gave her a half smile.

The words seemed to drain the last of Caresse's energy and her hand was lifeless in Diana's grasp.

'He loved us differently, I know that,' Diana went on, her voice soft. 'I know you were far more important—'

'He loved you because you were my daughter.' Caresse spoke in a low, final tone.

Diana shook her head. She knew she should stop, but she couldn't.

'It was my first love. My great love—'

'Oh, will you never get *over* that silly infatuation!'

'He loved me because I was like a smooth sweep of sand and he like a—'

'You were a child! You were only ever my child.'

'Yes. I was a child,' Diana said, trying to still the trembling in her hands.

'You're an ageing woman, Diana. You must move on.'

Diana looked at her mother, stricken.

'And *I* was your first love, Diana. That's what you forget. And you, an echo of mine. He couldn't stand that. It was about *me*, Diana.' Caresse shook her head. 'He wanted all of me to himself. I'm sorry if that misled you. If you misconstrued his nursery games as something more.'

'It was *not* a game. You just can't bear to admit it.' Diana laughed suddenly. 'You're smothering pride. Look at it head on – I dare you.'

'I don't even know what you're talking about.' Caresse closed her eyes.

'Admit it.'

'Admit *what*?'

'You can deny it all you like but you cared enough to burn every letter. I know what I *won't* find in Southern Illinois.'

The bells began again outside the window. The sound reverberated in the room.

'I was misused,' Diana said eventually in a low voice.

259

'Oh, Diana,' said Caresse softly. 'Who of us hasn't been?'

'You should have left me in Boston.' Diana stood up. 'Better a blind drunk than a blind visionary. I should have stayed on that boat. I should have jumped off that boat.'

'Oh move on, Diana! Move on. You mustn't do this to yourself any more. It's gone. Take his example, if you must. But do not feast on the past. It is death. Utter death.'

'Release me then,' Diana said simply.

'That, Diana, is beyond me. Whatever it is that troubles you is between you and your god.'

Roberto made his way across the courtyard, surprisingly empty and still in the midday heat. There was usually a woman of some sort dancing alone through the strict shadows or a man sleeping beneath a table, unwilling to be kept indoors. They all came to the meals, of course, but some liked to keep up the appearance of spontaneity. He looked up to Caresse's rooms and could hear Diana's voice. There was a sound of brisk footsteps, and then the distant groan of a door being closed. He stepped beneath the protection of a shaded arch and waited, the small package of sun-stamped books, which he had carefully wrapped in paper of cerulean blue in his study that morning, held loosely at his side. As he stood looking up at the brilliant sky he began to hum a low song that his father used to sing on hunting trips. He glanced at his watch and then up to the still shuttered windows of Caresse's rooms. She would not wake up for some time yet. Roberto made his way towards his study. He would put these out of the way and then continue with his paperwork before bringing the Principessa her evening soup.

Alderney, 1993

James climbed the stairs, switching off the lights as he went. Opening his bedroom door, he stood for a moment, looking at the bed.

Elena was sitting up, her eyes closed, and he watched her in her stillness, tracing the almost translucent lids with his gaze, noting the bruised tiredness beneath her eyes.

'Do you think the baby will look like me?' she said, opening her eyes unexpectedly.

He smiled tiredly as he undid his shirt. 'She'll be a lucky girl if she does.'

Elena placed an arm over her stomach, and closed her eyes again.

'Are you okay?' he asked. 'I mean, after . . .'

'Of course.' She attempted a reassuring smile. 'I don't let them in, remember.' Her smile faltered.

'Your bloody family.' He shook his head.

She looked suddenly nauseous and frowned, concentrating.

'What is it?' He looked at her.

'It's nothing, it's . . .'

He came and sat beside her, one shoe still in his hands. 'I think we should leave.'

'I think you should leave,' she said quietly.

'Elena, what do you mean?'

Elena felt the patter of guilt begin to fall in her mind like a fine rain.

Her eyes filling with tears, she said, '*You* should leave. Be free of all . . . this. I'm keeping us low, James.' She looked at him. 'I can feel it coming. You don't need to go through all that again. Not again.'

'You can say it as much as you like, for the rest of our lives if you will, but I'm not going to leave you. I'm never going to leave you,' he said simply.

'But how can you bear it?' She covered her face, unable to look at him. She was pressing too hard, he could see her fingers digging into the spaces beneath her eyes, and holding her wrists he gently pulled her hands away.

'Don't let this ruin all you've done. All those hours of work . . . You've escaped all that.'

She nodded and it was a lid closing on something.

He looked at her, taking her in slowly, bit by bit, his eyes moving from her tanned shoulder, along her collarbone, up the long neck. He took in her still surprisingly short hair, falling over one eye, the lovely slender face, as finely drawn as one of the Beardsley etchings whose sensuous lines and rutting figures she disliked so much.

'Bay seems to be curling into a smaller ball every night,' she said anxiously.

'She's fine, Elena. She's a child. She's fine.'

'She's always ill,' she said quietly.

'She exaggerates.'

'She's the same age I was when ...' Her voice faltered.

'Elena, she's *fine*.' Something in James's voice made her stop. Elena stared at her hands. Her words were ill-fitting, both revealing too much and concealing nothing ...

She got up, went to the night-filled window and looked out at the yellow moon that was being concealed by a ragged blanket of cloud.

'Diana said it was excessive to have more children ...' She half-turned towards him so that she was in pale profile against the dark sky outside.

'Your mother is vicious.' He shrugged.

'Doing it all again after all these years.' She gazed at the mellow round of the disappearing moon. 'The long nights.' She turned and looked at him with worried eyes. 'What if I can't do it?'

'Elena, you were born to be a mother. And while not sleeping for the next year is not exactly a joyous prospect, she will be. New life, Elena!'

'Can we even afford it?'

James looked at her ironically, and she ducked her gaze. 'My mother always said that once you had three, you might as well have six.'

'Please don't bring your mother in here.'

'It's life and it's beautiful,' James said firmly. 'As you always tell me, we've been given a gift.'

'Yes.' She nodded, head bowed, battling in her mind as she was stretched taut between gratitude and a cold-burning

263

rage. She looked up, ready for one more try, wanting him to protect her from the jagged thoughts.

'But perhaps we should have been more *careful*.'

'No, Elena. No.' There was a resistance in James's voice that silenced her and, trying to keep the serrated thoughts from touching the raw sides of her mind, she lay down and gently returned her hands to her stomach; becoming very still as she stared out at the clouded indigo of the night sky.

Paris, 1929

'Now look at that, Rat.'

She looked eagerly to where a woman was walking hand in hand with a small boy. Diana took in the hug of the skirt against her buttocks and the way the child pulled at his mother's hand.

'Those who cling are taken unwilling.' He picked up an oyster from the tray between them and held it out to her. 'I bet this little oyster thought he'd picked a good safe rock under the sea. Do you think he ever dreamt, Rat, listening to the wash of the water and with the moon spilling over him, of the twin horror of hand and knife?' He levered open the shell and revealed the translucent flesh.

Diana took it from him gingerly. 'Hold on.' He grabbed a half-lemon, its face shrouded in muslin, and squeezed, causing the pearlescent flesh to shudder slightly.

'Eleven oysters for your eleventh year. An important number, Rat. One and One comprise the gateway of duality.

Sun and Moon. Good and Bad. Man and Woman. Nothing will ever be whole again.' He handed her an oyster.

'Down it goes.'

Eyes wide, Diana tipped her head back and swallowed.

Alderney, 1993

The wind blew softly, lifting the short strands of Bay's hair, the same length now as her mother's. It was a sweet, warm wind and she closed her eyes, letting it wash over the curve of her exposed belly where she lay beneath the fig tree. She was like a curtain now, being blown backward and forward, no beginning, middle or end. The tree above her liked it too, she could hear its leaves saying so. Could she hear it in the grass? No, that was too small a sound. It seemed to come from somewhere she'd already been, this wind, or was taking her back to herself – the place she wanted most. She heard a window open but did not move. She was hidden in the grass beneath the wide rough green leaves, her feet lying either side of the tree's dry grey elephant trunk. This wind was her friend and she smiled at the waving leaves, agreeing entirely.

'Bay!' She heard the call as if it were from yesterday. 'Bay!' It was her father.

She sat up, squinting.

The men must have come to get her grandmother.

She wasn't even sick, Bay thought with disdain, as she did up her dress and stuffed her feet into her red jelly shoes. *She was just being a big baby.*

Wrapped in a tawny blanket and secured in a chair, Diana began her descent. Wearing short-sleeved white shirts, the outline of their vests just visible, the men's arms strained as they bore the weight of the seated body down the stairs towards the open door.

Standing with her two boys tucked against her sides, Elena reached out a hand to her mother as she went by, but Diana stared ahead like a seated statue of Sekhmet, her eyes fixed on something only she could see.

'I don't want skin,' Bay said to her father later that night, remembering the blackened hairs of a previous meal. 'I don't like it.'

'Bay, *please* stop saying no and *try* to start saying yes.' Her father's voice was hard and he pulled the plate away and slammed it down on the counter. Bay lowered her head until her chin met her neck, her chest rising and falling.

'You must try, Bay,' her mother said, taking the plate and carefully cutting the meat away from the fat. When she placed it back in front of Bay, the burnt skin was gone. 'We have to eat, my love. We must try and eat.' And Bay saw her mother smile at her father.

'Has Grandma gone for ever?' Jake asked.

'She won't come back here, no.'

'Can I have her room?' Tom asked.

'We're not going to be here much longer,' Elena said, glancing at James. 'Summer's almost over.'

'This has been a very difficult time for Mummy.' Their father spoke in an official voice and the boys nodded, sitting up a little straighter. 'A difficult time for all of us.'

Bay nodded with feeling.

'And, unfortunately, tomorrow Anita's coming for lunch,' James said.

'Why?' the children chorused. Anita had been married to their grandfather, a man who only existed to them in a small framed photo that their mother kept on her desk. Every time she came, their mother became sad and quiet.

'Anita wears skin-coloured tights even on the beach,' Bay said.

'Why are all the old women we know so horrible?' asked Jake.

'I hate them,' said Tom with feeling.

'My mother's not horrible,' said James. 'You all love your other grandmother.'

Elena concentrated on helping Bay load food onto her fork.

'And on the bright side, in a few days your Aunty Leo's going to come,' James continued.

'Why?' asked three voices, this time looking at their mother. 'She never comes.'

'Because she's going to help me sort out your grand-mother's things,' Elena said, wiping her mouth and taking a large drink of water.

'Will she wear her costume?' Bay asked.

'It's called a habit, Bay.'

'Did Aunty Leo not want to see Diana? Is that why she waited until she had left?' asked Jake, looking at his mother.

'I'm ... not sure,' Elena said, flustered.

'Aunty Leo doesn't like Grandma,' Tom said authoritatively.

'What makes you think that?' Elena asked in a careful voice.

'Because she said so. She said that when you're a grown-up you can choose if you want to see your parents.'

'Yes, that's true,' Elena said quietly.

'Why do you choose to see Grandma when she makes you sad?' Jake asked.

'Well . . .' Elena glanced at James. 'You must remember that your grandmother didn't have an easy time of it. She had a very painful childhood. Very . . . lonely.' She shook the air between her hands as though sifting the words so that they would emerge somehow finer.

'So was yours,' Jake said defensively.

'Yes.' Elena nodded reluctantly, putting her head on one side and smoothing a crease in the tablecloth. 'But everyone's pain is different. And your grandmother's childhood was particularly hard.'

Bay frowned down at her untouched plate and then across at her brothers.

'What was hard?' Tom asked bravely. Breathless, Bay waited.

'Your grandmother had to . . . she . . . was . . .' Their mother's words were full of holes through which the children could see nothing and the boys looked at their mother with matching frowns.

'That maniac Harry Crosby didn't help, for a start,' their father broke in, cutting his meat enthusiastically.

The children's eyes swept towards their father.

Elena widened her eyes. 'James,' she said.

270

He glanced at the children and then back at Elena. 'Sorry.'

'Who was Harry Crosby?' Jake asked.

Bay nodded, she knew. Her father had told her once while they were looking at the books on her grandmother's shelves. He had taken one down and showed her the black sun on its spine. A man that had flown too close to the sun . . . Her frown deepened as she tripped over the story . . . No, that wasn't right.

'He was married to your great-grandmother,' James said, putting his head back, controlling his words now.

'Why was he a maniac?' Tom asked, turning back to his mother.

'He was . . . selfish.' She stared at the table and then up at her son. 'Sometimes men can be very, very selfish.'

Bay looked at her brothers and father, and then, taking her mother's hand in hers, pressed it to her cheek, trying to comfort them both.

Rue de Lille, 1929

The small black box above her door buzzed and buzzed. Diana stood, staring up at it. Four times. A moment later the door opened and the maid came in. 'You're wanted upstairs,' she said with a jerk of her head.

'Who's there?' Diana asked.

'Only them,' she said.

'What time are they leaving?'

'Seven o'clock.'

'What are they eating?'

'Banana meringue.'

Diana nodded and went to her mirror. She tried to arrange her hair in a twist, securing it with pins. She turned and saw Hélène watching her. 'Must you stare like that? Haven't you a job to do?'

'Ah, here you are.'

Diana took her seat in the purple-painted dining room. Harry kept his eyes on the letter he was reading. Her mother stroked Narcisse's throat and smiled vaguely at Diana.

'Your hair looks pretty like that. Were you attempting a chignon?'

Diana narrowed her eyes slightly.

'I've realised that death isn't for graveyards.' Harry spoke without looking up from his letter. 'All those screams, covered in soil.' Diana watched him take some wine into his mouth and swallow it down. 'Cremation is clean. No worms, nor white bloated rats. Better to burn.'

'I don't feel like either of those today,' Caresse said. 'When the jasmine blooms like this all I want to do is bathe and wear white dresses.'

From far downstairs the sound of the telephone became audible.

A maid entered the room and went to Harry, murmuring something in his ear.

He looked at the clock. 'Tell her, in an hour.'

The girl nodded, and Caresse went on stroking the dog's throat.

The same maid re-entered the room with a huge tray loaded with a mountain of meringue, its tips burned brown, little rounds of banana running in rings round its edge. She set it down on the table and the three of them looked at it dubiously.

From the end of the table a gold lighter flew through the air and, making contact, destroyed the mountain so that it lay collapsed in an avalanche across the centre of the table.

'Banana bombe,' Caresse laughed, reaching out with her spoon. 'Eat it up, Diana, it will still taste delicious.'

Diana leaned forward, elbows on the table, and dipped a spoon in the mess.

'You look more and more like your mother, Rat.' Harry sat back and looked at them both.

'The Wretched Rat.' Caresse, amused, leaned back in her chair and licked her spoon. 'It's not a very nice name. Don't you mind it?'

'No,' Diana said, looking steadily at her mother, also licking the burnt sugar and cream from her spoon. 'Names are important.'

Roccasinibalda, 1970

The only noise in Caresse's room was the eager scratch of a pen making its way across paper.

'Now the next.' Caresse held her hand out to Roberto, who was standing at a discreet distance from the bed, his linen-suited body turned slightly towards the window. He picked up the last of the pile of papers and brought them over, before lifting the inked pages with the gentle care of a midwife and placing them on a table to dry.

With her breath coming short, Caresse's finger moved over the lawyer's typewritten words with difficulty, a faltering progress as though she were trying to decipher the strange symbols of a forgotten language.

'This bit here ... does that mean that it will all be secure?'

Roberto hurried across and hunched over the small figure in the bed, following her finger and nodding.

'*Sì, sì*, that's right.'

'I so want it to go on, Roberto.' She gazed up at him

through her thick tortoiseshell glasses, her arm resting along the length of his.

'Of course, signora. Principessa.'

She smiled at that, enjoying the joke, the best possible kind, one that recalled a choice with a happy outcome.

'Is it fair to do it this way, Roberto?'

He took in her eyes, eager with hope, and the soft hands talking anxiously to one another, and nodded.

'She'll be very angry not to get it all, you know.'

Roberto spread his hands. 'Disappointment can be an important part of growing up.'

'I told her about selling the archive to Illinois.'

He crossed his arms and inclined his head, listening.

'I don't know why I told her everything had gone already. It was a lie and it's been making me feel restless ever since.'

'It doesn't really concern Diana. It's your property to do with as you wish. Did you make the changes you wanted to for the publishers?' he asked smoothly.

'You mean the edits?'

'*Sì*, of course, edit. I forget the word.'

'Yes, I did. There was hardly anything to do. He wrote so beautifully. Such power. It was very hard reading some of it. Not something a wife undertakes easily.'

'It is a testament to your passion for his work.'

'Not just for his. For all good work. It must be brought into the light, shared with as many people as possible. Diana said she thought they should remain private. She was the same about the funny letters they exchanged while she was at school. He wrote to *everybody*, but I fear she mistook his affection . . .'

'She speaks of him with great love.'

'Love? Perhaps. Though she hardly knew him, Roberto. She was a child in the nursery and he *loathed* the domestic. But I suppose,' she said, staring out of the window, 'that it all looked rather different from her point of view. Things are so much bigger when we are children, and continue to grow ever more unwieldy as we become adult. Sometimes we need a parent's take to put things in perspective.'

'Of course.'

'Diana can be so morbid, left to her own devices.'

'She can be very dark, yes.'

'Well, darkness is good, Roberto. Darkness is light's counterpart. You can't have one without the other, or things get all out of whack. It's why I'm grateful for all the pain of my life. I feel it's scoured me out to make space for even more joy.'

Roberto murmured a tide of '*Sì, sì, sì*' as he prepared the next papers.

'And there's still plenty of sun in Diana. It's just her dogged determination to hang on to the past that's dangerous. She's wedded to yesterday and seems unable to understand that there are no answers there.'

'Yes, what's in the past is in the past.' Roberto nodded, looking rather relieved. Caresse glanced at him. She'd never pressed Roberto about Diana. They'd obviously made love at some point, but what Diana had done to make him quite so unable to articulate, Caresse could only imagine. Well, there were some things that could remain a mystery.

'And what shall I do about the university board's invitation to open the new wing of the library?' Roberto asked.

'When is it?'

'Early next year.'

'Tell them yes.'

Roberto hesitated. 'You are sure?'

'I said yes, Roberto.'

'And Dalí has written that he will not leave Spain again without Gala, but she has retreated to Púbol and so is, at present, out of reach.'

'Very well, I will go and see him there.'

'Of . . . course.' He glanced at her. 'I will write today. And now, the last . . .'

He picked up the final piece of paper and placed it on the table that bridged her covered legs.

She glanced at it and read her own dictated words, moving her aching wrists in small circles. Really, the body was very weak. It was the pen that was powerful. She pressed the fat nib into the paper and made a mark. More than the body, more than the sword, it was the pen that would decide the future when one was buried and the other ploughing the earth. *Yes, this is the real holy trinity*, she thought: *ink, hand and pen*. And with a glance at the painting of Diana that hung on her wall, she fixed her will with a simple scrawl.

Alderney, 1993

Elena looked over the neatly laid table, and brushed some crumbs from around her plate before her stepmother could see.

'Elena, I asked you a question.'

Elena stopped as though caught. 'Sorry, what?'

'It's *pardon*, Elena.'

'Our grandma says pardon is what housemaids say,' Tom said, staring at her.

Elena and James gave each other the ghost of a smile. 'Tom,' James said warningly. Watching her step-grandmother, Bay lowered her head beneath the table and held out a forkful of food to the little dog that sat next to her chair.

'Where is she staying?' Anita asked.

'She's at St Malo's.' Elena picked up her fork. 'It overlooks the sea, with that little chapel set beside it. I thought it might be nice for her to hear the sound of the bell in the morning.'

'I'm sure the bells will be a *great* comfort.'

'If nothing else they might remind her of last orders.' James smiled at Anita, who stared back at him blankly.

'Diana in a home.' She pressed her napkin to her mouth. 'I never thought I'd see the day.'

'Well, she was getting so confused that it seemed . . .'

'*Getting*? I think that's something of an understatement. Diana's been losing the plot since I met her.'

'She's not mad,' Tom explained. 'She just can't stop remembering.' Anita glanced at the boys as though noticing them for the first time.

'That's right, Tom.' Elena smiled at her blond-haired son. 'She's got a bit stuck.'

'It can be very tiring at the end,' Anita said, lowering her voice dramatically. 'I've always thought it's when relationships are really put to the test.'

'We're very grateful to you for looking after Anthony in the way you did,' Elena said, trying to make it sound as if it were the first time she'd said it.

'Someone had to,' Anita said. 'Thank heavens it wasn't Diana. Can you imagine!' Anita tried to get the small dog's attention with a flutter of her fingers but she remained by Bay's chair, transfixed.

'Well, since she's not here to speak for herself, I think it's probably better we don't,' James said.

Anita glanced at him as though this comment confirmed a long-held suspicion. 'I'll go and see her tomorrow on my way to the airport. I have to take the dog to the vet anyway and it's nearby. Bay, do not feed her from your plate!'

Bay stopped, hand in mid-air.

'Come here,' she called the dog with little kissing noises.

'Don't eat that, it will make you ill.' She lifted the bony dog onto her lap and placed her arms on either side of it.

'How is your garden, Anita?' Elena asked, placing a consoling hand on Bay's arm.

'My roses were particularly good this year. Pruned them all back to nothing. Most successful.'

A silence fell over the table, and the children glanced at their parents, waiting for them to speak.

'I could never have put your father in a home.' Anita spoke into the silence. 'He would have loathed it. It was a lot of work looking after him, of course, doing it all on my own, but I'm glad I was able to give him that, right up to the end.'

After a pause, Elena spoke. 'She asked to go, actually.'

'To a home? Diana?' Anita's chin sank into her neck in disbelief.

'She doesn't even go to the loo,' Tom volunteered, and Bay glared at him. Anita looked with distaste at the detritus of the children's meal collected around them and then down at her own neatly piled plate.

'Why don't we have coffee out in the garden?' Elena suggested. 'It's turned into a lovely afternoon.'

'Don't be ridiculous, Elena, it's far too cold. Particularly in your condition.' She nodded pointedly towards Elena's womb.

'Oh ... yes, you're probably right. We'll all stay. Oh, no,' she caught sight of the children's faces, 'you go and I'll stay. I'll stay here with Anita.'

They watched in silence as the children ran into the garden and James began clearing the plates into the kitchen. 'You spoil them,' Anita said.

'Oh.' Elena couldn't trust herself to say anything more.

She took a deep breath. 'Well, that's one thing you and Diana agree on.'

Anita raised her eyebrows. 'Your mother and I got on pretty well. She was intelligent enough to know when to play ball and when to stop.'

'It's good to know when to stop.'

'And why is Bay dressed like a Spanish harlot?'

'She chooses her own clothes, Anita. I think today's offering is a reaction against her new haircut.'

'It's rather inappropriate, for a child.'

Elena felt herself being washed in that old feeling, a grinding greyness that wanted her on her hands and knees. She closed her eyes and pushed upwards, towards the waves of flickering light.

'She doesn't know about all that yet, thank God.' She fought to keep her voice steady.

'You used to dress very provocatively as well.'

Elena stood to help clear the table and was glad of the heavy drape of the dress she wore. She did not look at her stepmother.

'I remember the dress you wore for your mother's wedding to David. The men could hardly keep their eyes in their heads. *He* could hardly keep his eyes in his head.'

'Well, I had the body for it,' she said in a bored voice that concealed the tremor that had started in her clenched hands. She picked up the water jug, needing to hold something solid, and realised it was a piece made by David. She held its curved glazed weight against her, like some kind of protection.

Anita laughed, once, and gave Elena an appraising glance. 'Your father always said you were too thin.'

Elena took hold of Anita's glass and filled it with water from the jug with a deep glugging sound. She placed the jug back down on the table and held the glass out to her stepmother, who took it without thanks.

Elena now picked up one of the children's plates and felt its underside coated with the grease from the plate beneath. She put it down again and roughly wiped her fingers on a napkin.

'Have you heard from David recently?' Anita cast the feathered question lightly, so that it quivered deceptively on the water's surface.

Elena said nothing for a moment, unwilling to be hooked. 'No.' She wiped each finger carefully. 'David remarried. He lives in South America now.'

'Nice young wife?'

'Yes, a very "nice young wife". They invited us to the wedding but we couldn't go as I was too pregnant at the time.'

'He was terribly fond of you, wasn't he?'

'He was kind to me,' Elena said carefully.

'Well, you were so close in age.'

Elena flinched. 'Not that close.' She shook her head.

'Complicated, that.' Anita said with a faint smile and wiped the tips of her own fingers on her clean napkin. 'I think I'm ready to go outside now. We can have the coffee out in the garden.'

She would go in and speak.

Elena stood in front of the walnut-panelled door, and raised her hand as though about to knock.

The hallway of the residential home was quiet.

'I wouldn't try and talk to her if I were you, Ele. I'd let it all

283

go.' Her sister's husky voice on the telephone came back to her. 'I don't know why you'd even want to keep the house. That strange island. All that pain dug into the land. I wouldn't choose to build my house on that.'

'But it might be healing, Leonie,' Elena had replied, a note of hope in her voice. 'Children playing. A new story . . .' Her voice faded. Neither spoke, and in the silence of the line between them a shadow had moved, too quick to catch.

'All those tunnels and bunkers full of urine and broken glass . . .' Her sister said after a pause. 'Sitting on the beach, knowing all that's underneath.'

'But the children love it. And they don't know about all that. It's a gift that they have somewhere to spend their holidays. We couldn't afford to go away otherwise.'

Her sister said nothing and Elena received the weight of her silence, her shoulders slumping.

'Ele, I have to go in a moment, evening prayer is starting. But I'd like to say this: I do think it would be better if it was sold. Better for you, I mean. Then you can plant somewhere new. Nothing good is growing there, I really believe that.'

'It's not as simple as all that, Leonie. The money's tied up in the house, it's kept safe by the trust Ivan built for it. If she sells it now, the money will all be swallowed up by death duties.'

'So be rid of it.'

'But it's all that's left.'

'It has to end somewhere.'

'And what about the children?'

'Let them move on.'

'It's their home.'

'Is it for them, Elena?' her sister had asked. 'Are you sure this is about them?'

Now Elena looked at the closed door in front of her and took a long, deep breath. Setting her face, she pushed open the door.

Her mother was lying back on the pillows asleep.

Forcing herself not to retreat, she put her bag down and pulled up a chair. But the eyes remained closed and, watching the rise and fall of her chest, Elena saw that her mother was in a deep sleep, the eyes moving quickly beneath the folded skin of the lids as though she slept in the guttering shadow of a windblown sail.

Elena remembered making her way across the wooden deck to where her mother was lying asleep in the sun, her tanned body cut by the white of her swimsuit. She'd lain down next to her on the sun-warmed wood, careful not to disturb her, and pressed her face into her hands so that when her father eventually came up onto the deck, stretching his long body as though he'd only just woken up, Elena's body had disappeared – swallowed back up inside her mother's clean white costume.

The eyes opened suddenly and they regarded each other in silence.

'I was asleep.' Diana squinted at her daughter, and then looked round, confused.

'You're in your new room.'

'I was dreaming,' she said hollowly and then was silent.

'You must rest.'

'My body can rest all it wants. My mind's been hunting.'

'Did you get anything?'

285

'Almost.' Her mother smiled, weakly.

'Is it all right here?' Elena asked, her eyes moving anxiously over her mother's body in its single nursing bed.

'Yes. Though whoever's in the kitchen should be shot.'

Elena laughed and reached into her bag to take out the books she'd brought. 'Now, I've brought you some of these. You mustn't worry about the others, I've taken care and they are all going to be catalogued and put in boxes.' Elena motored forward, trying to ignore her feelings of agitation.

'Too much detail.' Diana stretched in her bed like a big cat.

Elena looked at her. There was still time.

'Mum,' she put down the books and reached her hand out to touch the freckled arm, 'I want to talk to you about the house.'

Diana pulled her arm away as though burned. 'What about the house?'

'We need to talk about it while we still have time.'

'Time? Already carving it all up, are we?'

'No.' Elena shook her head 'No,' she said more firmly. 'It matters because it concerns the children.'

'*The children*. How very convenient. Well, you'll have to talk to Ivan about it. He's in charge of all that.'

'So you haven't made any changes?'

'I'm too tired to discuss it. Talk to Ivan. Though why you care about that house I can't imagine, it isn't worth anything.'

'The children have grown up there. And they associate it with you . . .'

'That is both an endearing and an awful thought. Let me tell you, Elena, I would not have placed my chips on this little rock if I'd been asked to take a bet about where I'd end up.'

'The children don't care about where or what it is . . . it's their *home*.'

'*My* home.'

'Think how you loved Le Moulin when you were their age.'

'I was never their age.' Diana sat back, putting some space between them. 'Besides, that was a house worth keeping. Rousseau died there, for God's sake.'

'But you won't benefit from selling the house,' Elena reminded her. 'It's in a trust for the children. A trust that you set up. Remember? Ivan has explained it to you. James has *tried* to explain it to you.'

'They've explained nothing. The only reason I even came to this godforsaken place and that that trust exists is because Ivan assured me it was the simplest way to avoid tax. It was always going to be *sold*, Elena. I have to *live*.'

Elena bit her lip.

'You're hardly going to starve, Mum. James and I have told you that we'll take care of it all. We'll take care of you.'

'I don't trust your husband, Elena.' Her mother now returned the gesture, placing a hand on her arm. 'We've never had any luck with our men. I have a bad feeling about him. One of my feelings.' She raised her eyebrows with meaning.

'What do you mean?' Elena looked at her mother fearfully.

'He is a liar, Elena.'

'No.' Elena shook her head, staring down at the hand clutching her wrist.

'All that cheerful boyish innocence. It's a façade. It's plain as anything that he plays around. All that charm is a deception.'

'No.' She continued shaking her head. 'It's not. In fact, that innocence is where I go to meet him.'

'He's stolen money from me, Elena, whatever the rest. I've been through the accounts. Both he and Ivan.'

'Money?' Elena said, pressing her temples against the headache she could feel building behind her eyes.

'It's all gone, Elena!'

'I know that, and I don't care. I do not care.'

'He's taken it. He's colluded with Ivan.'

Elena shook her head. 'You're imagining things. There is nothing to take. And Ivan is your friend.'

'No, he doesn't love me, he's been to see me once in two years and that was only to make me sign something.' Diana clutched the blankets.

Elena could not meet her mother's eyes.

'James is your friend. He's your son-in—'

'I have no sons!' As Diana spoke, her hands moved blindly towards her middle.

'He loves you. They both love you,' Elena said, trying to force meaning into the words with the intensity of her speech.

'Oh wake up, Elena, you don't get your childhood back, *despite* being born again.'

Elena looked at the body swaddled in the single bed and said nothing. After a pause, she spoke. 'So you're determined to sell it.'

Her mother nodded her head, once.

Elena sat back and folded her hands in her lap. *Ask, Elena,* she told herself.

'Before I go, can I . . . ?'

'What?'

'Can we . . .'

'*Speak*, Elena.'

And the question that she'd asked countless times in her mind seemed to take flight. 'Can I pray with you?' Elena surprised herself with these words.

'No.' Diana turned away. 'I don't want all that. I believed in a god once . . .' she said, 'and he shot himself.' There was silence and Elena closed her eyes, the unasked question still hovering above her, beating its wings.

'Perhaps all girls believe in God when they first meet their fathers,' she said quietly, and turned back to her mother. Diana did not move. 'Why have you never asked me?' she said finally, forcing herself to say it.

'Asked you what?' her mother said, shaking her head.

'About him.' Elena felt her throat tighten. 'About . . . him.'

But Diana only shook her head.

'Sometimes we have to live with things unanswered, Elena. It's the way life is.' Diana seemed almost sorry. She closed her eyes and did not speak for a moment. When she did, her voice was low. 'I don't blame you for trading in the one I gave you, he was a menace.'

Elena stayed very still.

'But I don't want any more fathers, heavenly or otherwise. Now, open those curtains, so I can look at the sun.'

Rue de Lille, 1929

'Diana?'

'Yes.'

Diana held the black earpiece to her head and felt the silence stretch over the long trough of the dark sea to New York.

She pictured her mother standing in a hallway, soft fur choking her throat.

'Are you there, Diana?'

'Yes.' Diana's hands clutched the phone. 'What's happened? Mama? What's happened?'

'He did it.'

'What?'

'He did it.'

'All alone?'

'No, not *alone*.' Her mother strangled the word and it hung limp between them. 'With *her*.'

Roccasinibalda, 1970

'Diana, it's time.' A voice spoke in the dark.

'Of course.' She sat up, pressing a hand to the side of her head. 'What time is it?'

'It's four in the afternoon.'

'Oh. All right.' She peered into the shuttered darkness. 'I'm coming.' The unseen voice closed the door and Diana lay back, watching the thin lines of light shaping the window as she tried to bring herself back to the day. Eventually, she rose and walked quickly to the windows, pushing open the shutters so that she was bathed in the low, yellow light of late afternoon. She turned to her washstand, wet a flannel and pressed the cool square to her face, breathing in the faint scent of neroli. She wanted to be calm for this, as cool and calm as a dark damp room. *Like a cellar*, she thought. No, not a cellar. She wanted to be like the inside of a cathedral. The pure, marble quiet of that cathedral in Granada. *Like a tomb*, said the inner voice. Oh stop it, she shook her head. She did not want to be like a tomb.

*

As she entered the courtyard, half-filled with shadow, she was surprised by the noise and the number of people. It felt as though the entire town was there and from beyond the walls she could hear the beeping of cars. As she pushed through the sweating bodies, people she'd never seen before, she could hear crying. This was absurd, she wasn't dead yet for God's sake, she was simply going to hospital.

'What the hell is going on?' Diana slammed open the door of Roberto's study. 'I've just been outside and there are men with cameras camped in a line and the entrance is crowded with fucking hysterical people.'

'It has fallen entirely out of hand, I quite agree,' Roberto said, closing the filing cabinet and leaning against it. Diana could see the sweat beading along his tanned brow and the wet patches at the armpits of his pale linen suit. 'I requested a single photographer, I never imagined so many people would come.' He glanced at the desk where the blue-wrapped package lay on top of a pile of papers.

'A photographer? You requested a photographer? My mother is at death's door and you thought you'd organise a photo shoot?'

'She agreed. Though she felt better then, admittedly.'

'Get them all away. This is a bloody circus, it's undignified.'

'She's coming down now, there is no time.'

'At least clear a path. Get some of your toy boys, lackeys, whatever they are to make way.' Diana stopped as she turned to leave. 'Are you packing?' She looked round the room.

'Yes.' Roberto nodded, quickly stuffing the package into an empty desk drawer. No time to leave a note with it as he'd wished. Ah well, she'd find it eventually.

'I'm accompanying your mother to Rome.'

Diana took in the room more slowly. 'And then?'

'Diana, there isn't time for this, we can talk in the city. Have dinner tonight, if you like. We need to get upstairs.' He began to usher them from the room.

'Let go of me,' she said, wrenching her arm free and going quickly to the dresser where the whisky had been kept.

'You are upset,' Roberto said quietly.

'I'm not upset.' She shook her head, refusing to look at him.

He went over to her. 'Come, your mother needs you. Let us go.' She could see he was softening towards her. That hunger was still there. She took a deep breath, causing her chest to rise up towards him and then fall away again. He glanced down, his expression gentle now, and she felt herself grow calmer.

'All right,' she said, and looked down at the floor for a moment. When she looked up she was going to let him take her. But as she swept her gaze confidently upward, she did not find him waiting there but already walking out of the door. She slammed her hand down on his desk and felt chaos begin to move through her.

They waited on separate benches in the dim green hallway of the hospital on Monte Trastevere. A door opened at one end and a slim young doctor, his white coat flapping as he walked, came down the hallway towards them. Both pairs of eyes watched his progress but as he passed it was Diana on whom his gaze lingered briefly. She seemed to remain perfectly still, but beneath her demurely cross-legged demeanour she had shifted position with a subtle arch of her back and she could afford to glance over at Roberto. It was his turn now to refuse to meet her eyes.

The door of Caresse's room opened and an older doctor came out. Lawyer and daughter both stood eagerly. He passed his eyes between them both, unsure of the correct order of things.

'She's stable but the heart is too weak for us to operate. We have given her morphine, but it's now a matter of time.'

'I'll go in.' Diana started forward.

'She's asked to see Signor Mansardi.' The doctor's eyes darted between them once more and then down at his notes, as though confirming this fact in writing.

Roberto moved past her and Diana could see the barely concealed effort to stop his mouth curving upwards in triumph.

'Principessa. You look tired.'

'That's another way of saying someone looks awful.' Caresse smiled wanly. 'But I appreciate your honesty. Where's Diana?'

'She's gone to meet her lawyer.'

'Already.' Caresse smiled, again. 'Well, I can hardly point fingers there, can I? Though of course you have become far more than that, dear Roberto.' She turned to him and took his hand. 'You will help her, won't you? I know she's a handful, but we all need support. You must try and work together.'

'In what way can I help her, Caresse?'

'In the way you've helped me.' She looked up, eyes shining. 'The world's a fickle place, especially for a woman. The Città della Pace will help that. And whether Diana admits it or

294

not, women are the source of peace.' She smiled. 'It will be a force for good in this world.' She closed her eyes and breathed, before opening them again. 'You will honour her, won't you?'

'Signora,' he sat on the bed, his throat husky, 'I am a man of my word.'

'Yes, you are.' She nodded and smiled but then tapped him on his arm with the back of her hand. 'But you are still a man.'

'Don't forget that the movement will need continued support too.' Roberto used his lightly warning voice and Caresse squeezed his arm.

'You need more faith. Where there's a will there's a way.' She was silent then for a moment, so that there was only the noise of the respirator collapsing up and down with slow steady movements.

'I tried so hard to get it right.' Her voice was high and distant, a bird arcing through the sky.

Roberto nodded and drew up a chair, a look of concern on his face.

'You did all you could, Caresse.'

'Did I?' She looked at him and there were tears in her eyes.

'You need to rest. You have done all you could. Don't worry about all that. It is so far in the past. Remember what you always tell me: all that has passed.'

And Caresse held his gaze, eyes wide, her hand clutching tightly on to his.

'Good evening, Diana.' Roberto approached the table where she sat with a group of friends on the rooftop terrace of the Hotel Eden. Behind her, the Roman skyline played across a violet sky that was sinking into darkness, and she sat before a large candle, glittering like an icon surrounded by dark-suited men.

'Excuse me.' She got up and the men at the table half-stood as she left. 'I don't think I have anything to say to you, Mr Mansardi,' she said as they walked a short distance away. She wore a black dress that wrapped round her body, falling open in a long gently undulating split. A light wind was blowing her hair slightly, forcing her to half-close her eyes.

'Diana, please . . .'

'The whole thing was undignified. She expected more and deserved better.'

'She gave me no instruction. And really her mind is elsewhere. She is going to another place.'

'Oh, don't talk about death in that reverent tone, I can't stand it. Why was the press there? Scrabbling like monkeys. They could hardly get her through. Jostled about. Women like to be in control of their appearance, you know. And who were all those people? I'd never met, let alone seen, half of them. All those boys of yours crying crocodile tears. Most of them had never even spoken to her.'

'Please, let's sit down.' Taking her elbow, Roberto guided her towards a quiet corner of the terrace. Diana shrugged him off and strode ahead. She sat down at the table and glared up at him.

'What would you like to drink?' he asked.

'Milk. What will you be having?'

'*Due Negroni*,' he said to the hovering waiter, who was staring at Diana with a mixture of admiration and alarm.

'This is where we came the night before I brought you to the castle,' Roberto said with a smile.

Diana eyed him for a moment. 'You've known me throughout my adult life, Roberto. We should be friends by now. But I can say with absolute certainty that I neither like nor trust you.'

'Why, Diana?'

'You're a hypocrite.'

'How?'

'You alter your behaviour according to your audience. I don't respect that. I'm not sure you have any beliefs at all, alongside which you have a wife and child whom you never visit and barely mention, while playing the pious husband to my mother.'

Roberto was silent. He had barely thought of his wife recently, secure in the knowledge that she and the child were financially assured and getting along happily in the apartment in Milan. He took a napkin and pressed it to his mouth, then folded it carefully beside his drink.

'And you are worthy to judge me?' he asked.

'I believe so, yes,' Diana said.

'You, an animal.'

'Better that than a vegetable, Roberto.'

'Tell me, Diana, why do you always refer to these "boys"? There are just as many girls in the Città della Pace.'

'I refer to the "boys" because that is what I see. You are not their caretaker. It sickens me to see it.'

'Your mother and I have run a very successful youth movement here for the past fifteen years. If you were only vaguely interested you'd know that many of the children have gone on to university, become artists, are working in the peace corps . . .'

'And the rest are for ever dissatisfied with the simplicity of their lives in those villages. It will be Milan or bust for them now, I suppose. Did it ever cross your brain that they might have been happy as they were?'

'You do not know what you are talking about.'

'Well, we can agree to disagree. The time has passed for *entente cordiale*.'

'Let us stick then to the subject of your mother.'

'What she really needs are her friends, Roberto. Her old friends. Where are they? Why aren't they coming? Have they contacted you?'

'Diana, calm down. Your mother is being well looked after.'

'By you,' she spat. 'An employee.'

'I'm sorry you feel that I did not treat your mother's departure from her house with dignity,' he said, drawing himself up coldly. 'It was not my intention. But she is now under the best possible care.'

'No one ever *intends* to do anything undignified, Roberto. No one *intends* to do any harm at all.' They glared at each other, their bodies tense. Diana shook her head and opening her small silk bag took out a lipstick. 'She gave you licence to do as you liked. I'm just ... surprised ... that it was the best you could do.' She clicked the lipstick closed and then got up to leave. 'I'd like you to set up a meeting for tomorrow morning. I'll be using my own lawyer, of course. Oh spare me the eyes, Roberto, I need someone clean.'

He spread his hands in acceptance. 'Of course, Diana. We can discuss the future of the house. There are many ...'

'House?' She laughed and threw back her head, causing

a nearby table to look towards her. 'That's not a house, it's a mistake.'

Diana made her way back to her table and smiling quickly at the gathered company accepted a drink from the man sitting beside her. His thick dark eyebrows were raised slightly.

'Your mother's lawyer?' he asked. Diana nodded, once, and took a deep drink from the glass she held in her trembling hand. The table continued to speak, the voices around them rising like a curtain on a stage set with a party scene. But the man by her side was silent, watching.

'What will it mean, Ivan?' she asked, turning slightly towards him, her dress falling open at her thigh. Ivan turned away from her and, placing his elbows on the table, squared his shoulders, so as to think. Honestly, this woman was like a scrambling device. He was glad she was marrying that artist. He couldn't afford this type of distraction on a permanent basis.

'What will what mean? Has he told you something?'

'If she's written me out of her will, what will it mean?'

Ivan looked at her. 'You know what it will mean in legal terms, Diana, I don't need to tell you that. But as for where it leaves you in the context of your relationship with your mother . . .' He leaned back and looked her in the eye. 'Well, that will be for you to discover. Every child has to learn that for themselves.'

'Mother.'

Caresse's eyes opened and Diana could see the light was fading. 'Where's Roberto?'

Swallowing a reply so sharp that her throat ached, Diana

sat down and drew a chair up to the bed. 'I wish you would move to the hotel. You'd be much more comfortable.'

Caresse smiled tiredly. 'Yes, I do love my room there. But I'm quite all right here. It won't be for long.'

'The nurse tells me you slept very well.'

Caresse nodded. 'Is Roberto all right? Is everything all right?'

'Yes, Mother. Everything's all right. Roberto's exhausted, that's all. He's taking some rest.' She did not mention that he hadn't turned up to the meeting. 'In the meantime, I thought—'

'He'll come back, won't he?' Caresse swallowed. 'We need to discuss things.'

Diana hesitated. 'Yes,' she said finally. 'He'll come back. You just rest a while.'

Caresse leaned back, still unsure.

'Mama, I want to discuss . . . how things stand. We need to decide while . . . while there's still time . . . what we're going to do.'

'You must talk to Roberto. He has all the plans.'

'Yes, I know you've lots of *plans*. I'm talking about how things stand now.'

'I don't know. I don't know. Roberto's handled it all, Diana. You must speak to Roberto.'

'But it's in my name?' Diana felt panic begin to lap at the edge of her thoughts.

Caresse was silent.

'Mama.'

Caresse turned her head slowly towards Diana and she could see that her mother was drifting.

300

'I had the nurse read to me last night. It was so lovely.' She closed her eyes. 'The window was open and I could see the moon and all the lights of the city down below. This ancient, layered place. I thought of all those people inside all those buildings. The many heads lying down. Those who were alone with only their thoughts beside them and those sharing a pillow; I wanted to reach over all of them and bless them. Tell them all that I've done and hear all that they will do. It made me terribly sad that I won't meet them all. That there are still so many places, full of so many people, I will never know, that will never know me. Perhaps one day I'll know everyone and see it all contained in one.' She opened her eyes. 'That would be best. I would like that. I'd like it all to be held in someone's capable hands.'

'And I'm sure they'd all like that too.' Diana gave a thin, weary smile.

'I would like to return to my youth ...' Caresse said. 'To Boston and that world of fine smells and long drawn-out hours. The wind pouring down those sandy beaches, taking me back to my mother's arms. That's what is happening, that's where we are going. I will be young again and then will disappear back into the great cosmic egg of abundance. I will go back to that first act of love.' Caresse looked at her daughter. 'And it will all carry on.'

'I was planning to go out to dinner ...'

'Go, go, eat a wonderful meal with a delicious man. Giulia is going to sit with me, I've lots to think about.'

'There are many telegrams at the hotel,' Diana said. 'The front desk is practically buried. Many people are sending their love.'

'How kind of them. Are they coming?'

'Yes, of course,' Diana lied. 'I'll bring the letters and telegrams to read to you in the morning.'

'One more thing,' Caresse said, as Diana stood to leave.

'Yes?' She turned.

'Don't put me in the ground, Diana. I want to burn, like him. I want to burn and then fly free.'

Alderney, 1993

Bay lay in bed with her book, listening to the murmuring sound of her aunt's voice and her mother's in the room next door. They'd been sorting through her grandmother's things all day and though Bay had helped, as soon as it had got dark her mother had sent her to have her bath and get into bed.

Bay was beside herself, she had said. Absolutely beside herself.

Lying under the covers now, Bay agreed; she was hardly able to turn the pages of the book that lay open on her chest, revealing the picture of a house whose side had been cut away so that she could see the open rooms from top to bottom.

When her aunt had arrived that morning Bay had breathlessly shown her to her room, waiting to see what Leonie would say when she saw the single bed with its neat quilt and solitary pillow; the bedside table, prepared by her mother, with a small vase of flowers from the garden and a picture of some holy hands.

'You have a single,' Bay had pointed out, but her aunt had

only smiled. Sitting down, they had together tested its comfort with a few bounces.

'Would you like to help me unpack?' And Bay had nodded, unable to stop looking at her aunt's simple grey dress that covered her completely, and the matching cloth that hid her thick blonde hair. She still had her face though, and it was as pretty and open as a window.

'What do you wear in the bath, Aunty Lola?'

'Nothing,' her aunt laughed, as she opened her small bag and took out a nightdress and placed it in the chest of drawers.

'I lost another tooth.' Bay stretched her mouth so that her aunt could see the castellations of her lower teeth.

'Our bodies change.'

'I had blood in my mouth when it came out.'

'Growing up can be a painful business.'

'Would you like to hear a joke?' Bay asked.

'Yes.' Her aunt turned and looked at her.

'What's the dirtiest piece of furniture in the house?'

'I don't know, what?' her aunt said, as she placed a single book whose pages were edged in gold on the bedside table.

'The bureau, for it never changes its drawers.'

But her aunt had only smiled, not laughed like her father had. 'That's one of your grandmother's jokes, isn't it?'

Bay had nodded.

'Yes,' her aunt said, 'she had lots of those.'

'Do you live in a church?' Bay asked. She could remember visiting her aunt once, after Inés had died. A quiet green place where Bay had played in a walled garden while her mother cried under the shade of a big tree and her aunt listened. The other women had moved silently around the garden, their heads all covered with simple grey cloths.

'It's called a convent.'

'Grandma said that bed is her church.'

'Well, no one can accuse her of failing to regularly attend.'

'Bed is more comfortable than pews,' Bay pointed out.

'I prefer a hard edge. Too much padding stops you being able to feel things properly.'

'I don't like feelings.'

'Some are nicer than others.' Leonie nodded. 'But it's important to let them all have a turn.'

They looked at one another for a moment, and Bay saw her mother in the shape of her aunt's eyes.

'Are you married?' Bay asked suspiciously.

'No.'

'Are you going to have children?'

'I've chosen not to.'

'Do you have a single or a double?'

'Single what?' Her aunt looked at her quizzically.

'Bed.'

'Ah, a single. With a good, firm mattress. Much better for your back.'

Bay glanced at the door. 'Do you have lovers?' she asked quietly.

'No.' Her aunt took a little longer to answer that. 'But I do love, Bay. I am learning how to love.'

'Thank you for coming, Leo.' Standing among the boxes in Diana's bedroom, Elena looked gratefully at her sister, who

305

sat with her hair uncovered on the edge of the large bed. 'I don't know if I could have done this without you.'

'It's the least I can do, Ele.'

Elena could not meet her sister's frank gaze. 'I don't really deserve that kindness,' she said, looking down at her bare feet, wishing, as always, that the nervous movement of her heart would calm itself in her sister's steady presence.

'Yes, you do. We all do.' Leonie looked round. 'What on earth happened here? Her rooms were always immaculate.'

Elena gazed too at the waste of clothes and dust-covered detritus littering the surfaces. The canopy of the bed had been pulled with violence, and now sagged loose of its frame.

'She wouldn't let me clean in here.'

Leonie nodded, saying nothing.

'I'd have been completely overwhelmed, trying to do this alone,' Elena continued. 'James is hopeless, hopeless! He just wants to keep everything.' She laughed and then bit her lip and lapsed into silence.

'What's *in* all these boxes?' Leonie asked, opening one and looking inside.

'Paperwork, mostly. From her lawyers. That awful man Ivan Denning.'

'I thought he was the best of a bad bunch.'

'Yes, but that's not saying much.'

'What shall we do with it all?'

'Burn it?' Elena gave a hollow laugh.

'Bonfire of the profanities?' Leonie asked with an arch smile that only remained on her face for a moment.

'We can dance around it like we did when we were children,' Elena said.

'Those meaningless rituals of hers.' Leonie shook her head. 'Belief without God. A somewhat empty gift.'

'Do you remember her room in Ibiza?' Elena sat beside her sister on the bed and ran her hand over the huge embroidered mantilla that covered it, stopping at a large stain that had leached across it turning a pale pink rose a murky brown.

'The lion's den,' Leonie said.

Elena had the sense that her sister was about to speak further, but stopped herself. She waited, hoping it was clear that she encouraged the words. But none came.

'She would have been so much happier if she'd stayed there,' Elena spoke the familiar thought, and it trailed uselessly in the dust-filled air.

'I don't know about that. As within so without. Only Diana could have chosen an old concentration camp as her place of retirement.'

'There is more to this island than that,' Elena said reproachfully. 'It can be very beautiful here.'

'It's okay for something to be awful, Elena.'

'I'm aware of that, Leo, but . . .' Elena stopped herself.

'Well, you did always like to stay close.'

'Is that a dig?' Elena said, looking hurt.

'No.' Her sister looked at her, with a clear, open face. 'It's just how I see it.'

Elena was silent.

'And I probably go too far the other way. Diana might have seen my vows as an act of violence but they were only an attempted retreat. I *thought* I'd found the perfect escape in my cell. Little did I know what was in store,' she laughed.

Elena nodded.

'You know it was Caresse who first suggested I go and stay in a convent? I still don't know how she knew of the nuns up there in Big Sur. I often wonder at her understanding that I needed the emptiness of that place. The seclusion of those great fogs covering everything like so many ghosts and the rage of the fires that burned them away. A clearing out of all that had served its purpose. Soft and brutal. Blackened corpses of trees. No understanding of why. And then, the little shoots of green and the endless rains.' She paused, thoughtful. 'And the abbess there was extraordinary,' Leonie went on. 'Calm, scrawny . . . A bit like Inés.'

Elena smiled.

'Surprisingly sexual, actually.'

Elena's smile turned to a frown. She turned away from her sister and began to tightly fold her mother's soft woollen jumpers.

'Yes, Elena, sexual. She wasn't afraid of acknowledging that side of life.'

'But she didn't . . .' Elena glanced at her sister, her fingers getting lost in the baby-softness of the wool in her hands.

'Have intercourse?' Her older sister gave her an old smile. 'No, of course not. But it was a great help to know that I would not be shamed for what had been. She was very frank.'

Elena knelt and placed the neatly folded jumpers in a box. She sat back on her heels. 'Do you miss it, Leonie?'

Her sister shook her head. 'It's like entering a quiet room after the din of one of those awful parties.'

Elena couldn't prevent herself from looking down at her own heavy stomach.

'When I married Victor, that hunger paced inside me. I felt contaminated by its restless urge. Utterly contaminated.'

Elena glanced at her sister's wrist where the faint scar emerged from the sleeve of her habit.

'It came from within me, lived inside me, wanting more,' Leonie continued. 'Always wanting more.' She shook her head and began to gather up books into small piles. 'I remember once being with a man and before it was even over, already planning to see another.'

'Yes.' Elena nodded, eyes wide. 'I mean, I can imagine how hard that must have been for you.'

Leonie stopped and for a moment it seemed as though Elena was rowing away from an island leaving her stranded on the empty stretch of sand. Her face hardened. 'Yes,' she said, her eyes not leaving Elena's face. 'I'm sure you can.'

Elena turned her head away and gazed towards the window.

'Victor was just as damaged,' Leonie rolled a leather belt into a neat loop, 'and far too old to want to change anything. Though it got me away from her, which was the point I suppose.'

Elena's stare was fixed, and Leonie looked at her in profile for a long time.

'Elena, what is it?'

'Nothing,' she said, and the sisters lapsed into silence.

The room seemed to fill with Elena's unspoken thought, the air between them getting thicker and thicker with it, until Leonie's voice broke through. 'Elena. Speak.'

'It . . . it's what you said.'

'Which bit?' Her sister spread her hands.

'Contaminated,' she said quietly. 'You said that you felt contaminated.'

'Well . . . I suppose I did, to an extent. What's the matter with that?'

Elena waved her hand over her stomach, the other arm holding it protectively.

'What do you mean?'

'Sometimes, I wonder if . . .'

'If? You can speak, Elena.' Her sister laid a hand on her shoulder and Elena turned her head towards her.

'Perhaps I shouldn't . . .'

'Shouldn't what, Ele?' Leonie looked at her in bewilderment and then, sitting back as though taking in an enormous picture so that its disconnected images began to make sense in their entirety, shook her head, a frown creasing her forehead. 'Oh no, Elena, no.' She went down on her knees and, reaching forward, placed her hands gently at her sister's middle.

Elena did not move. 'But what if it builds, Leonie?' she said, her voice constricted. 'What if it gets stronger?'

'But I was talking about me, Elena. It's different, we're different.'

'Is it? Are we?' Her sister looked at her searchingly.

'Yes, of course.' Leonie nodded with feeling. 'We had different fathers, for a start.'

Elena stared at her sister and then down at her lap. 'They were as bad as each other,' she said quietly. She glanced at Leonie to see her reaction and saw she'd gone still, one hand placed on the floor as though steadying herself. Her sister was silent for a few moments and then reached over and took hold of a heavy stack of papers.

'You are eating properly, aren't you, Ele?' Leonie's sure voice moved them back towards safer ground.

Elena shrugged irritably. 'Of course I'm eating. I'm pregnant.'

'What does your doctor say?'

'As soon as the baby comes, I should start taking the pills again.'

'And you say?'

Elena was silent.

'And you say . . .'

'I say *all right*.'

They were silent for a while, moving around the subject as though manoeuvring in a small cabin.

'Why did Anita come here?' Leonie asked in a new, lighter tone, as she half-turned and began sifting through a drawer stuffed full of photos.

'She wanted to let me know that she'd thrown away the things Anthony left me.'

'What things were they?' Leonie said.

'Nothing much. The good furniture all went to a cousin up in Northumberland. Man to man, clean and cold. But I would have liked to give his tools to the boys . . .'

Leonie grew very still. 'I didn't keep anything from my father,' she said after a pause. 'And I wouldn't want anything from yours either.'

Elena watched her. 'Anyway, life's much cleaner without all those things. Best not to let luxury sink its teeth in.'

'I wouldn't call a few tools "luxury", Leonie.'

'It's not an attack, Elena.'

Elena observed her sister's familiar face, revealing some

of Diana's curves, but cut with the sharp brow of that very old Frenchman whose enormous house she'd never wanted to visit.

'I'm sorry I didn't come and see you when you were in hospital.' Elena spoke in a rush of feeling. 'And I'm sorry I've never said that till now.'

Leonie looked her in the eyes. 'I know she told you not to come, Elena.' She shook her head. 'Inés wrote and told me that.'

'Inés told you that?' Elena said, eyes shining.

'Yes. And I know that Diana was incapable of answering a cry for help.'

'She wasn't taught how to,' Elena said, twisting her hands.

'Your soft heart.' She smiled ruefully. 'The way you'd cry for the birds as she cut short their flight with that unanswerable gun.'

Elena was silent. 'I was scared of birds. Would probably have killed one myself if it had got into my room. It was those horrible men beating their sticks in the woods, forcing them out of their hiding places, shouting so that they had to fly into danger.'

'But you stayed by her side, even while she did the things you loathed.'

'You think it's weak,' Elena said in a low voice. 'You both do.'

'It's not weak, Elena,' her sister laughed softly. 'Holding it together – all that violence and all this beauty' – she gestured at her sister's pregnant stomach – 'it's far from weak.'

'Beautiful words, Leonie.'

'No, Elena,' her sister said fiercely. 'Not beautiful *words*. Feel it.' She sat forward again and pressed her hand against her sister's heart this time. 'This is where it is happening, Elena, right *here*, where you love. The heart is our burial ground, it transforms what we give it. Death back into life. But you *have* to feel it. You have to feel it with as much pain as when those children left your body. The heart will devour the loss, the pain of the feast will wash you clean.'

Elena did not move. Her sister's hands were strong and warm and she had never been able to be held by them for long.

'That's Bay calling.'

They listened and there was another plaintive cry from the room next door.

Her sister looked at her for a long time. 'You are free to leave, Elena. You always have been.'

'It's not because I don't want to talk.'

'Go, Elena.'

'I'll be right back.'

'Go to her,' Leonie said. And, getting to her feet with difficulty, Elena walked from the room.

Roccasinibalda, 1970

Diana opened the door and entered her mother's silent rooms, a glass in her hand. The shutters were held open and the faint trace of tuberose was fading with every hour of her absence, pushed out by the cold empty air blowing in from the hills. The castle was quiet now, most of the people gone. She looked at her watch. Just after ten. She listened. And there it was. The ringing of the death bell, pulled by Bruno who'd asked to do it, tears streaming down his lined face, every hour throughout the coming month. She sat and listened to the low clang breaking the strange silence. The life was fading out of the place as quickly as the mark of water on sun-warmed stone; what had only just occurred was being forgotten. *Because all things come to an end*, Diana thought. *What else could this have ever been?*

She looked into the bathroom, a simple table and a bar of soap, the movement of the door causing her mother's dressing gown to slip from its hanger onto the floor in a heap of collapsed colour. Diana picked it up and felt the silk, cold and fine in her fingers, and returned it to its hook. She had not seen her mother's naked body for some time. The long legs always striding, the hands always moving and those beautiful, feted breasts that had lived on in many men's minds as an example of God's kindness, as high and heavy as love itself. Diana had always envied those. Hers were nothing like so remarkable; she cupped one with her hand, testing its firmness. Still pretty good though. Her hand ran downwards over the encased curve of her stomach, patting it thoughtfully as she walked back into the bedroom, where she stopped. Hanging between the two windows was her portrait. She glanced at the bed, and realised now that it must have been the first thing her mother saw when she woke up.

Diana moved her hands into a similar pose and walked in a small circle. She did not know what to do.

She sat heavily on the bed, picturing the church and the people whose names she barely knew, outdoing one another in loud and theatrical grief. Diana had sat throughout, neither kneeling for the prayers nor standing for the liturgy, incanting her own words as strange as the markings on the stolen obelisk that stood at the centre of the gurgling fountain in the piazza outside the church. At the end of the long, wearing day, only her mother's ashes remained in a yellow urn shaped by David's hands. He had not questioned her decision to stand alone on the battlements and tip it forward so that the grey dust had flown with a sudden gust of wind and disappeared into the clouded sky.

The girls had stripped the bed and remade it so that a smooth expanse of white linen stretched over its surface. She lay down gratefully, still wearing her shoes, and pulled the satisfying weight of the covers over herself, glad of their substance, drawing her shoulders towards each other in some kind of conclusion.

Rue de Lille, 1930

'Life goes on, Diana. I have to live.' Caresse continued to button up the long black silk gloves that matched her new hat. Mourning suited her.

The housemaid came in. 'Monsieur Dalí is here. And Monsieur Pound is waiting also.'

From the hallway came the sound of the telephone. It had been ringing incessantly for days now.

'Tell them I'll be just a moment.' Caresse stood and checked her reflection, watched by Diana where she sat on a chair, knees brought up to her chest.

'I've found a new artist.' Her eyes met Diana's in the mirror. 'A true Surrealist. Mind like a hot wire on a raw nerve. When you go back to school I'm going to take him to America. I've already lined up a press conference for him when we arrive. Talent like that needs as much exposure as possible.'

'You're going back?' Diana asked, biting her lip.

'No, not going back.' There was a faint tremor in her mother's voice. 'Moving on.'

Roccasinibalda, 1970

'Do you know where Diana is?' David asked one of the women, glad to finally find someone.

'*Nello studio dell'avvocato*,' she muttered and pointed towards the end of the corridor and then turned to go. As she went she called over her shoulder, '*Stai attento, giovane artista. Ci troverai una leonessa, ed è a caccia di sangue!*' She disappeared into the long darkness of the hallway, her footsteps echoing.

Entering the room, David found Diana sitting behind a carved wooden desk surrounded by shelves and dying plants, paper littering every surface. A cut-glass decanter of whisky stood unstoppered at her elbow, and her sleeves were rolled up, her hair tousled as though she had been disturbed in the middle of a wild dance.

She glanced up. 'You!' she laughed, and her eyes glittered.

He nodded, and put his bag down. 'Yes, me. I decided to come back and see you before I fly tomorrow. The show finished early in Rome.'

'You came back for me,' she said. 'I'm touched.' She

beckoned him towards her with one hand, while riffling through the papers with the other.

'What is all this?'

'A mess.' She smiled up at him and then pressed her cheek against his stomach. 'I had to meet with the lawyers this morning.'

'You should know your daughter has arrived.' David looked down at her. 'I was told to tell you.'

Diana pushed him away and turned back to the desk.

'The firing squad. All I need.' Diana glanced at him. 'Did you see her?'

'No, someone just passed the message on.'

She nodded and continued looking at the papers.

David placed a hand on the cool plaster of the wall and stared out of the window, frowning. Why had he lied? He'd seen the girl walking across the courtyard below him, her long bare legs pushed into a scuffed pair of sandals, a man's shirt belted at her slim waist. She'd stopped when she'd got to a pillar and placed her hand on it, just as his hand was now pressed to the wall, crossing one foot behind her to scratch her leg with the toe of her shoe . . .

'Apparently, she's here with a man,' he said over his shoulder.

'Good,' Diana murmured absentmindedly. 'Well, if you see them, tell her we'll eat at nine. You'll have dinner with us?'

'Yes. I want another night with you before we part.'

Diana leaned back in her chair and looked at him frankly. 'I'm beat, David. This has been a real bitch of a day.'

'Wasn't this Roberto's study?' David looked around. 'Where is he?'

'He's gone.' She stood up and threw her arms wide. 'It's all gone.'

'What do you mean "gone"?'

'Gone to the dogs.'

'Diana,' David said, alarm in his voice. 'What's happened?'

'I met with the lawyers this morning and it seems Caresse handed control of what's left of her estate to Mr Roberto Mansardi under the proviso that he be responsible for ensuring the continuation of the Città della Pace.' She spoke in an official voice, her hand tracing the words in the air. 'He drew up all the paperwork, so you can imagine the size of the loopholes he left himself to jump through. He'll no more stay here encouraging world peace with these mountain people than I will. Though at least *I* didn't ever pretend I would. As for the political movement – well, it will join all the other little surges of spirit that have waved through the centuries.'

'And what about you? What did she leave you?'

'This!' She spread her arms and laughed bitterly. 'Three hundred and fifty-two empty rooms. A mausoleum full of homeless poets, hiding themselves in the walls. Thank you, Mother.'

'Well, we should be grateful to these walls for giving shape to our meeting.'

'Forgive me, David, but gratitude is not quite what I'm experiencing at present.'

'And what about your daughters?'

'Joint ownership of the contents.' She held up a handful of papers. 'But clever Roberto has been hard at work. There are some very happy art dealers in London raising a glass somewhere. He's been selling off anything of value steadily

319

since he got here.' She waved a hand at the empty wall space behind her. 'Oh, there'll be *something* for them. I'll make sure they get it.' She drained her glass.

He watched her drink and then nodded at the littered desk. 'What will you do with all this paperwork?'

'Burn it, in the way I was taught. I'm joking, David, there's no need to make that face. No, Ivan will deal with it.' She ran her hands through her hair. 'Mother of mine, I suppose I expected nothing less.'

'And what will you do with this place?' David asked, looking round him in wonder, running his fingertips over his jaw.

'I'm going to sell it, of course. And I don't' – she held up a hand – 'need you to speak.'

David frowned. 'You might not need me to speak, Diana, but I will.'

She flashed him a warning look, but said nothing.

'I think you should wait. You're clearly . . . upset. And you might feel differently about it after some time has passed.'

'You'd stay here?' she asked, disbelieving.

'Perhaps.'

'I thought you said that we "had to be in London". That it was "non-negotiable".'

'I do need to be in London – don't get me wrong, Diana. And I probably am being overly romantic. It just seems rash to give up something so beautiful. All your mother's work. The roof.'

'Please don't even *mention* that fucking roof.'

'I'm concerned you're acting out of some kind of—'

'Some kind of what?' Diana said, throwing herself into her chair in exasperation.

'Grief . . . Rage . . . I don't know.'

'When my mother followed her instincts, everyone applauded. When I do the same, everyone seems to gather in thin-lipped horror.'

'But this is a decision made in death, Diana. It's not life-affirming. It's not a yes.'

'I don't ever want to hear that silly phrase again. This is a yes to me. Whether the shadow is thrown by a castle or a person, I don't want to stand in it. I'm shedding all ballast. You're welcome to stay here and play with the ghosts, but I'm moving on.'

He nodded, almost imperceptibly.

'David, the life I have created for myself is one that I find beautiful. My ideas, while perhaps less grand than my mother's, are just as interesting to me as this chaotic . . . schema. My mother's desire for transcendence will not be at the expense of those left in the material realm. In fact,' her voice rose, 'like all the others, what you're doing is admiring the fucking flowers while I'm buried six feet underneath a load of someone else's bullshit. My mother has gone, so forgive me if I want to breathe again!'

David was silent.

Diana raked her hands through her hair. 'Besides,' she said quietly, 'I couldn't afford to keep it, even if I wanted to. Have you any idea how much money my mother spent on this place? She must have been at her pipe when she was doing the figures. And *all* the provisions she left for its upkeep have gone with her beloved Roberto.'

'But you have some of your own money, don't you?' David said, frowning.

'I have enough to get by, but it's no great shakes. Ice to make a few cocktails from what *was* a glacier.' She sighed and pushed the papers away from her. 'I'm tired of fighting.' She looked at her nails.

'But, Diana, you always fight.'

'Yes, I like a good scrap,' she said thoughtfully. 'But my mother chose to trust Roberto with what was left of her money. The law is clear on that. And it was *his* money anyway.'

David looked at her quizzically.

'Harry's. He didn't leave me anything when he died. Not so much as a note. Though he did bestow a small fortune on a street-boy named Bokhara from Tangiers. The Morgan Bank had quite a time trying to track him down. I think they might still be at it.'

'That must have been very painful. I'm sorry.'

'You're sweet to say sorry.' She looked at him and smiled. 'You know, David, I'm not sure what happened this morning, but as those lawyers were speaking it felt as though something that has been gnawing at my insides just died. I thought I'd feel rage, spitting rage when this happened. So all right, I've been yelling at the staff and hustling people about, but that's nothing really. Just getting the blood flowing. And I know I should rail at the clouds and write hundreds of letters, but right now all I want is to leave this place and never see it again.' There was a knock and they both turned. A young woman stood in the doorway, staring levelly at them both.

'Elena, my God, you're here.'

David stood still, as though he had unexpectedly seen a lone deer in a clearing. Unseen, his hand moved, tracing the curve of her neck.

'You haven't put on any weight,' Diana said, without going forward to meet her.

'I'm well, Diana, thank you. How are you?' The girl crossed her arms, and glanced at David.

'Leonie hasn't come?'

The girl shook her head. 'She's in California now.'

'You've been speaking?'

Elena shook her head again. 'Inés told me.' Her chest was rising and falling quickly. 'Where shall we sleep?'

'And who is "we"?'

'James and I.'

'Wherever you like. It's like the fall of Rome around here, so make your bed where you can.'

'We want somewhere quiet.'

'So you can make lots of noise?' Diana said slyly.

The girl stared at the floor. 'Yes, that's right,' she said quietly.

Diana laughed and then glanced at David, who was gazing out of the window, a faint muscle moving in his cheek.

'Elena, you haven't met David.' He turned, holding Diana's eyes in reproach, and then went forward to shake the girl's hand.

She took his gently, and her hand was cool in his grip. 'It's nice to meet you,' she said. 'I'm going to go and have a bath then. If there's nothing you need help with here?' She looked at all the papers on the desk.

'No.' Diana turned her hands in two elegant circles. 'It's all taken care of. See you at dinner.'

Elena nodded and, without looking at David, left.

Diana and David were silent for a moment after she'd gone.

She cut him a glance. 'Are you still going to stay for dinner?'

'Yes.'

'And then tomorrow you're going to London.'

'As we agreed.'

She nodded.

'Will you be all right here?' He took her wrist and pulled her towards him.

'Yes, yes. I'll be fine. The sturdy Boston cousins are on their way to help too.' She tried to raise a smile. 'Relieved, I suppose, to end this saga. The tearaway can tear no more. Not that they'll get *me* back to the country club.' She smiled. 'My flight's booked for Saturday. We'll be free before we know it.' She turned to face him; aware of the glare of the bright desk lamp, she moved slightly to the side so that the light was behind her.

'I want to be with you, Diana.' David caught her face in his hands. 'I want to marry you.'

She looked him in the eye, her heart beating quickly.

But she knew not to ask a serious question without first being sure of the answer.

Lying in the big marble tub in the shadowy bathroom that adjoined her room, Elena listened. James was next door, lying on their bed staring up at a vaulted ceiling that might as well have been stars. She could tell the effect of this place on him and was glad they would not be staying long. It would be hard for him to go back to their little flat with the damp on the ceiling and the cramped galley kitchen. She closed her eyes and pictured their bed with its Indian cover and the mismatched lamps on each side; the small sitting room with the framed posters on the walls and the knotted rug they'd bought together in Nepal. The room seemed perfect to her until she came to the dark wooden chair taking up too much space in the corner.

It was a gift from her father and Elena had allowed it to become covered in books and coats so that only its legs remained visible. He had brought it himself a month ago, unstrapping it from the roof of his Mercedes as she watched, standing on the pavement in her bare feet.

'Well, you never bloody ring any more, Elena. And you haven't been answering my letters or calls since your mother and I finalised the divorce.' He pushed past her holding the chair, his still strong frame in the unexpected ease of jeans and a soft cotton shirt. 'So the mountain has come to Muhammad.'

She had taken him for lunch at the little Italian café that she and James ate in most days. She knew the elderly couple who ran it and that there would be people around. James had wanted to come, but Elena had refused and, kissing him on the cheek, walked out of the flat alone to where her father was waiting.

Inside the steamy café, her father was fascinated by the busy crowd of labourers and pensioners sipping bowls of minestrone. She'd ordered simple plates of pasta for them both. 'Wipe-clean menus,' he said, turning over the curling plastic in his hands. 'Both useful and vile, rather like your new stepmother.'

Elena had concentrated on working the spaghetti round her fork and pretended not to hear.

Her father had eaten his food with enthusiasm and on

finishing ordered coffee from the elderly owner with a small tilt of his hand, then sat back and lit a cigarette, pushing the packet towards her. She only ever smoked with him, and as she leaned forward to take one without wanting it, she caught the faint smell of lemons.

'I used to come to a café like this when I was training as an engineer. Run by an old cockney. The food was appalling.'

She said nothing, trying not to grimace at the taste of the cigarette.

'I bet the men here can't believe their luck, having you walk in.'

She pressed the cigarette into the ashtray until she was sure it was completely out.

'I want to give you and James a gift.' He squinted at her through the smoke. 'You know I'm having to sell the London house to finally be rid of your mother.'

She stared at him, dreading whatever this new offer would be.

'I'm moving back to Yorkshire, and Anita and I would very much like to give you the huntsman's cottage. It's not too close to the main house, so you can have your privacy.' He watched her face, but she did not move. 'You used to like it when you were a child, and perhaps you'll have some of your own one day.' He flicked his eyes in the direction of her stomach and as it churned Elena was glad that she'd left most of her food. 'I admire your vow of poverty, but one day you may well find you want to get out of this dump and get some fresh air.'

Elena stared at the table. She could picture the great stone house set in the middle of the deer-strewn park. The network of rooms and corridors, separated by hidden doors set into the walls. Her father's housekeeper walking grimly around the bottom floor of the big house, hitting a gong for mealtimes. Her father striding along the corridors with some dead thing in his arms to give to the cook. She remembered the hostile cold of the dining room in which her grandparents sat at either end of a long table communicating to one another through their servants. The piles of lewd magazines in the loos that felt like being locked inside her father's head.

'No.' She looked up at her father.

He put his head back and raised his eyebrows, like a driver meeting an unexpected animal in the road.

'No?'

'I don't want . . . to be rude, but no.'

Elena turned over in the bath, her cheeks burning at the memory. Had she really said that? She sat up and pulled open the window above the bath so that the night air rushed in, cooling her body. The dark blue of the sky was pricked with stars.

She could smell jasmine.

'We'll eat in here, it's too gloomy in that vast empty hall.' Diana ushered James into one of the smaller ante-rooms where a candlelit table had been set for four.

'What about all the other guests?' Elena asked, following them in, David behind her. She had tied up her long hair and wore a white cotton dress that hung simply to her ankles. Her sharp shoulder blades moved beneath her skin as she walked, so that it looked, David thought, as though her wings had been cut away with two quick flicks of a blade.

'They can all fend for themselves this evening,' continued Diana. 'I want to have an *intimate* family meal.' She smiled victoriously at them all. 'Now,' she gently guided James towards a chair, 'I want you by me. We're having porcini risotto and then wild boar, shot a few weeks ago by my friend Giancarlo. It should be perfect.'

As they sat down, David turned towards Elena. 'Your mother's ability to hang meat rivals any butcher I've known. It's quite an alarming art.'

But Elena was looking up at the frescoes on the ceiling above them and seemed not to hear. James looked at her expectantly for a moment, an open expression on his handsome face, but when she still did not notice he reached across and gently touched her hand, bringing her attention back down to the table.

'What?' She looked at her mother.

'David was talking to you,' Diana said, looking between them both.

'I'm sorry, David, what did you say?' As she asked, James and Diana began to busy themselves with the pouring of wine, chattering brightly.

David smiled at Elena and shook his head. 'My comment wasn't important.' His eyes were kind and Elena turned herself slightly towards him.

'My mother tells me that you're an artist.'

'Yes.' He smiled, and Elena liked the way he seemed able to laugh at himself.

'Struggling?' she asked.

'Depends on the day. And the time of the month.'

Elena looked at him quizzically.

'I've always had a woman in my life and the moon affects us all.'

'And now you have her.' Elena nodded across the table to where Diana was telling a story to a laughing James.

David watched her across the table. 'A woman indeed. Unlike any other.'

'Have you got what it takes?' Elena asked.

'Well, what I've got she certainly takes,' David laughed. 'No, that's not fair. We take it out of each other.'

'I was just telling James about the disastrous journey I took around the Channel Islands when I sailed there to visit my lawyer,' Diana said loudly. 'The wind was ferocious and everyone was sick as dogs, apart from me up on deck in the rain eating cod's roe.' She smiled at David, who knew the story. 'They are the strangest little islands. Pretty, but rather chilly.'

'Weren't they occupied in the war?' James said.

'Yes, and one, Alderney – I think the most attractive – was entirely fortified. The whole place is dotted with brutalist forts and an entire network of underground tunnels. It's most unusual.'

'The beaches there are meant to be beautiful,' James said.

'Yes, they are rather fine. Very peaceful. I was sitting in a pub one evening with all the salty sailors and one told me that when they returned to the island after the war, the lobsters they caught off the north end were the biggest they'd ever known them to be.'

The table looked blank.

'Well, that was where they dropped the bodies.'

Elena put down her fork.

'But do tell us about the state of your affairs, James.' Diana's tone became light. 'You had grand plans when I last saw you in Ibiza.'

He sat forward to take the glass she'd just filled. 'My grand plans have been chucked out the window. Somehow or other I've had my attention diverted.' He smiled at Elena. 'I'm not sure I'll ever be able to work on anything with undivided attention again.'

'Let's see how long that lasts.' She gave an acid smile in return. 'But you'll have to do something for money, James. Elena's hardly going to be able to support you both by writing esoteric texts about the tradition of silence.'

Elena looked at Diana in surprise. She always sent copies of her work to her mother, but never imagined that she actually read them.

'Actually, Elena and I have a plan. Perhaps just a dream.'

David raised his eyebrows. 'And what is that? I always keep an ear out for other people's plans. Some are very useful.'

'Well, you're welcome to this one, David,' James laughed. 'Though I would imagine you're kept pretty busy.'

'Day and night!' Diana laughed, and David noted the way Elena winced as she drank her water. She had not drunk any of her wine.

'So what is the big plan?' Diana said with a raised eyebrow.

'Well, my cousin died recently and left me some money,' James said. 'So ... I've decided to start a bookshop. I love books, always have, and got a spectacularly bad English degree to prove it.'

'A shop?' Diana asked, looking at Elena. 'Elena, darling ... really? I can't see you behind a till.'

'Why not?' Elena looked seriously at her mother.

'Because you're not a shop girl. You're . . .'

'What am I?'

'Well, you're my daughter for a start.'

'What kind of books?' David asked, with a nod at James.

'Rare books, particularly fine first editions. With a focus on the inter-war period.'

Diana looked uncomfortable. 'And where will you get these *books*?'

'I've been collecting for a while now. I have to say, when Elena told me about Black Sun I was terribly excited. What a story. Though I was hardly surprised. I knew there must have been something extraordinary behind such a woman.'

'I disagree with you about that, James,' Elena said quietly. 'I think experience has more power over our lives than our blood.'

'I'm not sure.' James took a mouthful of the risotto. 'I think the majority is written within. My God, this is good.'

'It takes a happy man to say so,' David said to James. 'Most people need the hope of changeability.'

'My mother always said that we can give birth to ourselves,' Diana said, shaking her hair back. 'And I think she was quite right.'

'Of course.' James spread his hands wide. 'I don't deny the ability to change. Elena and I are working hard to change certain things.'

Elena glanced at him and gave him a small shake of her head.

'What do you need to change?' Diana's eyes narrowed as she looked at Elena. 'What's wrong with the way you are?'

'I don't *need* to change,' Elena said quietly. 'But there are some things . . .'

'Such as . . .'

'Well, the main one is that we've decided to get married immediately.'

Diana looked at James. 'Aren't you meant to take me out for a whisky to ask my permission?'

'I'm afraid I don't believe in all that, Diana.' James held up his hands. 'Elena doesn't belong to anyone – she's taught me well,' he laughed. 'We just want to make our vows sacred as soon as possible.'

'Sacred in what sense?' Diana said, crossing her arms. 'Marriage is a fine thing, don't get me wrong. But sacred? I'm not sure about that.'

'I believe it's sacred,' Elena said quietly.

'Vows made before God can't be broken,' James agreed. Elena winced.

'I think you'll find they can. But you're not getting married so you can have a guiltless fuck, are you?' Diana said with a raised eyebrow. 'There's no need for any of *that* around here.'

Elena stared down at the table.

'We just want to start our life together. We've found a flat below Inés in Batter . . .' James felt the pressure of Elena's leg against his and his voice trailed into silence.

'How cosy for you all,' said Diana slowly. She turned to her daughter. 'Well, don't expect a big wedding, Elena; there's no salt left in the cellar.' She spread her arms wide. 'So it will be *sopa de papas* at Inés's. Do let me know if I'm invited.'

'We don't want a big wedding,' James said. 'We honestly don't expect anything at all, Diana. Apart from being happy.

I can't deny I fully expect that.' He smiled at Elena and she met his eyes briefly, before turning to her mother.

'But what will you do, Diana?' she said, eager to change the subject. 'How long will you stay here?'

Diana glanced at David, but he was silent. 'I need to stay here to organise the sale.'

'Of this place?' said James. 'That must be terribly painful.'

'Quite the opposite, actually,' Diana replied.

'Did Caresse ... want you to sell it?' Elena asked tentatively, straightening her knife and spoon so that they were in line with one another.

Diana swept her gaze over to her daughter and Elena's eyes widened. But she held her mother's look.

'What your grandmother wanted was for me to be free. Freedom was her greatest desire in life. So that is what I am doing.' She pressed her napkin to her mouth and then laid it to rest, a faint red stain pressed into the white linen.

'What a thing, to sell a place like this.' James shook his head, gazing around. 'I've hardly seen it and have already fallen in love with the very stone it's made of.'

Elena shot him a warning glance.

'It's beautiful, isn't it,' David said. 'I had a similar feeling when I first came. It seemed extraordinary that one should be able to come and actually live somewhere so alive with the past. Many of the rooms haven't even been reopened. Did you know there's a snow cellar? It's dug so deep into the foundations that a previous Cardinale could store ice and snow there through even the hottest summers.'

'Unbelievable,' James murmured.

'I'll tell you what's unbelievable – the bills. The artists' hotel is sadly closed for business. It'll be back to the chilly garret and studio for the lot of them.'

David stared at her. 'Diana, I am one of those artists.'

'Yes, but you're good. I have plenty of time for someone making work that means something. But half the people here are no more artists than I'm Georges Braque. I think this kind of thing makes people lazy.'

'But the role of patron is as old as money itself,' James interjected. 'It seems a good use for the stuff.'

Diana looked the boy over. 'You can use yours to patronise whoever you like, James.'

'So where will you go now?' Elena broke in.

'We'll be in London for a time. David needs to be there for his work.' Diana turned back to her daughter. 'And you never know, perhaps like you two there'll be a quick tying of the knot.' She did not look at David.

'And what about Ibiza?' Elena said. 'You're not going to sell that, are you?'

'No, of course not. We'll go back there eventually.' Diana smiled, and David nodded thoughtfully, his hands clasped round his knee.

'It's all to be discussed.' He smiled at Elena and James.

Diana laughed suddenly. 'You see, Elena, marriage is no cakewalk. Men can be very difficult. Very difficult indeed.' She gave James a sly wink. 'But prepare yourself, darling. We women can be quite the adversary. Our methods have no centre and no circumference. It's hard not to find yourself quite surrounded.'

Rue de Lille, 1931

'Darling, how are you?' Her mother's voice soared through the telephone.

'Fine.' Diana frowned.

'Are you happy to have done with school?'

'Oh, yes.'

'How was the sale of Rue de Lille?'

'Fine.'

'And Le Moulin du Soleil?'

'Fine.'

'Has Maxime been a great help?'

'Yes.' Diana slowly unfurled a smile at the man standing in front of her.

'He's such a faithful friend, it's terribly touching that he should offer to collect you from school and help you with all of it. I know you understand that I had to come. The moment was just *ripe* and the show has been a complete sellout. New York is wild for Dalí. Washington tomorrow.'

'Yes,' Diana said. 'Maxime is proving a great comfort.'

'The Astors have thrown a terrific party for me. They don't want me to sink into gloom. Dalí has been terribly well received and I had a great success with his press conference on arrival. I wore a provocative suit with lamb chops on each shoulder. The press went berserk when we got off our plane. The photographers wanted me to . . .'

Diana let the phone drop as she leaned back in her chair and lifted her feet onto the desk, and the man got down on his knees before her.

Alderney, 1993

Cast in the switching blue light of the muted television, Diana lay in her bed. She'd asked them to leave it on. Somewhere a telephone was sending forth its shrill call. Was no one going to answer it? It might be him calling. Her hand searched the bed, looking for the black handle, as smooth and curved as the big black Daimler. She answered the telephone. Hello. And the earpiece was warm against her face and a rich deep voice was pouring his need into her head, making plans for later. She breathed deeply and let the sound drown out other thoughts. Her lovers liked to hear her low laugh winding along the curled wire. They were always glad she called.

Darling, are you there?

But the wind changed direction and she was being sucked out on a dark tide now, dragged backwards. Here was another voice, low and broken, cracked over the solid fact of death.

He did it.

Her mother wringing life from all words.

He did it.

The hand reaching for the breast beneath her coat, playing over its warm curve. Opium-drenched, struggling to form the words. *Do it, Harry, do it to me*, the young woman's voice rose to a singing hymn. He did it and she was silent.

And Diana sliding down the wall by the telephone until she lay in a small heap on the floor.

And now her mother drawing a hand out of her black silk glove and her thumb working the lighter so that fire began to eat the pile of paper she had gathered. The whole lot disappearing quickly into hungry flames. Diana staring, speechless, as her mother stood with one hand on the mantelpiece, chest heaving.

'There!' was all she said.

Diana looking round her rose-papered room as though drunk – the handprints all around her bed – and then, to work.

There was no frenzy like it. She knocked and smashed and tore at all that had stood, she kicked and ripped and bit until her teeth ached. She scratched at the walls and her face and the low neckline of her mother's black dress, wanting to expose her too, wanting to get *at* her, until she sank to the floor. Her mother, face set, stepped over her and walked from the room, leaving the door open behind her.

She could feel someone behind her holding her tight and she turned, reaching arms towards them, as her nightdress twisted and got caught up leaving her dangerously bare. Firm arms pulled the material down and she was concealed by cotton as plain and kind as her daughters' faces. She smelled the pillow and frowned. It had been washed with cheap soap. She would have to talk to the girls.

Perhaps, she thought, drifting downwards again, she was a little addicted to her mistakes. Someone pushed her head up and did something to the pillows. Always trying to sharpen herself – she felt a sharp scratch on her arm – always cutting, always hurting. Her head was laid back down and she was tucked in tight. Everything hurt. She followed the aching line of thought downwards.

But people want *to be cut free*, she thought as she reached blindly for her glass and somebody held her head and helped her drink.

We must *all be set free*.

Roccasinibalda, 1970

The next morning, wearing a new dress, feet tied into a pair of pale blue espadrilles, Diana wound her way down one of the cool stone stairways. As she entered a large room whose shutters had not been properly opened, she looked around, suspicious of the stillness. The half-restored frescoes had been left with ladders leaning against them, and someone had forgotten a pile of papers at one end of the long table. She moved quickly through the room and then across the brilliant square of a small courtyard until she finally entered the cool of the main hall. The doors were, at last, closed. She checked her hair in the huge mirror that hung before her and, sensing something, turned and saw Ellis standing behind her. He looked and smelled as though he had not washed for days. Her lip curled.

'You know.' His voice was cracked, as though he'd been shouting. 'You might not have liked what your mother was doing here. But this was good.'

'I never doubted that it was good, Mr Porto, but it was not

real. This was a dream, another one of my mother's surreal dreams.'

He grinned at her. 'You look like a dream. How old are you now? Forty? Fifty?'

'Old enough to know not to answer that question.'

'Shall we take a walk?'

She looked up, surprised, then glanced at her watch. 'Yes, all right. I was waiting for David, but I can't find him anywhere.'

'I saw him walking up the hill earlier with your daughter and her guy.'

'The three of them?'

Ellis nodded. 'She's very thin. A broken wishbone.'

Diana pressed her dress down over her sides.

'Painfully beautiful. You all are.'

Diana said nothing.

'Let's walk through these rooms and say farewell to those that haunt them,' Ellis said. 'May your mother's presence be a welcome addition.'

Diana nodded and they began to walk. The courtyards were quiet now, and only the sounds of the birds in the walled garden could be heard. The wind moved too, gently blowing Diana's hair over her forehead so that she had to push it back with her hand. They stood at the edge of one of the gardens, where breakfast had always been served, and looked out at the surrounding hills, and then turned and looked behind them at the steep stone walls.

'She had no friends here,' Diana said quietly, almost to herself. 'No real friends.'

'Perhaps she felt new friends were as good as old.'

'But they weren't.' She looked at him. 'I don't mean you, Ellis. I'm not trying to be cruel. But none of them came to see her in the hospital. To say goodbye. She died alone, Ellis. After all that *talk*, she died alone.'

'She moved on, Diana. She liked to move on. I'm not sure you can have both roots and wings.'

Diana said nothing and they turned and walked back along a shaded cloister. The poet began to murmur as they walked, half-whispered lines of verse.

Diana took his hand. 'Where will you go?' she asked softly.

'Back to New York, most probably.'

'We could have dinner when I'm next there,' she said, and her smile was almost shy. 'I know a wonderful place in Brooklyn where we can eat.'

He shook his head ruefully. 'Ah, little girl. Tenderness after the kill. I know the feeling well.'

Diana frowned. 'Little girl?' she said.

He stepped forward and kissed her, pressing her hands against the wall. The smell of him was overpowering and Diana felt she might gag. But he was strong and his desire was enough. She lifted her skirt and was pushed against the wall as he fumbled with his belt.

It was over quickly, his dark greasy head pressed against her neck. She kissed the top of it tenderly, holding him close to her, trying not to breathe. She stroked his back and feeling the worn wool of his coat beneath her hands, began to cry.

Alderney, 1994

'Let's pray.'

In the front seats of the car her parents bowed their heads and after a moment of silent tussle the boys behind them did the same. Sitting in the back, Bay cradled her cut flowers as carefully as her mother held the new baby.

Now Bay made her way down the aisle of the almost empty chapel, her brothers walking behind her like too-late grooms, their shoes tapping smartly over the stone. It sounded as if they were almost catching her up, and Bay quickened her pace as she made a straight line towards where her Aunt Leo sat in a pew unnecessarily marked *Reserved*. The family sat down and Bay watched her aunt first kiss her mother, pressing their foreheads together in silence, and then bend down and kiss the baby, held close to her mother's chest.

Leonie welcomed Bay into the crook of her arm, and as Bay pushed against her she felt the familiarity of her mother's shape. The evening before, Leonie had lain with her in the narrow bed reading her a story while her mother tended to the new baby in the other room. Her grandmother's room had been emptied and cleared, the wind billowing the fine curtains into ghosts that blew in and out, filling the room with cold, clean air.

The last time she'd seen her grandmother, she was lying in a small bed in that close-smelling room. The curtains were closed even though it was day, with only a single lamp spreading shadows up the walls. Her mother had not pulled open the windows as she normally did so that they could all breathe, but left the room in half-darkness, keeping Bay's hand tightly in her own. In the gloom of the bedroom, Bay could tell that her grandmother had changed, and as she went forward to kiss her cheek, saw that she was like a sandcastle – half washed by a wave to a softened mound. Not knowing where to look, Bay stared instead at a black-and-white photo of a little girl holding a dog in one hand and a whip in the other.

It was a stroke, she had heard her mother say to her aunt, and she'd lain in her bed and run her fingers gently up and down her arms, stroking and stroking, until she buzzed under the covers and had decided that she would like to die of that too.

Bay felt her aunt looking at her and leaned closer, rubbing her cheek against her arm.

Leonie kissed the top of the child's carefully brushed head and felt the ache of love as she looked down at the folded white socks and red jelly shoes that kicked back and forth, the bony knees, and the hand that rested with no intention or awareness along her own thigh. Last night she had read to the child, feeling sleep stealing into the room until the small body became heavy with it, and as she'd put the book down and pulled the covers up tight, she'd been cut by the first sharp stab of loss.

The organ began to play and everybody's gaze was drawn towards the back of the room as the men carried the wooden coffin down the aisle. Bay turned further round and saw a man she didn't recognise take his seat in the back row. He had wild hair and his eyes met Bay's with a jolt so that she quickly turned away, heart beating against the stiff wool of the cardigan her mother had buttoned her into that morning. She felt her mother also turn and Bay watched as she inclined her graceful neck and smiled at the man. Bay looked up at her father, but he was hovering near the front, ready to deliver his speech. She cast another quick look behind her. The man went on watching, and Bay turned her head slowly too, just as her mother had done.

At the front her father, in a navy suit and pale tie, his soft dark hair waved back from his forehead, was speaking.

'Diana's life was extraordinary, troubled, warm and dangerous, as well as brave and sad and filled with great kindness, generosity and style.'

Bay sat a little straighter as the words settled over the family. By association with her grandmother, she also felt grand; full of that feeling, she risked a final look back and saw that the man was now looking at the coffin, his hands pressed over his mouth.

'All living things are subject to death,' her father went on, 'and Diana was not afraid of meeting this part of life. May she rest in deepest peace with her maker and her friends.'

*

345

From inside the car, Bay watched her mother and the man with tangled hair walk under the trees in the dripping graveyard, until they turned a corner and she lost sight of them.

She leaned forward and wrapping her arms round the front seat, brought her head close to her father's, who sat in the front seat with his eyes closed, the sleeping baby in his arms.

'Where's Mummy going?'

'Hmm?' He turned to look at her.

'Who's that man she's with?'

'He was married to your grandmother.' He smiled at her and then closed his eyes again.

Bay sat back in silence and resumed her watching.

'It's all right, Bay.' Her father spoke gently and his eyes found hers in the rear-view mirror. 'He's a friend.'

Elena walked slowly past the graves almost lost in a phalanx of brambles and nettles, clutching her arms tight round herself. 'I'm so glad you came, David.'

'I had to come,' he said. He kept his head bowed as he walked, his hands deep inside his pockets. He had aged in the way of knotted rope, his form and purpose hardening and just beginning to fray, the curly hair spun with greys. Looking down, Elena saw clay dug deep around his thumbnail.

'Can you not stay? James and I would be so happy if you did.'

David shook his head. 'Claudia and the children are waiting for me in London, we fly back to Rome tomorrow and you know what she's like about Diana. It caused a small blaze that I flew to be here.'

'But will you meet my children?'

David was silent and Elena looked away, annoyed that she'd forgotten his refusal to be pulled in any direction but his own. Hearing the click of a lighter, she glanced over and saw the length of a finely rolled joint between his teeth.

'What are you doing? You can't smoke that here,' she said, her voice swinging upwards in alarm.

'"Can't"?' He looked at her with gentle amusement, but he pinched the lit end and slid the joint neatly into his top pocket, squeezing her arm. 'All gone.'

'I'm sorry ...' she said after a pause. 'I don't mean to be tense.'

'I know.' He put an arm round her. 'I know. You can't help it.'

She allowed herself to relax against him as they walked. As David spoke, his voice was low.

'Did she know that she was going?'

Elena nodded, once.

'Did she fight it?'

Elena walked in silence before she answered. 'She asked to watch the sun going down. You could see it from her window. She stared at it for quite a while, propped up straight by the nurses, and then she lay down.' Elena swallowed. 'She was determined that she was somewhere other than where she was. Would only refer to the nurses as her "girls".' David laughed softly.

'When I asked if she was scared – I know she hated that question, but I so wanted to know – all she said was, "Leaving's easy, Elena. It's staying that's been a bitch."'

'She never trusted being comforted,' David said.

'It was never safe enough,' Elena said.

'Perhaps,' he looked down, and then up, holding her eyes. 'My God, Elena, when I look in your eyes, they're the same shape as hers and seem to hold something similar. I still don't understand what it is that flows between you, but whatever it was that dug into your mother went so deep that every new day could only ever run back to the past.' Elena dropped her gaze and ducked under the dripping branch of a tree, the leaves moving across her face with the cool drag of a water-dipped finger. She closed her eyes, her face raised to the dappled light.

'When I used to ask her what her childhood was like, it was not because I wanted to understand her, but because I wanted to absorb more of all that surrounded her. I was so in love with the idea of Caresse and that castle.' David sat down on a bench, not seeming to notice the wet wood, and looked up at Elena. 'I loved Caresse, she was an ideal, and I couldn't help but see things from both of their points of view. Diana *hated* that.'

'You were meant to pick a side.'

He nodded. 'I've often wondered whether I should have given her the loyalty I knew she craved beneath all that talk. But I don't know if it would have made any difference.'

Elena was silent.

'She needed there to be three in the bed, it was an obsession, and though I told her countless times that I didn't want other women, she wouldn't believe it. And then she introduced me to Claudia and, well . . .' He fell silent too, squinting out across the gloom of the graveyard.

'I remember her hand' – David took Elena's in his – 'tracing a long crack in the wall by the bed and her voice coming

348

towards me like a thread in the dark, telling me a grim love story I wasn't sure I even believed. All about Paris and her childhood. Her stepfather. About being taken out at night in her nightdress and throwing gold to drunks and setting birds loose. She guarded those memories carefully, but that night she offered them to me like a child showing a grazed knee. She wouldn't let me touch it. Wouldn't let me help. She only wanted me to listen. She only ever wanted me to listen.'

'It's hard to do that,' Elena said.

'Do you think I was a coward to leave her in the way that I did?' He looked up at her, beseechingly.

'You were a coward to leave without saying goodbye.'

'But it was all she would understand, Elena. It had to be final.'

Elena met his gaze. 'But she was so alone, David. At the end, she was so very alone. If she'd stayed in Ibiza, she would at least have had her friends around her. But she followed you back to London and then ended up here with no one.'

'She made her own choices, Elena. Compelled by who knows what, she moved her pieces.'

They were both silent for a moment.

'I need to get back,' Elena said and, standing, turned to leave.

'She loved you, Elena.' He caught her hand.

Elena bent her neck as though trying to pull free of a harness. 'Perhaps. But I don't think I ever managed to hollow myself out enough to match her deep self-regard. Though I tried.' She laughed and shook her head. 'My God, I tried. I thought it might get easier towards the end. That she might enjoy some of it. Spend time with the children . . .'

David shook his head. 'Elena, your mother didn't die from that stroke; she died the first time she walked into a room and none of the men looked up. All she knew was how to seduce, and however good she might have been, sex is not a lasting legacy.'

'Children are,' Elena said defiantly. But beneath her words there was the weight of something uncertain in shape, a living thing caught in a tied sack.

'Oh, Elena.' He smiled at her sadly. 'My heart broke when I first saw you and the wound of knowing you cannot heal.' He pressed her hand to his mouth. 'You and your sister are strong. Teach your children to be like you. The rest will make itself known in time.'

Alderney, 1994

Elena sat with her back pressed against the anti-artillery wall that protected the long beach, her face raised to the sun. It was a hot morning, the sky hard and blue above the sea. She had set their camp down in the middle of the beach, tucked against the shelter of the long curved wall, and holding the baby carefully in her arms beneath a white muslin, she watched as the children ran down to the water's edge.

Strange, the way they had grieved.

The news of their grandmother's death had been accepted as something natural, even welcome. But the passing of the house ... they had wept as though something was being cut from them. She closed her eyes and remembered the way she had cried when she had realised that Ibiza was gone. A telegram opened in the small kitchen of their flat, Jake on her hip. And yes she had wept, watched by her wide-eyed son. Not for the house, of course, but for the memories stranded there. She took a deep breath and looked down at the baby rooting at her breast. Undoing her shirt in a simple movement, she settled her to feed. She recalled Inés's hands guiding her own as Elena sat in the hospital bed after giving birth to Jake, her first.

'Like this.' And Inés had held the back of the small dark head and brought it firmly against Elena's breast. 'Now he knows peace.' The old woman gazed with satisfaction at the meeting of the two. 'And he will never love another in the same way.'

'Do you ever wish that you'd had children?' Elena had asked, fixing her large eyes on the lined face.

'No.' Inés had shaken her head. 'Because then I would not have been able to have you.' And with both hands she had brought Elena's head towards her lips and kissed her forehead, murmuring a prayer into her hair.

Diana had also come. 'You can get someone to do that for you, you know,' she said as she'd watched Elena struggling. 'Or use a bottle.'

'I want to do it myself,' Elena said.

'You'll ruin them.'

'It's what they are for, Diana.'

'That, darling, is something of the chicken or the egg.'

And now too, Elena thought of her grandmother, sitting up in a huge wicker sun chair, body still as slim as a girl's, her legendary breasts concealed beneath a striped blouse cut arrestingly across her neck.

'Your body is a temple, darling little Elena. You must get used to people wanting to worship in it . . .'

She felt James sit down next to her and smiled at the familiar sensation of her husband's arm against her own, waiting a moment before she opened her eyes onto the sun-stretched beach.

'How was it?' she asked, examining the curve of his ear as

he leaned across her and moved the muslin aside to look at the little face now screwed up against the light.

'The end,' he said, squinting down towards the sea. 'I've finished packing up the last of the books.'

'Thank you.' She rested her head on his shoulder. 'Are we going to have to keep them all?'

'Yes.' He smiled down at her.

She nodded.

'Elena, there was something else.'

'What?'

'I found some diaries. I think they're the ones Diana often spoke of. Harry's.'

'Where?' Elena shook her head, confused. 'I sorted through all her things.'

'In a package wrapped in rather lovely blue Italian paper, along with a typed manuscript of hers. A sort of botched memoir of her childhood in Paris.'

'I didn't know she'd written that.'

'It seems to have been abandoned halfway through. I tried to read some, but it was hard to make sense of any of it.'

Elena frowned.

'But the diaries are clear: 1923 to 1930.'

Elena rocked the child gently from side to side.

'Do you want to read them?' James asked, after a pause.

'No.'

'Are you sure?'

She nodded.

'They could be worth a lot.'

Elena gazed towards where the children were playing at the water's edge. 'I don't want them.'

'What shall I do with them?'

'Do whatever you want.' She turned and their eyes met. 'I trust you.'

Bay came down into the kitchen to find her father sitting at the kitchen table. Early morning light filled the room. He was writing a note. He had his coat on.

'Where are you going?' she asked.

He stood up. 'For a walk.'

'Can I come?' She put her head on one side.

He looked at her for a long moment. 'Yes. Of course.'

'Are the boys awake?' she asked, as he got down her coat and helped her into it.

'No,' he said, and craning her neck to look at the zipped up tent in the garden, she felt thrilled.

'Here.' He held out her shoes and quickly knelt to do up the buckles.

Then, getting to his feet, he picked up a package from the table, tucked it under his arm and offered her his hand.

They drove in silence up to the steep cliffs at the north end of the island. At the headland a large fort stood watch, its four storeys bulked like a closed fist, and Bay was glad that her father took the path that led away from it, moving instead along a winding path that led towards the cliff's edge. She and her brothers had explored its dark rooms and stairwells many times, but today, alone with her father, she wanted to keep to the grass and the small white flowers that released a frantic honey smell as they passed.

They gradually approached the edge and Bay felt the wind pull at her coat with sharp tugs. She gripped her father's hand tighter, hardly daring to look below her at the sea moving insistently against the foot of the cliff, preferring to keep her eyes fastened on the horizon.

Her father let go of her hand and she clutched his leg instead, fearing the fall, watching as he took the package from inside his coat.

'How far do you think I can throw it?' he asked.

'Very far!' she said, smiling up at him.

'Do you think I can throw it so far it won't come back?' he asked.

'Yes!' she cried.

'Stay there,' he said. And stepping backwards a few paces, he ran forward and with a wide arc of his arm sent the package spinning through the air in a long curve down towards the sea. The water was too far away to hear the splash.

They both stood and looked, searching the water's surface for any sign, the only sound the hiss of the sea at the foot of the cliff.

'For the lobsters,' her father said, smiling down at her, and taking her hand in his, he led her back the way they had come.

Acknowledgements

For their generosity and inspiration, I would like to thank: Serena Colchester, Charlie Colchester, Lorraine Cavanagh, Sean Cavanagh, Polly Drysdale, Caresse Crosby, Harry Crosby, Marjorie Taylor, Alexander Colchester, Benjamin Colchester, Zachary Colchester, Talitha Colchester, Zoe Colchester, Jonty Colchester, Chloe Fithen, Felicity Rubinstein, Juliet Mahony, Rowan Cope, Gillian Warren, Nicole Bahbout, Ksenia Alexandrova, Emily Wingate, Daniel Dawson, Tish Wrigley, Bruce Parry, Lisa Chan, Geoffrey Wolff, Sybille Bedford and Gregory Corso.

SCRIBNER